*This is not the usual type of book that I read but I was fascinated and could not put it down. The author did so much research that it felt like I was reading a true story of a family and how they lived during that time! I wish the author could write faster so I could get my hands on those next ones...keep them coming!~* L. B. Collins

*This is a unique and interesting read. I couldn't put it down–almost missed my flight!* ~ J. Simmons

*Just like The Dreamer – The Beginning, once I started reading Dreamer II – The Gathering I could not put it down. It is so interesting with a great personal story line. And I love all the historical information. After reading the first two books of this series I cannot wait to get the third one! Keep it up!* – Patti Stribling Lauer

*I read this book and thoroughly enjoyed it...so exciting that you can't put it down. Kept me on the edge of my seat. Great writing.* ~ J. Stuller

*I've read the whole Clan of the Cave Bear series by Jean Auel, and I was bummed when it ended; you got the ancients going again in totally different happenings and people's! I will probably read all three again. Can't wait for book four!*

~ John G. Smith

# Books in this series:

The Dreamer ~ The Beginning (2016)

The Dreamer II ~ The Gathering (2017)

The Dreamer III ~ The People of the Wolves (2018)

The Dreamer IV ~ The Cave of Bones (2019)

The Dreamer V ~ The Blood-Red Skies (2020)

The Dreamer VI ~ The Outsiders (2021)

The Dreamer VII ~ The Challenge Circle (2022)

The Dreamer VIII ~ The Talking Stones (2023)

# The Dreamer VIII

# THE

# TALKING STONES

The Dreamer Book Series

By E. A. Meigs

Dreamer Literary Productions, LLC

2023

For information regarding this novel or permissions
to reproduction selections from this work, please

visit

Dreamer Literary Productions at:
www.dreamerliteraryproductions.com


ISBN: 978-1-7350558-8-6

First Edition

Cover photo by my friend Paula Krugerud
www.PaulaKrugerudPhotography.com

I dedicate this book with much love
and gratitude to my Mom.
It was my great good fortune
to have had you in my life.

 Fonts used in this novel 

Papyrus was created by Chris Costello in 1982.

Garamond was designed by Claude Garamond in the early 1530's.

# The Dreamer VIII

❧

# THE
# TALKING STONES

*The Dreamer VIII ~ The Talking Stones is the final installment in an ongoing saga that follows the life of a young Neanderthal man. The story takes place at a time in history when much of the world was experiencing brutal climatic changes and man's position within Nature's food chain was indeed perilous. The Dreamer VIII is written as a stand-alone novel, meaning it is not necessary to have read the preceding volumes to understand the plot, but for the best reading experience it is recommended to do just that. An updated version of the original Introduction is included for those who are new to this time period.*

## Introduction

This tale takes place approximately 40,000 BCE (Before Common Era), when the last Ice Age was well underway. At the peak of the Great Glacial Maximum, nearly one-third of the Earth's surface was hidden beneath a thick layer of ice. A substantial percentage of the planet's moisture was frozen solid, causing the oceans to recede and coastlines to become greatly expanded.

At that time the Eurasian landscape consisted of vast wind-scoured tundra and small pockets of woodland populated by at least three groups of people: the Neanderthal, Homo sapiens (in this case, the Cro-Magnon), and the Denisovan. These populations probably coexisted in parts of Eurasia for a relatively short period of time, geologically speaking. It was likely that they lived a seasonally nomadic lifestyle. We can only guess at what their lives would have been like: their languages, their social behaviors, their spirituality. Due to the passage of time and the impermanent nature of most materials they would have used in their day-to-day lives, there is little to tell us about their existence besides the tantalizing clues left by their remains, their tools, their art, their burials, and . . . their refuse.

Analyses of fossilized Neanderthal skeletons show that the males averaged five feet, five inches to five feet, six inches in height. The tallest Neanderthal men found to date were five feet, nine inches. The females were five feet to five feet, one inch. Their bones were about one-third stouter than ours. They were heavily muscled and had tremendous upper-body strength. The Neanderthal had the largest brain size of any known humans. Initial DNA testing showed that they likely had fair coloring: red to auburn hair, green or hazel eyes, and pale, probably freckled skin. Later genetic research on Neanderthal individuals found in different parts of Eurasia revealed that some had brown hair, brown eyes, and dusky skin. It is now considered likely that the Neanderthal had the same variety of skin tones, hair and eye coloring as do modern Eurasian people.

The Neanderthal roamed the Earth for roughly 200,000 years (longer, if you include the proto-Neanderthal) before their trail went cold around 37,000 to 42,000 BCE. That said, the Neanderthal may have persisted to eke out a living for some time afterward. However, since most modern humans outside of sub-Saharan Africa share between one and four percent Neanderthal DNA, it would appear that the Neanderthal are still with us even now, albeit in diluted form.

Homo sapiens may have first appeared in the European fossil record as early as (approximately)

200,000 BCE, but more conservative estimates range from 40,000 to 65,000BCE. The previously mentioned Cro-Magnon have been dated to 42,000 to 47,000 BCE. They were named for the rock shelter in which they were discovered in the Dordogne Valley in France in 1868. At one time, early anatomically modern humans in Europe were often referred to as Cro-Magnons, but that term has since fallen out of favor. However, since these novels take place almost entirely on the ancient lands we now know as France, my Homo sapiens characters actually are Cro-Magnons.

Over a period of tens of thousands of years the predecessors of the Cro-Magnon migrated out of Africa, gradually making their way into Eurasia. The men averaged about five feet, nine inches in height, but it is thought that some taller individuals may have been upwards of six and a half feet. Like the Neanderthal, their brains were also bigger than those of today's people. They are believed to have had dark coloring: brown to black hair, brown eyes, and shades of skin ranging from tan to brown. (Blond hair and blue eyes are a relatively new development in modern humans, having first appeared about 6,000 to 12,000 years ago, long after the pinnacle of the Ice Age, but possibly coinciding with the end of that last glacial period.)

This novel reintroduces the Denisovans to the series. Not much is known of these people at this time. What little information we have comes from a few teeth, a handful of bone fragments, a number of artifacts, and what can be gleaned from the study of their DNA. The physical characteristics of the bones suggest that the

Denisovans were a sturdy people, perhaps with a build resembling that of the Neanderthals. Their teeth, on the other hand, were quite large, about one-third bigger than that of either the average modern human or Neanderthal. We might then surmise that they probably had a heavy jaw to accommodate those teeth. DNA from a finger bone disclosed that it was taken from someone with dark hair, brown eyes, and brown skin.

When we consider the artifacts that have been attributed to the Denisovans, it must be acknowledged that they were an intelligent, skilled folk. Their needles (dated to approximately 50,000 to 60,000 BCE) look much like our needles of today. A bracelet of green stone shows that they had sufficient technology to drill holes and to shape and polish stone. We can only hope that further discoveries bring us more data on these intriguing people.

*  *  *

It is my humble opinion that after so many years of existence in a world that often presented extreme challenges, these intelligent beings would have been at the top of their game in leveraging the available resources to ensure their own comfort and the continuation of their species. Some indications suggest that early man was potentially much more advanced than is generally credited, and it is my guess that we will continue to be surprised by what is revealed when ongoing and future anthropological studies peel back layers of time as we search for ourselves within the lives of our ancestors.

*  *  *

An animal index is presented at the end of this novel for the convenience of those unfamiliar with the animals of Ice Age Europe. It gives basic information about most of the creatures mentioned in this book. It might be useful to know, for example, that a wisent is a species of European bison, and that the animal North Americans refer as a moose is called an elk in Europe.

* * *

This is a work of fiction and it is not intended to hold up to scientific scrutiny. I merely seek to tell a story that is set amid this ancient backdrop. I have peopled it with those whose lives — when broken down to their most basic elements — would not have been so different from ours: sharing care and concern for loved ones, enduring all life's hardships, and reveling in serendipitous moments of love, beauty, and joy when they grace us with their presence.

 **Chapter One** 

*It is dark. A small circle of light illuminates the path as I tread the uneven ground. A chunk of rubble dislodges from under my feet and suddenly I pitch forward, landing hard on the crumbling surface.*

"Tris, your hair is showing threads of white."

These words tore me from the depths of my Dream.

"I think I fell asleep," I mumbled to my mate, Morning Star, on whose lap my head was now cradled. It was a mild afternoon, and we had been enjoying a bit of respite from our busy day. "How long was I napping?"

"Not very long. I did not realize that you were in fact dozing until you startled when I spoke," Morning Star told me. Then, brushing loose strands of hair from my face, she changed the subject. "It has been a while since I have re-bound your hair. It needs to be done again. Did you hear me say that you're starting to go white? I can see white threads amongst the red."

"That is probably true on both counts. I would not be surprised to know that my hair is coming undone and that it is beginning to betray the number of my years," I said.

Just now, I was only too aware of my age. It was for certain that at thirty-two winters old, I was no longer a young man. And Morning Star, at thirty winters old, was not the sprig of a girl with whom I had become paired so many years and so many children ago. Nonetheless, she was still the most beautiful woman I had ever seen. Her face may have become thinner and more careworn, but the mere sight of it was enough to warm my heart. I considered myself to be lucky beyond any reasonable expectation to have as my mate the only woman I had ever loved. More than that, to also have her love in return. She was my partner in life. She knew me, perhaps even better than I knew myself.

Morning Star continued to pillow my head with her lap, tenderly caressing my face.

"You must be tired," she said. "Da told me about the hunt. It sounded like a trying one."

"It was fruitful, that is all I care," I replied. "No one was injured, and we brought home a lot of meat, a huge hide, and lots of other materials, besides. We can go back later to retrieve the head and antlers if anyone wants them."

I had taken part in an early morning hunt, and we had brought home a young giant deer buck. There had been four of us: me; my Puh; Morning Star's father, Black Wolf; and Fish Hawk, who was mate to Morning Star's sister Petal. We first saw the stag as it leisurely grazed by a stand of birch.  The breezes had picked up shortly after dawn and the birches shivered and swayed in the hearty gusts, distracting the animal from our downwind approach.  He did not sense our proximity until it was too late; thus we each managed to strike him with our spears.

Rather than bring him down, the injuries we inflicted upon the deer seemed only to spur him into action.  The beast had been sleek and well fed on summer foliage, and he was strong and fleet of foot.  He left a blood trail for us to follow, and we soon found him where he had expired near a thicket, where he may have hoped to find a safe haven if he could penetrate its tangled growth, what with his spread of antlers.

Giant deer are exceedingly large creatures.  Even after gutting the beast and removing the huge head with its considerable rack of velvet-covered antlers, and then loading the body on a hastily constructed travois sled, we knew it would be an arduous journey homeward.  The heavy carcass caused the sled poles to dig into the softer patches of earth, to become hung up on roots, and to collect an assortment of dried and fresh plant matter that we occasionally had to clear away from the underside of the vehicle so it did not impede our progress.

After returning home, we skinned and butchered the animal.  Then, having worked up an appetite, we had feasted on thin strips of the organ meats, which had been roasted over hot coals.  Most of the remaining flesh would be cured on smoking racks, but for now, those of us who had taken part in the hunt had settled down to digest the copious amount of meat we had eaten and indulged in a well-earned rest.

I looked up at my beloved mate and she smiled at me. I returned her smile.

"You will be relieved to know that the remainder of the buck's carcass is currently being divvied up into assorted foodstuffs and goods," Morning Star said, continuing a halfhearted attempt to reorder my unruly hair. "So there is no need for you to rouse yourself right away."

"That is good," I responded. I did not want to move. "The heat from the sun feels nice. And it is especially nice to lie here like this." I lifted a weary arm and reached to touch Morning Star's face. My shoulders, arms, and back still felt the aftereffects of the day's toil.

"It is nice," Morning Star concurred. "It has been a hectic season, and we are not as young as we used to be." Morning Star let out a rueful laugh. "But I will not complain. As always, I am ever grateful for all we have."

"Where are our offspring?" I asked, suddenly noticing the quiet and their apparent absence.

"Do not worry," Morning Star began. "Fox has gone fishing with Oak, Mror, Bewok, and Weasel, and our older girls have taken the little ones to visit with Mama. The baby will soon be hungry, so I am expecting their return at almost any time."

Our eldest was scarcely a child anymore. Fox was now a fourteen-winters-old young man who was nearly as tall as was I. He shared my dense, curly, red-gold hair, pale green eyes, and freckles, and he gave every appearance of also inheriting my height and sturdy build. I sometimes wondered if he would also inherit my ability to Dream, as I had from my great-grandmother. Fox showed no signs of being a Dreamer as of yet, but time would tell. For now, Fox spent most of his days in the company of his two closest friends, Mror and Oak. Our daughters, of whom there were six, ranged in age from three to thirteen. We had one more son, who was just an infant. There had been two additional sons, but they had not lived to celebrate their first winter. This one, however, was now a lively eight-moons-old baby, and we were hopeful he might survive to live a long and healthy life.

"Your mother is very kind to allow them to descend upon her household," I observed.

"She is, indeed, but she loves to have them stop in," Morning Star responded. "They are good company for her. Da is seldom home, and when he is home, they scarcely talk. My brothers do not often visit since they became paired two summers ago and then settled with their new mates near the Gathering Hall." Morning Star sighed and went silent for a moment. I speculated that she might be thinking, as I often did, that it was her mother's own domineering nature that caused her brothers to flee so that they might finally be free of Little Fawn's interference and overprotectiveness. "Poor Mama is lonely," Morning Star went on. "All but one of her children has left home, and my youngest sister, Dewdrop, will probably be paired and leave to set up housekeeping before too long. Besides, now that Mama is not able to do much work anymore, she must rely on others to help with chores. Fortunately, our children do not mind lending a hand."

"I hope they are not disturbing your father. No doubt he will be trying to nap after this morning's strenuous activities," I said, referring to our hunt.

"No doubt. But you know Da. He can sleep through almost anything." Morning Star giggled at this. Then, taking on a more serious tone, she added, "I wish you slept as well. You are almost always an uneasy sleeper."

I did not like to divulge much about my Dreams to Morning Star. There was no point in causing her unnecessary concern. This vision of a dark, rock-strewn place had been part of my Dreams for years, but I had no idea what it represented. I had a sense that I was looking for something, but what could it be? My Dreams might show me scenes from the distant past, the present, or far into the future, but I had no inkling of when or where the event in this Dream was taking place. It looked like a very dilapidated cavern, one that either had not yet come to be inhabited by man or beast, or had not been in use for a very long time.

"You look troubled," Morning Star told me.

"Do I?" I replied. "I do not think I am."

Morning Star's warm hands stroked my forehead.

"Your brow is furrowed," she said. "But I will not press you. I know you have much to occupy your mind. There is much to be done before winter. Just rest for now."

I closed my eyes, enjoying the soft summer weather and the sensation of Morning Star's fingers lightly tracing the lines on my face. Some of the lines were scars, and some were simply the etchings left by time and years of exposure to the elements. Moments like these were rare and ever so precious to me.

It was not to last very long. The quiet was disrupted by a loud whooping sound, no doubt emanating from Fox's latest pet, signaling their impending arrival. The previous year, Puh, Black Wolf, and I had taken our teenage sons on a hunt, during which we had stumbled upon a hyena den. The mother must have retired from her pack to give birth in this lair, and when she sensed our presence, she charged from the cavity she had dug from an earthen bank and came at us with her formidable teeth bared. We had attempted to retreat, but she would not allow us to simply withdraw. Perhaps she was so relentless because she feared we would take advantage of her absence at a later time and do harm to any potential cubs. We were forced to kill her.

Upon inspecting the hyena's body, Fox noted her engorged teats and surmised that she did indeed have a litter of little ones. He wanted to check the inside of her den, so we retraced our steps to the hyena's home. There, we found a number of wolves, which must have been awaiting just this opportunity; in fact, it was probable that the mother hyena had been harassed by these wolves in the recent past. Many of the wolves carried a deceased or still-squirming cub in their maw. They promptly ran off as they heard our approach, taking their prizes away to be consumed at a more private locale.

It was understood that this was the way things worked. For one to live, another must give up its life. Nevertheless, Fox seemed unusually dismayed. When we turned to leave, a pitiful whimper escaped the den. Fox was at the den's opening in an instant; he knelt and reached in, pulling out a plump hyena cub. Fox begged to keep it, and I reluctantly relented, but only because I did not think an unweaned cub would survive for very long without its mother. However, I had underestimated Fox's animal-rearing skills. Now, we had a full-grown hyena with which to contend.

A hyena's gender is ambiguous; all hyenas outwardly appear male. The most noticeable difference, except in a pregnant or nursing hyena, was that the females tended to be the larger of the two sexes. We could not tell for sure if it was male or female, but given the size this animal had obtained, I guessed it was female. Fox simply named her "Ena," and she followed him everywhere. Morning Star would not allow the animal in our home, so Ena lived outdoors, but she never strayed.

I sat up with a tired groan, watching for the boys' approach. Soon, I could see them as they raced across the field that spanned the distance between our compound and the lake, their long hair flying behind them and their faces alight with glee. The boys were clad only in loincloths, and they each held a string of fish that swung to and fro as they ran.

"We three will always be together! And as long as we are together, we can do anything!" Fox called out to his companions.

I smiled at his exuberance. Fox looked like me, but he had Morning Star's spirited nature. Ena loped along beside them, keeping Fox within her sight at all times. When the boys reached us, they proudly displayed their still-dripping catches.

"Look, Puh-Puh," Fox said to me. His voice had deepened and it was rather husky in tone. "I caught three trout." He then held the fish toward Morning Star. "See, Muh-Muh?"

"You did well," I said, congratulating Fox. "Mror, Oak, those are some very nice fish." The other boys just smiled broadly and nodded at my words.

"I see," Morning Star responded to Fox. "Where did you leave Bewok and Weasel? Did they not come back with you?"

"They are following, but they are walking." Fox answered in a manner that bespoke a disdain at their elderly ways. Both men were about the same age as me. "They would not run."

Ena stood beside Fox, drooling as she often did, and looking up at him adoringly.

"I gave Ena a few of the smaller fish to eat," Fox told us. He then cast a glance around. "Where is everyone?"

"If you mean your siblings, I am expecting them at any moment" Morning Star replied. "They are visiting your grandmother."

"Oh." Fox then turned to Mror and Oak. "Let us clean our fish and set them up over the fire pit. Some of the coals from the midday meal should still be hot."

The other boys again nodded their reply and they departed, fish still in hand, with Ena at Fox's heels. As I watched them walk away, I reflected on how much my son had grown. He was tall, and he already had the beginnings of a beard. He would still need several years to finish filling out, but he was well on his way to manhood.

"They will no doubt eat all those fish just as soon as they are cooked," Morning Star said with a laugh. "It is just as well, since they are usually seeking sustenance sometime in between the midday meal and evening sup."

We continued to chat amicably until we saw our daughters exit the home of Little Fawn and Black Wolf.

"Ah, here comes the rest of our family," Morning Star announced.

"Willow, Fawn, do not run ahead!" Pony, our thirteen-winters-old daughter called to her younger sisters, who trotted in the lead, giggling at some mischief.

Pony was the eldest of our girls, and she was toting her baby brother, Eagle Owl, while her next-youngest sisters Raven and Lily walked sedately at her sides. Our newest addition to the family was known to us simply as *Owl*. I took a moment to feel pride and to marvel at these children; each so beautiful and amazing in his or her own way. Perhaps all parents felt this way, but I liked to think it was more than the simple miracle of life and Morning Star and I bringing the next generation into the world – that somehow our love made our family special.

Morning Star and I had come from two different peoples: me from a clan of Old Ones, and she from a tribe of The People from the East. I was but a boy when I first became captivated by the lithe little girl who would one day be my mate. At that time, I had not realized that a man and woman from two different peoples did not generally become paired or what trials we would face should we choose to do so. It was never far from my mind that our family existed only by incredible good fortune.

Unlike Fox, our daughters and our youngest son mostly took after their mother. All but nine-winters-old Lily had Morning Star's shiny black hair, tawny skin, and dark eyes. In contrast, Lily had reddish-brown hair, pale skin, and hazel-colored eyes.

I had left the naming of our children to Morning Star. The people of my clan were given real names, such as my Puh was Tor and I was Tris. The People from the East named their children for things. For example, Morning Star's father was called Black Wolf and her mother was Little Fawn. Our offspring's monikers did not matter much to me, so – with only a little trepidation – I left that to my mate. Our newest infant, little Eagle Owl, was named for one of Morning Star's revered relatives. Six-winters-old Willow was named for Willow Woman, who had been our dear friend and the former Head Elder of The People. Additionally, she was Oak's mother – and, until her death, she had also been Black Wolf's paramour. Morning Star's mother, Little Fawn, was rather put out by this choice, so the next daughter, who followed only a year later, was called Fawn after her grandmother, even though it was not usual to name a child for someone still living.

Within moments our daughters stood before us, and little Owl began to writhe in Pony's grasp. He let loose a hearty wail and leaned toward his mother. Morning Star laughed as she took the baby from Pony's arms.

"Are you hungry, my love?" she asked Owl. "Thank you, Pony. You girls must be getting hungry as well. You may see to building up the fire, if you would like."

"Will we eat some of that big deer?" eleven-winters-old Raven asked.

"No doubt we will," I replied.

"And possibly some fish, if Weasel and Bewok have caught enough to share with all of us," Morning Star added. We had already watched the boys cook and consume theirs. To me she remarked, "Why do you not try to get some more sleep? At least until the evening sup."

"I just might," I said, grinning, thinking on how nice it would be to have a good nap.

I leaned back against the wall of our home, contentedly watching my mate nurse our baby as she simultaneously instructed the girls on collecting tinder to revive the now-dying coals and gathering firewood from our wood cache. Our youngest daughter, Daisy, was but three winters old, and she tagged along, eagerly trying to help but usually presenting more of a hindrance. When her elder sisters had managed to coax small flames to life, Daisy placed green leaves on the little fire; it caused an acrid smoke to fill the air and nearly extinguished the flames. I called to Daisy.

"Come to me, Daisy – sit," I said to her, pulling her onto my lap when she came within arm's reach.

Daisy obligingly settled onto my lap and snuggled against me, placing her thumb in her mouth. Morning Star chuckled.

"I predict you both will be asleep before long."

* * *

I awoke from a dreamless slumber when the tantalizing aroma of cooking food infiltrated my senses. Daisy was still in my lap, snoozing soundly. I did not wish to disturb her, so I just sat quietly, observing the various activities that were going on around me. The skies had begun to darken as the sun moved closer to the horizon, and the fire within the hearth had been raked down to a bed of red coals, over which our dinner cooked.

Morning Star was at the hearth with a number of women, but when she turned and saw I was awake, she left the meal preparations and approached Daisy and me.

"Are you feeling renewed by your nap?" she asked me.

"Indeed, I am," I said with a smile.

"Good. Now to make you look more like yourself." Morning Star disappeared into our home and emerged with a forked stick she used when she worked with my hair. "Turn around so I can access your back, and I will tame and rebind your hair."

I did as bidden, still holding Daisy. Morning Star knelt at my back and began to untie the leather thongs that kept my hair in place. This was a laborious process. We Old Ones did not traditionally cut our hair, except to trim off a short length once a year. We believed our hair endowed us with a unique awareness of the world around us, and to cut off any substantial length was to lessen that insight. Therefore, our hair grew to be very long. Most adult women of the Old Ones wore their hair corded and bound and pinned to the back of their heads, while most men wore their hair corded and bound into a thick rope that hung down our backs.

Morning Star was well practiced at this. She diligently untangled the now-matted bundle of hair and divided it into manageable sections. As was the nature of curly hair, it wanted to re-curl upon itself, so working with the direction of the curl, she twisted each section into a cord. Then each cord was gathered up and lashed into a neat rope that was easily long enough for me to sit on. In fact, rather as if I had a tail, I had to be careful I did not sit on my hair wrong and thus cause my head to be suddenly yanked to the back or side.

Fox had returned by now, and he sat nearby, solemnly watching his mother and me.

"Perhaps my hair may be bound this summer," Fox said to us.

The binding of a young man's hair was a sign of adulthood. Most people of the Old Ones were considered adults at fifteen winters old, but a male might earn this status earlier if he made his first big kill before that time. I glanced at Fox.

"That is possible," I agreed.

I did not want to tell him that I had become a man at his age, and that his grandfather, my Puh, had also become a man well before his fifteenth winter. I did not want Fox to feel pressured to make his first kill before he was ready. He was both large and strong for his years, but he was also rash and impulsive. These were not traits to which most hunters aspired. A good hunter must be patient and must wait for his best opportunity. To rush into a potentially risky situation was not only less likely to successfully bring in meat, it was also more likely to injure those taking part in the hunt. A poorly struck animal posed a serious hazard to all involved, as it might kill you before you could dispatch it. Thus, I wanted Fox to be not only big enough to take on the tasks of a man, but mature enough, as well. I sympathized with Fox, because I still remembered how I felt at that point in my life and how eager I was to be an adult.

"But you just brought in a huge deer," Fox said somewhat sullenly. This meant he would not have the chance to earn adulthood anytime soon. "We will not need to hunt again for a while. But Ena found a blood trail this morning. Perhaps we could follow it and see if we might come upon wolves scavenging a carcass. Muh-Muh said she would make a new winter coat for me, and a wolfskin ruff on the hood would be nice."

"It would," I agreed. Wolf fur does not frost over as many furs do, making it a valuable commodity. Fox had outgrown his coat, and doubtless others could make use of the fur and the wolf meat, too. However, by the time we reached any potential carcass, it would be well picked over. The likelihood that any wolves would still be interested in anything left would be slim. That being said, I saw no reason to mention my thoughts on the topic just now. I liked to encourage Fox to share his ideas without criticizing him unless it was necessary. "Let us speak of it when everyone joins us for the evening meal."

Fox nodded at this, evidently content to wait for a group discussion.

Gradually, more of our neighbors arrived to take their places around the hearth. This was one of my favorite times of day. During the warm-weather months we always gathered each evening to take our nightly sup together. Then we could look forward to socializing, getting caught up on the day's happenings, and making plans for future projects and forays.

Now that our food was cooked, we built up the fire once again. The sun had set, bringing about deepening shadows, so now there was just the firelight to brighten the circle of faces around the hearth. The sounds of our voices rose and fell over the undercurrent of chirps and hums from nearby amphibians and insects. The wind had lessened to a gentle breeze that occasionally caused the flames to dance and sparks to take flight. Flitting fireflies blinked from the surrounding woodlands, lending a magical air to the scene.

As I gazed at everyone around me, I thought on all those who used to be among us; those who were now gone. Some had moved on, others had passed on. I keenly felt the loss of my uncles, Inlee and Trae, and my aunts Soosha and Soonie, and our good friend, Slow Bear. They had managed to reach advanced years, so I could not begrudge them their well-earned rest, but I missed them terribly. Also, my faithful dog Raena was no longer here. She had lived for twelve years – a long time for a dog – but no matter if she had lived twenty, it would never have been enough. She was a good and loyal dog, and even though we now had Ena, she was not really dog-like. Ena was devoted to Fox, but she barely tolerated anyone else. I would have liked to get another dog from Black Wolf's dog breeder cousin, Gray Elk, but I had not the heart to give to another dog just yet. Someday I would, but not yet.

I then saw Fox shift in his seat, and it reminded me of his proposed hunt. I caught Fox's eye and smiled at him. The corners of Fox's mouth twitched upward and his eyes took on a hopeful glow.

"Fox and Ena made an interesting discovery today," I announced to the group.

Attention was turned my way, but I gestured to Fox to continue.

"Yes," Fox said, eagerly taking up the story. "Mror, Oak, and I were fishing with Bewok and Weasel this afternoon when Ena began to call out from somewhere in the nearby brush. Then she ran up to me and she nudged me with her snout, as though she wanted me to follow her. So we ventured just far enough to find several large bloodstains on the ground, hoof tracks and paw prints, and then a blood trail leading away into the forest. We did not want to leave our fishing gear unattended, so we did not go any farther, but my thought is that it appeared to be a fatally wounded animal, possibly a quite big one, such as an elk, maybe. The body might attract wolves, and we could use some wolfskins. I thought we could pick up the trail and follow it."

Fox abruptly ended his tale. A brief silence ensued while everyone presumably absorbed this news. Black Wolf shook his head, causing the many stiff braids that sprouted from the top of his head to jiggle.

"I am sorry to disappoint you, Fox," he said, "but even if we were to set out right now, by the time we found whatever had been injured, whom or whatever had done the injury is bound to have already taken most of the meat off the animal, leaving only scraps for scavengers. Did you see any wolf tracks? Wolves may have been the perpetrators. If so, they are long gone."

Fox's face fell, and his posture slumped at his grandfather's assessment of the situation.

"It was a good idea, Fox," my Puh said, having seen Fox's dismay. "We can still take a look, if you would like."

I did not relish the thought of going on another excursion so soon, but I was glad for Puh's suggestion.

"Yes, perhaps after we have recovered from today's hunt you can show us the blood trail and we can go from there," I added, trying to soften the blow.

"By then, nothing will be left and there will be no wolves . . .," Fox said heatedly, biting off his words when he realized it was pointless to press on. Part of him may have realized that his grandfather Black Wolf was correct, but another part of him, possibly the stronger part, urgently wanted to pursue a possible wolf hunt anyway. "Never mind," he muttered angrily.

I stiffened at Fox's rude behavior. It was unthinkable for a young man to address his elders in this way.

"Would you like to rephrase that, Fox?" I asked quietly, but in a tone that brooked no nonsense.

Fox seemed momentarily abashed.

"I spoke in haste," Fox responded. "Take no notice of what I said."

At that, with all the dignity a chastened fourteen-winters-old boy could muster, Fox rose from his seat by Morning Star and me. I felt sympathy for him as he marched around the assembly, Ena matching his step. Fox then resituated himself with Oak and Mror, probably seeking their company to soothe his ruffled feathers. Nevertheless, I was perplexed by his behavior. Did I act like this at his age? Puh sat to my left and I saw that he had also watched Fox walk away.

"Puh," I said, "was I like this when I was growing up?"

"No," he answered, shaking his head. "Although you were certainly impatient to get on with moving up to the next stage in life, you were considerably more subtle about it."

I pondered this. While it was comforting to know I was not alone in thinking that Fox was indulging in an excess of drama – the kind of fuss I would have been embarrassed to display at any age – I wondered how best to address it.

"I just do not understand him," I confessed to Puh. "His emotions are all ups and downs."

Puh was silent for a moment. He pointedly looked across the fire at Fox's other grandfather, Black Wolf, but he did not say anything. Black Wolf had been a steadfast friend to Puh since their boyhood, but if Black Wolf had any foibles, his most prominent was his volatile temperament. Also notable, were his unusually lofty height and a deep voice that could reach rumbling depths that would make even the biggest boar bear proud. At times Black Wolf seemed to employ his rages strategically, knowing that his size and his fury were apt to cow any opponent into submission. Of all his children, Morning Star was the only one who also had his fiery nature, but on the occasions when it surfaced it was always for good reason. Her two brothers and three sisters were all rather placid in disposition; this I considered to be something of a wonder, knowing that Little Fawn was almost as excitable as was Black Wolf.

"When Fox has had time to think about it, he will realize that such a hunt is not likely to gain us any wolfskins, or anything else, for that matter," Puh assured me. "He is not stupid; he is simply stubborn. Fox does not want to give up on his plan just yet. It may help to involve him in some other project in which he can refocus his attention."

"I like that idea," I said. "After a day's rest, I will be ready to embark on another hunt. The more experience he can acquire, the better."

Puh nodded. We sat in companionable silence, observing our sons and Oak as they were taken up in an animated discussion, Ena sitting close to Fox, her eyes glowing as they reflected the firelight. Fox was doing most of the talking while Oak listened with interest and Mror looked on, appearing thoughtful. Oak and Mror were a year younger than Fox, but they were already far more serious and sensible than he.

As the son of Black Wolf and the now-deceased Head Elder Willow Woman, Oak had been raised in his mother's household until the time of her death, so he was tutored almost from birth to conduct himself with poise and confidence. Oak was a winsome young man, but he had a quietly commanding presence. I thought he would make a good Head Elder when his time came. For now, Black Wolf acted as Head Elder in Willow Woman's stead, but only until Oak became an adult.

Mror was Puh's youngest son and my half-brother. Puh had taken a new mate, Ria, after my mother passed, and Mror was their only child. Ria had not conceived with her previous mate, and she had never expected to bear any offspring.　　Therefore, Mror was doted upon by his mother, but that did not seem to spoil him.　I found him to be a quiet and intelligent boy; and in stark contrast to his two very large companions, Mror was small and wiry of build.

Fox's mood seemed to improve as he talked.　I could not hear his words among the din of many ongoing conversations, but he was beginning to smile once more, and his bearing became more relaxed.

I was relieved at this.　I glanced over at Morning Star and our younger children.　They were in good spirits and enjoying the meal.　However, Morning Star had taken note of Fox's outburst.

"I gather you men will be making sure Fox finds some excitement in the next few days," she said to me.

"I believe so," I responded.

"That is well," Morning Star commented thoughtfully.　"He chafes because he feels he is being held back."

Morning Star then returned her attention to the baby on her lap.　I pushed my concerns about Fox from my mind.　Little Owl was bright-eyed as he watched the ongoing meal.　Owl sometimes clapped his hands, a new trick he had just learned. Morning Star occasionally took a bit of partially chewed meat from her own mouth and placed it in his so he could explore new foods.　He would not be weaned for at least another year, but in the meantime he would be given soft morsels to exercise his gums and help nourish him until he was ready for solid foods.　I was pleased that he ate so well.　Owl was a robust infant; already he was more than an armful for my petite mate, who somehow managed to birth and raise large children.  Even Pony and Raven were taller than their mother and outweighed her.  They often helped to care for their younger siblings and assisted with the household chores.

Morning Star then jarred me back to reality.

"Perhaps a bunch of you could take the boys someplace where you could *accidentally* lose that animal," she said.

I knew she meant Ena.  Morning Star had never liked the creature, even when Ena was a pup.  She did not trust a hyena of any age.  And actually, neither did I.

"If I did not believe it would make him even more rebellious than he already is, I would think it a good idea," I replied.

"Yes," Morning Star agreed with a resigned sigh.  "He should have named her *Shadow* instead of Ena; she certainly sticks to him as closely as his shadow."

"She gives him unconditional love and he loves her in return," I began.  "I am sure he feels the stresses of hovering at the precipice of adulthood, and he wonders if he will fare well during the coming hunts. Any hunt may be the one that will provide him with his first kill. Ena, on the other hand, provides comfort to him. She just lives to be near him. She does not judge him, or watch him, except to anticipate his next movement so she can match it."

Daisy was busy eating, but she paused to remark on our conversation.

"Ena stinky," Daisy commented frankly.

"That she is, my little Daisy," Morning Star concurred. "I hope Fox does not ask to bring her in this winter. She was just half-grown last winter; this year she is fully matured and much larger than Raena ever was. I do not want her in our home. She does not have the nature to live with the family. I fear she will bite one of us. I liked his pet crow, Kaw, much better than Ena. It is too bad Kaw did not follow us to our new home. Perhaps if she had, she would have satisfied Fox's need for a pet."

"I miss Kaw, and I am sure that Fox does, too. But I am inclined to think Ena will not like to be penned up with us for the winter," I said in an attempt to allay Morning Star's fears. Even Raena had found our rooms to be too warm and preferred to sleep by the doorway, where the air was cooler. Ena had an extremely thick fur coat, and I felt sure she would also quickly overheat in a fire-warmed structure. "With luck, the issue will never arise."

We did not dwell on the subject for too long. There was too much to divert our attention, what with all the many children of various ages to keep track of, both our own and those of our friends and relatives. I did not know it was possible to reside among such a large group, outside of living in a village. But this was a happy time, a time of plenty. One look at our families was proof of our good fortune. Everyone appeared well fed and healthy, and there were oh-so-many children. In lean times, things could be so dire that the old and the young perished and the strong did their best to hang on to life. I was grateful that we had relocated to this place. Here, we had all we needed to not just sustain ourselves, but to thrive.

Black Wolf then left his seat and came to join us. He folded his long legs to a sitting position by Puh and Ria.

"Our boys are certainly enjoying themselves," Black Wolf said, motioning over to where Fox, Mror, and Oak were chatting. "I am glad. Fox did not appear pleased that we would not track that blood trail."

"He was not, but he will get past it," I said.

Black Wolf nodded.

"He will," he agreed. "He is young; he will have forgotten all about it by now. When he is our age and he has just had to drag home most of a giant deer, he will understand. I am not too proud to admit that I am bone-tired. The only thing that might spur me into pursuit just now would be a two-legged being, rather than four."

"Might?" Puh teased.

Black Wolf laughed.

"*Might*," Black Wolf repeated. "Probably. If she were *sweet*."

"*Da!*" Morning Star cried out, feigning shock – but she was well acquainted with her father's proclivities and frequent dalliances.

I myself was more surprised that he was insisting on *sweetness*, or any other quality. Except for his faithfulness to Willow Woman, I had not known him to practice any particular loyalty or be terribly discriminating in his choice of partners. This was the main reason for the long estrangement between Morning Star's parents. Just the same, Morning Star did not appreciate that kind of talk in front of her children.

Black Wolf just grinned.

"A nice fat bird would suffice," Black Wolf added. "A *sweet* fat bird."

Morning Star rolled her eyes at him.

"Da!" She said again. "That is enough of that."

"Have it your own way," Black Wolf said, rising to his feet. "I bid you all a pleasant evening." And he walked away, limping just a little after our long trek, but still grinning.

 **Chapter Two** 

*Bits of rubble crumble and roll under my feet as I walk in near darkness, guided only by the mysterious orb of light that advances with me along the cavern's long corridor. The tunnel and the black void ahead seem to go on forever.*

I was mildly surprised that this Dream had visited me two days in a row. I was somewhat relieved that unlike the previous vision, there was no unsettling feeling of falling. I had teetered a bit on the stones, but I had not lost my footing. I had just walked and walked through a long and murky passageway. I did not know where I was going, but I had a sense of purpose, as though there were an anticipated objective that was just out of sight.

The next morning began very pleasantly. I awoke from my Dream before anything too untoward had taken place, and seeing that there was no light yet filtering in through the window opening, I knew there was no hurry to start the day. However, my full bladder inspired me to rise, if only for a short while, to go outdoors to empty it.

I always missed Raena, but I especially missed her at times like these. Throughout her life she had accompanied me on these nighttime or early morning jaunts. It was not only her presence I missed, but also her alertness to any possible threats. Even in her old age, her perceptions had been far keener than mine.

As I walked outdoors, I noted that the moon was low and the stars were slowly being blotted out by the hazy glow that hovered at the eastern horizon. I gazed toward Ena's shallow lair, where her nose and forefeet could often be seen within the shadows, but at this time it was still too dark to see her.

When I returned to our warm bed, Morning Star sleepily wrapped her arms around me and snuggled her face against my neck. I pulled her closer, enjoying the feeling of her body touching mine. The day would not begin for some time. We were ever eager to make the most of moments such as these. The children would awaken soon enough, and then there would be a constant stream of tasks ahead of us to keep our family fed and clothed.

When little Owl's whimpers reached our ears, we were by then lying peaceful and contentedly entwined with one another. Morning Star stirred.

"That is my cue to arise," she said, withdrawing her arms from around me.

"One more kiss," I requested.

Morning Star obligingly leaned in to press her lips against mine.

"Many thanks," I told her, smiling. "I must say, this has been a much sweeter way to start the day than stalking a buck as I was yesterday."

"I am glad you still think so, even after all these years," Morning Star responded, smiling back at me and giving me a last quick kiss.

"I will always think so," I promised her. "Of that I am sure."

Morning Star peered out the window opening as she quickly dressed.

"The sun is shining. I think it will be a nice day. It will be a good time to harvest grasses for bedding and making baskets; perhaps we can do that later," Morning Star said conversationally.

"Yes, that would be a good idea," I agreed. It did not sound too taxing a chore. I still was not eager to undertake any long hikes. Any restored energy I had gained overnight had already been spent in the morning's activities with my cherished mate.

Morning Star left me to tend to Owl, so I dressed as well. I could hear the other children beginning to rise for the day, too.

"Muh-Muh, what will we eat this morning?" Raven asked her mother.

"If ants have not gotten into the berries we picked yesterday, we can have some of those," Morning Star answered. "Then we will have smoked fish."

I came out of our chamber to see my mate nursing our baby while attempting to dress Daisy as our tousle-headed girls rubbed the sleep from their faces. It then occurred to me that Fox was not among them.

"Where is Fox?" I queried.

"I do not know," Morning Star said absently. She turned toward her daughters. "Have you seen your brother this morning?"

The girls exchanged glances and then shook their heads.

"I just woke up," Pony informed us with a shrug. "We have been asleep before now."

I thought back to when I had arisen earlier this morning. Had I seen Fox's slumbering form as I went by his sleeping nook, which, like his siblings' bed chamber, was just off the main room of our home? I could not remember if I had noticed him lying in the semidarkness.

"He must be outside. I will check," I said, and hastily ducked through the low doorway. After all, it would make sense that Fox would start the day with a full bladder as well. He and Ena may have taken a few steps into the forest to relieve themselves.

The sun shone brightly, and scarcely a cloud dotted the sky. Birds sang their songs in an enthusiastic welcome to usher in the new day. Other than that, there was little sign of life around our compound just yet. I scanned the dirt at my feet for Fox and Ena's tracks. The earth was fairly well compacted here, so there would not be much sign of their passing.

It was then that Puh suddenly appeared at the doorway to his home. His eyes bore traces of unease and he appeared to be perplexed. His mate, Ria, and my youngest sister, fifteen-winters-old Mi, soon followed. Mi was the last child of Muh and Puh still living at home, and she was as of yet unpaired.

"Puh, what is it?' I asked anxiously.

"Mror is gone!" Puh exclaimed.

Puh had always been a calm and self-assured man. I had seldom seen him in a state such as this. Ria and Mi also appeared shaken.

"*Gone?*" I repeated. A sudden chill wracked my body and I involuntarily shivered. "I just came out to look for Fox. He was not home when we arose."

Morning Star now joined us.

"Perhaps they went fishing?" she suggested.

"Mror would not go without telling us, and he knows better than to go to the lake by themselves," Ria replied.

"We must check with Black Wolf and Little Fawn to see if Oak knows what they are up to," Puh said, now decisive.

This made sense. Oak would certainly know if the boys had plans to do something. But before we could take a step, Black Wolf also exited his home, looking troubled. Black Wolf was wearing only a loincloth, even in the cool morning damp – but then I supposed his copious body hair might have helped to keep him warm. His coat of black fur was dense enough to almost completely obscure the tattoos that adorned his arms and legs.

"Is Oak with you?" Black Wolf called out to us in a panicky voice. "He was missing when we awoke and his pack, belongings, and spears are gone!"

I had not thought to look for Fox's pack or spears.

"I will see if Fox's are gone, as well," I said, quickly ducking back into our home, where my daughters looked at me quizzically.

"What is it, Puh-Puh?" Lily inquired.

"Did you find Fox?" Pony added.

"No, I did not," I replied, noting that Fox's possessions were not in their customary places. Even his collections of feathers, bones, and rocks were absent.

Daisy was sucking on her thumb, but she pulled it out of her mouth long enough to speak.

"I am hungry, Puh-Puh."

"I know," I said, picking her up. Daisy leaned her head against my bearded cheek, continuing to suck her thumb. "Pony, would you retrieve the berries your mother spoke of?"

Pony nodded, and disappeared into our storage area, soon returning with a covered basket. She removed the cover and displayed the contents to me. It was half-full of blackberries. No ants were in evidence.

"Many thanks, Pony," I said. "Would you see that your sisters get a share of the berries? I will take some for Daisy."

Pony again nodded, while I took a small handful of the fruit for Daisy, and then carried her with me outdoors to the group of people still standing near our entryway. Daisy happily popped a berry into her mouth, enjoying the sweetness and dribbling a little of the juice down her chin. I was glad she was oblivious to the crisis. By now, Puh had determined that Mror's things were also gone.

Puh began to search the grounds, seeking any sign that might betray which way they may have passed. More of our neighbors left their homes and joined in the search. As Puh and I walked together, our eyes constantly scanned the ground.

"I know they are trying to help, but I wish they would stay away," Puh murmured.

"Yes, their tracks may obliterate any traces of the boys' travels," I concurred. "All we can do is stay ahead of the others and hope they do not accidentally erase the signs we seek."

"Look over there," Puh said suddenly, pointing toward the meadow where many of our loved ones had previously been interred.  The tall summer grasses amongst the stone cairns still glistened with dew, and many of the stalks were bent, showing fresh trails through the field.

As we approached the lea to further investigate, the others began to also venture in that direction, including the compound's various children and dogs, who delighted in chasing one another through the last wisps of cool morning mist.  There was no point in holding them back from running through the meadow; the boys' straight trail and Ena's more wandering path as she canvassed the area were unmistakable.  Daisy pointed at the cavorting children, saying *Run! Run! Run!*  By now, I was also wearing some of her sticky berry juices.

"Where are they going?" Morning Star questioned. "There is nothing for a long way in this direction, except lots of woodlands."

"That is the way home," Puh replied simply.

"*Home?*" my sister Mi echoed. "Our old home?"

"Fox has always said he wanted to go home," I mused grimly. "We must go after them."

"You must first have something to eat," Morning Star insisted.

"Yes, we must eat and make ready to leave," Puh agreed.

We all turned for our homes so that those of us who were about to embark on this journey could prepare ourselves, but then movement overhead caught my gaze. I looked skyward, where several vultures wheeled in lazy circles. This was a sober omen. Perhaps they were merely drawn to the remains of whatever creature had left the blood trail Fox had spoken of yesterday, but I squelched a rising sense of worry over the fate of my son and his companions. It would do no good to speculate on the numerous misadventures to which they may have fallen victim.

* * *

Puh, Ria, Black Wolf, and I quickly finished dressing and collected gear and weapons for this impromptu trek. Morning Star stuffed me as full of food as she could before she and the children bid me farewell. The look in Morning Star's eyes haunted me as we set off at a fast pace. She had held me tightly and kissed me, before staring into my eyes and saying, *Bring him home.*

"We will find them and bring them home," I promised, but the terrible memory of my brother Dak niggled at the back of my mind.

Dak had been a Second Son. With the Old Ones, Second Sons are those who are usually relegated to staying home to protect the family while the father and oldest son hunt. Dak did not want to stay home, and one day while Puh and I were away he slipped out. Puh and I returned to find Muh frantic. She had also begged Puh and me to bring Dak home. But what we eventually found was

Dak's remains. He had been attacked and eaten by wolves. He was brought home, but only to be buried.

I could not let myself dwell on that.

Clan members Bewok and Weasel also joined us; they were paired with my sisters Twie and Saree, respectively. Bewok came to us from The People of the Wolves tribe. Their culture was vastly different from ours, but the Wolfmen had been good friends to us for a number of years before Bewok became paired with Twie. Like all the Wolfmen, Bewok was covered from head to toe with highly stylized animal tattoos, each one representing a successful hunt. Bewok was good-natured, and he had adapted easily to our ways. We did not ask him to give up anything, but without drawing attention to it, he stopped wearing his wolfskin cloak and grew out his close-cropped hair. Twie was a sensible and affectionate mate, and they made a happy pairing.

Weasel had come to us from one of the People from the East's tribes. He had come and gone from our compound many times before finally asking to settle in with us a few years ago. He had begun to court my sister Saree, then newly of age, when she was fifteen winters old. I was surprised that she would consider him. Saree was then technically nubile, but she was dainty and girlishly slim. Her red-gold curls and pale green eyes were strikingly disparate to Weasel's coarse black hair and dark eyes. Weasel was twice her age, and large and hairy. Owing to an affinity for fighting as a vocation and a form of entertainment, his face showed the abundant effects of such a brutal pastime. He was missing all his front teeth, leading him to use novel pronunciations. For example,

Saree came out sounding more like *Aye-wee*.  But Saree did not seem to mind.  She seemed to have no trouble focusing on his finer qualities, such as his kindness, good humor, loyalty, and his steadfast devotion to her.  They already had one little girl, and she was expecting their second child by autumn.

* * *

The dew had evaporated in the sun's warming rays and the day's heat increased as the six of us hiked steadily. Fortunately, our quarry's trail was easy to follow.  If they were indeed on their way to our old compound, they might make the journey in four or five days, depending on how hard they pushed.  I hoped they would not move too quickly so that we could catch up to them all the sooner, but it appeared they were eager to complete their journey.

Black Wolf generally liked to sing when we were on the trail.  It not only helped to pass the time, but it gave any people or creatures in the vicinity ample notice that we were approaching. This day, however, he did not sing, and he scarcely spoke.  His face was set in a stonily determined expression, but then I supposed mine was too.  At odd moments – as when we could briefly pause to examine a footprint or discarded item, such as bones from yesterday's buck, which they must have taken to sustain them over the start of their trip – Black Wolf would sputter *Rascals! Imps!*

When nightfall came, we still had not caught up with them.  We continued to walk, but we debated what to do. Clouds were gathering, threatening rain.  That did not concern us as much as the fact that the clouds would hide any moonlight that might illuminate the way. Reluctantly, we decided to make camp for the night before all light had disappeared.

Puh began to strike up a fire while Bewok, Ria, and I collected deadwood, and Black Wolf and Weasel set up a lean-to from a hide tarpaulin and a number of fallen branches. As I gathered wood, I realized the level of my thirst and hunger. I had been so set on covering the most distance possible that I had neglected to realize that I was quite parched, and my empty stomach was churning. The others must have been feeling the same, because as soon as we settled by the fire, we brought forth our water bags and opened our packs for the dried stores to eat. They were not very filling, but they were light to carry and dense with nutrients.

We did not talk much; each of us was occupied with our own thoughts. How could those boys have taken off like this? What foolish notions had filled their heads, apparently winning out over more sensible judgments? Did they not know the risks they were taking and the worry they were causing their loved ones? It was a heart-wrenching situation for all of us, but Ria was absolutely beside herself. Puh had tried to talk her out of accompanying us – after all, she was in her late forties by now, and this could be a long trek. We were traveling light so we could travel with all possible speed, so there would be few comforts. But Ria had insisted she would not be left behind in the search for her only child.

I heard a fox bark in the distance, and then an owl called, soon answered by the deeper reply from her mate. Fox and owl, the same as the names of my two sons. I sighed and wished I would fall asleep. It was going to be a long night and an even longer day on the morrow.

* * *

Puh gently nudged me awake the next morning. The night had seemed to go on forever, but I must have succeeded in dozing off. I took note of the gray sky. It was cool, as it was most mornings, but at least it had not rained. The winds were steadily increasing. Perhaps the rain would begin soon. I hoped it would hold off until we found our sons, because a heavy rain would wash away many of the signs we looked for to follow their trail. A wet trail was harder to make out. The tracks, if any remained at all, would be less distinct. Even though we were fairly sure we knew their destination, it was reassuring to see signs of their passage.

We took down our camp without making a fire and, not wanting to waste time, we broke our fast with more dried foods as we set out. We were so engrossed with pursuing the boys that we were startled when we came around a bend in the trail and found a number of red deer as they grazed. The deer jumped, and so did we. One of the deer barked at us – a sound that somewhat resembled a cough – and then they scattered in all directions. I rebuked myself for my inattention and resolved to be more aware of my surroundings. When I thought of it, I realized that I had seen the deer's droppings and signs of their feeding, but they had not registered in my mind. These were things to which I should have been more attuned. A glance at my companions' faces told me that they were also affected by this surprise encounter. We were fortunate that it had been a herd of deer and not a she-bear with cubs or some such creature.

It was then that the skies opened up. The rain pelted us.

"*Rascals! Imps!*" Black Wolf exclaimed.

"What?" Bewok said, confused by Black Wolf's outburst at the rain.

"We would not be out here getting soaked if not for those imps!" Black Wolf sputtered.

"With luck, the rain will slow them down," I said hopefully.

"I hope you are right, but I fear it may hurry them," Puh responded.

"The faster we move, the warmer we will feel," Bewok pointed out, as always offering a cheerful perspective.

It was a dreary, wet day. Many of the animals sought shelter, but we did come across one damp bear that took one look at us and bounded off, and another herd of grazing deer. These were fallow deer, and this herd also boasted many fawns. The frolicking little ones were slower to leave, but like the deer we had encountered earlier, these too vacated the area.

"I wish we were hunting," Ria said, fingering the tip of her little bow, which she carried slung over her shoulder, along with her quiver, under a cloak to protect them from the rain. Her bow was not big enough to bring down red deer, but it might have killed some of the smaller fallow deer. "We could have brought down a number of animals."

"The boys might be thinking the same thing," Puh said. "It could be they will try their luck. I have been pondering the notion that they hope to make their first kills and become men."

"That would make sense," I agreed. "Fox has been very vocal about that lately."

"*Impatient rascals!*" Black Wolf interjected.

"All boys are impatient to become men," Weasel said. "I was."

"Did you ever run away?" Bewok inquired, wiping the rainwater from his face.

Weasel shook his head.

"No," he answered. "But I had other distractions. I was learning how to become a fighter. Hunting was not so good where we were. It was more likely that a man would make a name for himself as a fighter, rather than as a hunter, and win meat and other goods. And besides, my father had picked out a mate for me, and I wanted to do as he wished so he would not withdraw me from the proposed pairing."

I had not heard of a parent withdrawing an offer to allow a couple to be paired, once the deal was sealed; that must have been something unique to his clan. However, the pairing had been doomed, anyway. Weasel's first mate had passed in childbirth.

Weasel was an adequate hunter and tracker, but he was an even better fighter, and I could attest to Weasel's prowess as a combatant from personal experience. Some years ago I had been asked by the former Head Elder, Willow Woman, to take part in a Challenge. The question at hand was whether or not to allow all clans and tribes to take part in The People from the East's annual fall Gatherings, which were formerly restricted to members of The People's tribes.

This was hotly debated before it was suggested that the matter was settled by a bout in the Challenge Circle. Willow Woman would pick her contender while the opposition would choose theirs. Willow Woman had chosen me, and as she was my friend, I would have done anything she requested of me. The opposition had chosen Weasel, and while he did not have a particular opinion on this matter, he was curious to see how he would fare against a man of the Old Ones.

Weasel was one of the largest, most robust men of The People I had ever seen, but while I was slightly shorter, I was still the heavier of us. I won, not because I was an adept opponent, but because we Old Ones do not battle with closed fists, as do The People. Weasel was simply unable to put up a defense against this unknown method of fighting. That being said, Weasel was a man to be reckoned with. It was fortunate that he was so affable, and he seldom set out to do harm to anyone under most circumstances.

Night fell again, without our seeing Fox, Mror, or Oak. We came upon a rock overhang where it appeared they had spent the night, and a pile of droppings that probably belonged to Ena. We guessed they were hers since they contained some bits of bone, but no fur and not as much bone as one would note in a wild predator's excrement.

The rain went on without letup, and in the evening we built a small trailside hut framed with saplings, thatched with leafy branches from nearby trees, and topped with our tarpaulin to keep out the worst of the damp. It was too wet to make a fire, and we were sopping wet, ourselves. The shelter was too small to hold the entire lengths of our long spears indoors, so the weapons were laid one on top of the other, their spearheads sticking out the door opening. There was also no room to lie down – but considering that we had little more than our body heat to keep us warm that night, no one minded being crammed together. Or at least no one voiced any complaints.

Ria might have had some reservations about the sleeping arrangements, but I noticed that Puh curled up tightly around her. And at least she could use her cloak as a blanket. No one else had chosen to bring their cloak. While I was glad not to subject Morning Star to these hardships, I missed her terribly. I slept poorly, awakened as I was by shivering off and on all night.

The morning brought improving conditions. The rain was by then just a light drizzle that came and went, while patches of blue skies peeked through the clouds now and then. Again, we decided not to build a fire to warm and dry ourselves before hitting the trail once more; we simply packed our gear and left, nibbling dried stores to fuel our bodies for the day.

"Black Wolf, you are limping," Ria said to him. "Take this. It may help."

Black Wolf had been scowling with pain, and probably with annoyance as well, since he was still incredibly put out that our sons had absconded. His expression softened and he surrendered a brief smile as he took the small sack from Ria.

"Thank you," he responded. He dug out a bit of the sack's shredded willow inner bark and began to chew. The taste of willow's inner bark was known to be vile, but it was also known to help deaden pain. Black Wolf's feet had caused him agonies for years. He generally suffered in silence, but after a time on the trail his limp would become more pronounced.

Just now Black Wolf looked pitiful indeed; he and Ria were the same age, but in many ways he had not aged as well as she. There was a time when Black Wolf looked younger than his years. His skin had been relatively unlined and his thick hair as black as a moonless night, but his beloved Willow Woman's demise had seemed to cause Black Wolf's years to suddenly pile upon him. His hair and beard were now streaked with white, and his lean face was etched with deep creases. On top of his outward appearance, Black Wolf's many years of trekking long distances had damaged his exceedingly large feet, and today he was using his spear to aid each torturous step.

I wondered how many more long journeys he would have to endure before he would be one of those who remained on or near the compound for the rest of their lives. Given that he was temporary Head Elder until Oak took on the role, it was likely Black Wolf would have to go to the Gatherings, far to the South, for some time to come.

I also thought on our pace. At this rate we were unlikely to catch up with the boys before they reached our former home site. I was sure I was not the only one who was acutely aware that we needed to find our errant offspring as soon as we possibly could, before they came to grief.

When we made a stop to rest at midday, Ria seated herself by Black Wolf's huge feet and, without asking, she placed one in her lap and began to massage it.

"Tor," she said to Puh, "you take the other foot." Ria smiled at Black Wolf. "We will do what we can to make this more bearable for you."

Puh did as he was bidden. Black Wolf seemed embarrassed to be the recipient of such care. He was speechless for a moment.

"I can manage," Black Wolf said, finally finding his tongue. "I will walk faster this afternoon. It is just that we had gone after that deer the day before and my feet were already sore." Black Wolf popped more of the bark into his mouth and began to chew it resolutely.

"I know you can manage," Ria said soothingly. "Let us do this. No one can get through life alone; we all need one another from time to time. Besides, I remember plenty of occasions when you have helped me. Do you recall when I unexpectedly went into labor with Mror? You and Tor delivered him. If you can do that for me, I can rub your feet for a bit." Ria suddenly became somber, recollecting the birth of her missing son. But then she forced a smile and went on. "Relax for now."

Black Wolf seemed to take heart at this.

"Thank you," he said softly. "And yes, I do remember that day. It was a summer day, like this one and we had been deer hunting."

Bewok began to laugh at the memory.

"Karno was aghast," Bewok said of his Wolfman friend, who had also been present at the birth. As I remembered, Karno's vivid and colorful description of the event to his comrades had been quite amusing. I too grinned as I replayed the scene of Karno's reenactment in my mind. But we Old Ones did not laugh aloud, as did the Wolfmen and People from the East. We believed that to make noise when you laughed or cried was to draw attention to yourself that might lure a predator to you.

When we were ready to recommence our hike, Ria quickly adjusted Black Wolf's many braids while he was still seated. His normally stiff braids were looking rather droopy and dispirited after the previous day's rain, but she greased them lightly and straightened each one out so they once more resembled the *spider hat* coiffure for which Black Wolf was so well known.

When we set out again, I thought it seemed as though Black Wolf had a bit of a spring in his step. We were able to move at a faster pace now. At each stop Black Wolf's sore feet were massaged, and he chewed more of the bitter bark. But just the same, although we continued to see signs of their progress, we did not manage to find Fox, Oak and Mror.

 **Chapter Three** 

Despite our having pressed hard to cover as much distance as possible, the fourth day arrived and we still had not found them. The only good thing was that we had also not found evidence that they had met with any dangerous beasts. I was impressed that they had come so far without adult supervision. Their camps had been situated on high ground, among live trees, so there was less chance of having a rotten tree or branch fall on them, and in areas sheltered from the weather. They had replenished their water bags at fast-moving streams.

I did not know how much food they had brought with them, but I speculated that they must be very hungry by this time. Trail food never quite fills the stomach, and three active growing boys require a lot of fuel. I had seen no signs that they had departed from the trail – not even once. So it did not appear that they had attempted to try their luck at hunting. They seemed to be steadfastly trekking with all possible expediency toward our former homestead.

As the afternoon wore on, I began to smell traces of smoke. My companions picked up on this as well and we exchanged quizzical glances. I was relieved when three people and one very large creature came into view, albeit in the distance. I could not yet make out faces, but the thatch of bright red-gold hair on the bigger of the two red-haired individuals and the presence of a sizable hyena could only signify that we had come upon our boys and Ena.

We all smiled to have finally found them. Our quarry, however, were not all entirely pleased. Except for Mror. He grinned broadly at the sight of us, and he rushed up to his parents, throwing his arms around them.

"Muh-Muh! Puh-Puh!" Mror cried out delightedly. "How happy I am to see you all!"

"We are pleased to see you, as well," Puh replied, wrapping Mror in a tight embrace.

Tears streamed down Ria's cheeks.

"I was so afraid you might be hurt. Or worse!" Ria told him. "Why did you leave?"

Mror now appeared remorseful.

"I am sorry to worry you," he said. "I . . ." But then he bit off his sentence abruptly.

Fox had been squatting by the fire, but now he stood up, wearing a decidedly defiant expression. He did not approach us but let us continue to close the gap between us. Oak also stood, but unlike Fox, he appeared apprehensive. He knew his father's explosive temper and, while he did not seem frightened, he did seem to expect that he was going to face consequences for his actions.

"*Imps! Rascals!*" Black Wolf muttered, as he had innumerable times since we had left home.

Oak now came to his father's side and took his arm in a formal greeting, in the traditional way of The People.

"Hallo, Father," Oak said solemnly. "I am sorry you have made this journey. I can see your feet are hurting you. Come sit by the fire." Oak brought Black Wolf to a huge fallen tree, where they had chosen to break their trek. A large root made a comfortable seat, and there Oak ensconced Black Wolf. Black Wolf was obviously fuming. He was so angry had had not yet been able to form words. Oak took note of this. "I know you are irate, Father, and rightly so. I would not have put you out like this, but we – um – I did not think anyone would pursue us."

"*Rascals!*" Black Wolf shouted this time. "Not pursue you? Are you not my own son, future Head Elder to your people?" Black Wolf was trembling with fury.

Oak hung his head with quiet dignity.

"I can see that I was wrong," he admitted. "I humbly beg your pardon." Oak then turned to look each one of us in the eyes. "All of you," he went on. "I very humbly beg your pardon."

"Yes, Muh-Muh and Puh-Puh, I am ever so sorry," Mror added. "And to the rest of you, too, I am so very sorry."

I was not surprised that Fox had not yet acknowledged us. He stood, his stance wide and arms crossed. It struck me just then how much he looked like a man, even though he was still so young. I went to him, where I met his cold gaze. I did my best to remain calm, but I was torn between wanting to hug him tight and never let him go or hit him for the distress he had caused all of us. I had no question as to who had instigated this poorly conceived adventure.

I then took notice of all the feathers that were blowing around the site. A freshly killed, naked bird was skewered and roasting over coals at one side of their fire.

"You are roasting a grouse, are you not?" I said, pointing to the bird.

Puh nudged Black Wolf.

"There is your fat bird," Puh said, pointing to the grouse, recalling Black Wolf's afore-mentioned desire.

"Not the kind of bird I had in mind," Black Wolf grumbled darkly. Evidently he was not yet ready to see humor in anything.

Fox was taken aback at my words. He seemed to have anticipated I might say something harsher, or at least commented on his sudden departure from home. Fox studied me for a long moment. I wrestled with my conflicting emotions, but I maintained an unperturbed visage.

"Yes," he answered at last. "Mror threw his hatchet at it and killed it. We were hungry and thought we would camp here for the night."

I looked around.

"There is plenty of deadwood to keep your fire going until morning," I said blandly.

"That was my thought, too," Fox responded, still looking at me warily, as though he expected an outburst from me at any moment. Fox drew in a breath, and then he said, "I am not going back. I am not a child. I know how to survive on my own. I am going to live at our old compound. You cannot make me go back."

I wanted to shake him and rail at him about how unrealistic his plans were, but then Puh broke in.

"You do not have to camp here," Puh said.

"What do you mean, Grandpa?" Fox asked Puh, using a more respectful tone. "This is a good camp, is it not?"

"It is," Puh conceded, "but the old homestead is just a short distance away."

"How far?" Oak questioned.

"Not far," Puh said, motioning down the trail. "I can hear the stream. That means we are almost there."

"Close enough to carry the grouse and cook it there, Puh-Puh?" Mror queried.

"Yes," Puh said with a nod. "Bring some of the coals with us. There are some big sheets of bark on the ground we can use to carry them."

Oak, Fox, and Mror set to work picking up the best sheets of tree bark and used them to scoop up the red coals, while Puh and I put out their fire and pushed sand over it to keep it from rekindling in our absence.

"Grandpa, how did you hear the stream?" Fox asked Puh. "I did not hear it. I still cannot hear it."

Puh shrugged.

"I was listening for it," he said simply.

When we arrived at the stream, it was then just a short walk to the compound. I had not visited our former home in many years, and it looked more dilapidated than ever. Trees and brush sprouted up in odd places, and the central hearth where we had once gathered for our evening meals was overgrown with tall grass. The coals had lost some of their heat during transport, but the boys set them down on top of the grasses and then broke up the now-smoldering sheets of bark over the top. After a little fanning, the coals reddened and little tongues of flame licked the bark. I gazed around us for deadwood to add to the fledgling fire.

A small blaze was quickly built up, sending white smoke skyward as the green grasses within the hearth burned, and the grouse was resituated over the renewed coals. We continued to collect firewood while the bird began to roast once more. I was somewhat dismayed to see lion tracks on a few of the patches of bare earth. As I scoured the area, I noted a well-scavenged carcass near the compound, partially obscured by the foliage at the edge of the forest. I supposed that was what had enticed the lions here, and I was glad to see it was picked clean; there was nothing left to interest a lion. In fact, there was hardly meat enough on it to draw flies. Ena, nevertheless, was quite interested. She settled herself on the scattered remains and began to gnaw the semi-disarticulated skeleton, loudly cracking open the bones with her strong jaws.

My thoughts were racing; we should open up one of the old dwellings and make it habitable so we had a place to spend the night. Also, I needed to find a way to persuade Fox to return home with us. I guessed that Mror and Oak would readily come back; perhaps that would be enough to change Fox's mind. He must know he could not stay here by himself.

I ventured a glance at Fox. His head swiveled as his eyes searched the branches of the nearby trees. All at once, he cawed like a crow. Other birds sang, but there was no reply in kind. Fox cawed and cawed. Still, there was no answer. Fox's shoulders slumped.

"She is not here," he murmured, still looking to the skies, his face betraying his angst. "I had hoped Kaw would be here."

"She would be very old if she were still alive," I said gently.

"I so wanted to see Kaw." Fox's voice broke with these words. "I have missed her so much. She has always come to visit me every time I have stopped here."

"You have Ena, now," Oak said, also trying to comfort Fox. "Ena loves you."

At that moment, all that could be seen of Ena were glimpses of her rump and tail through the brush, as she enthusiastically crunched the bones of whatever unfortunate beast had perished there. Black Wolf settled himself by the hearth, at last able to get off his aching feet for a while. We left the boys and Black Wolf to tend the roast and the fire while the rest of us worked to clear away the heaps of rocks and tree trunks we had left blocking the entrance to Puh's old home. Each of us had placed substantial barriers over the entryways to our homes to prevent animals from taking up residence, just in case we might need to return some day. Even the chimney openings were covered by huge rocks.

We had removed our packs and set aside our spears and had just begun to tackle the heavy debris when I heard Fox say, *Oh, look!*

"What is it?" I asked, tugging at a section of tree trunk that was well-mudded into place. I blinked as dirt from the freed tree trunk sprayed my face as it jarred loose.

"It is a baby!" Fox exclaimed.

"*Baby*?" Ria repeated. "What kind of baby?"

We turned in unison to see Fox crouched by the partially collapsed home that had once belonged to the Wolfmen. They had hastily constructed it for a brief stay at our compound. It was the only dwelling that had not been walled in, since it was only a small temporary structure.

"Come on, come out," Fox said in a soft voice. "I will not hurt you."

"Fox, perhaps you should come away from there," I suggested, my voice rising in alarm.

"It is just a baby," Fox responded, reaching into the opening. "Oh, do not bite me!" he admonished the unseen creature. "Oh, there are more! There are lots of babies!"

It was then that I heard the sounds of twigs snapping. Not quiet crackles, like those made by a being walking on dried sticks, but violent fractures – as though a bear were breaking through the brush at a dead run. All manner of small animals leapt into action, entering the compound in a mad dash to avoid an undesirable meeting with this oncoming beast.

As a group, we spun to face the sound, and suddenly a lioness was in our midst. She pounced from the forest's edge and landed near the Wolfmen's old home. Her hackles were up, and her teeth were bared; all the while she uttered a series of low growls. The lioness ignored us and the roasting meat and the fire. Her eyes were focused on Fox, who was still kneeling at the entrance to the collapsed dwelling.

Fox also turned to face the lioness. He had no weapon other than the knife at his belt, which he slid from its sheath.  The rest of us were also divided from our spears, since we had been wrestling heavy objects from the doorway when the lioness appeared.  The lioness now crept forward toward Fox, still snarling, her body slung low to the ground.  I debated whether I could reach my spear before she could strike; it could be that my movement would distract her enough to give Fox an opportunity to escape.  I feinted to my left, causing the lioness to jerk her head around – and then, as she attempted to follow me, I darted to the right, throwing myself in the direction of my spear.

However, my ruse did not keep the lioness's attention.  When she saw that I was moving away from her cubs, she returned her focus to Fox, and she moved to leap at him.  Fox raised his knife to meet her.  Now I had my spear in hand and sprinted up from behind the lioness; when she heard my footsteps, her attention was once again distracted.  For an instant, she looked between Fox and me.  The others had also regained their spears, and they, too, began to move toward the lioness.  But suddenly, Ena burst forth from the brush.

Ena's great weight hit the lioness at the shoulder, bowling over the creature.  We watched in awe at the hyena's ferocious attack, despite the lioness's larger size.  A female cave hyena is bigger than even the biggest wolf, and significantly heavier and more powerful. Nonetheless, a lioness might be as much as twice a hyena's weight, and this one had the added incentive of having young offspring nearby. The lioness grappled mightily with Ena, fur flying from both animals while their dripping blood stained the earth.

"Ena, *no!*" Fox cried out, frantic at the sight of the horrible battle. "Ena, get away!"

Ena's thick fur offered some protection from the lioness's teeth and claws, but still, she had already suffered numerous lacerations and puncture wounds. She bled freely from several places. Ena's strength was beginning to flag. Finally, the lioness pinned her to the ground by her throat.

"Ena, get up," Fox called to her, distressed. *"Please get up, Ena!"*

"We have to kill her while she is thus occupied," Puh said to us.

I nodded.

"Ria, you stay with the boys," Puh instructed. Even had she wanted to join in, her bow was too small to do any real harm to a lion.

The rest of us descended upon the lioness, thrusting our spears into her ribs, where we might hope to hit the lungs or heart. The lioness dropped Ena and wheeled to face us, but she was mortally wounded and soon collapsed. From start to finish, the entire encounter had lasted only a matter of moments.

We stood, panting, taking in the bloody scene. Fox had seemed frozen in place, but now he came to life and he rushed to Ena. Poor Ena was still alive, but only just. Fox sat on the ground, cradling her enormous head in his lap and stroking her ravaged fur as blood oozed from Ena's torn throat.

"Oh, Ena . . . Ena," Fox said, weeping.

Ena was wheezing and struggling to breathe as she lay in Fox's arms, gazing upon him with a look that spoke of a complete and unfettered love. Then her labored breathing ceased and she went still, all but her twitching paws.

I knelt by Fox and placed an arm around his shoulders. I wanted to say something, but I could think of no words that could match the magnitude of the sorrow now afflicting him. Fox pivoted in my embrace and he, too, put his arms around me, sobbing silently in the way of the Old Ones. I held him tightly; I did not know what else I could do but just be there for him.

"Tris," Puh whispered.

I looked up at Puh, and then at the grim faces that surrounded us.

"I know," I said. We all knew.

"We cannot stay here," Puh said, vocalizing what we were all thinking.

"I know," I said again.

Just then, Puh looked in the direction of our burial grounds, and I realized he wished to visit the graves of our loved ones; my Muh, Gran, and many others. I very much wanted to stop there, too. Puh seemed particularly pained. We did not often come this way, and I guessed he did not like to miss the chance to honor and mourn our family members. But there was no time.

"There is probably at least one litter of cubs in that broken-down hovel," Black Wolf pointed out. "It is likely that more than one lioness makes their home in this area. And where there are female lions, males will eventually come to seek them out."

Bewok shuddered at the thought. Years ago he had been attacked by a male lion, and he still carried vivid scars from the ordeal. Lionesses will often go off to find a secluded place to have their litters to protect the young cubs from the males. The males will sometimes kill the cubs if they can, to encourage the lionesses to go into heat again. Nevertheless, the males would continue to search for their missing mates and, if luck was with the cubs, they would survive their first meeting with the father.

I hated to press Fox, but it was imperative that we leave here as soon as possible.

But I did not need to. Fox lifted his face from my shoulder and wiped his eyes and nose on the back of his hand. He looked around him – the two dead beasts and the group of forlorn people standing at his side. He nodded and stood up. Fox squared his shoulders.

"I suppose we cannot bury Ena?" Fox said, fresh tears streaming down his cheeks.

"I am sorry Fox, we cannot," Puh answered. "We must go now. Lionesses often stay together in extended family groups, and I fear that one or more lionesses will have heard the fracas or smelled the blood and will return any moment."

Weasel and I pushed dirt over the fire while Fox returned to Ena and hugged and petted her one last time before we took our leave of this place. Then, with Mror and Oak carrying the spitted grouse between them, we promptly began to walk toward home. I kept an arm around Fox's shoulders as we marched, but before the compound was lost from sight, Fox turned briefly for a final look at his friend. An air of desolation hung over the scene. Fox sighed and brushed away his tears, and we walked on.

When we reached the stream, we stopped just briefly to top off our water bags and Fox and I washed the blood from our bodies. Some of the lioness's blood had sprayed on me during our attack as she fought with Ena, but Fox was covered with Ena's blood. He was also wearing a lot of the fur that had been ripped loose by the two battling animals. It would not do to carry with us the strong scent of blood and freshly killed hyena, as it would only attract predators.

Watching for signs of lions, our group trekked steadily along. I could still feel my heart beating strongly within my chest. Every sudden sound made me jump. Poor Fox seemed downcast, indeed. He no longer wept, but the paler tracks from his tears were highlighted against his dirt-stained visage. Even after bathing at the stream, he had somehow neglected to thoroughly clean his face. Given Ena's dreadful end in the lioness's jaws, we had ample motivation to keep us moving at a fast pace. With the realization that we would not be able to stop to finish roasting the grouse before it spoiled, it was soon cast away.

I was happy that we were able to make it all the way back to our previous night's camp before evening fell. We were amazed to have covered so much distance in such a short time, but it can be astonishing how fast and far you can go when you believe lions might be hiding behind every bush.

Our camp was a quiet one that night as we sat around the fire, each lost in thought. Oak and Mror were very solicitous of Fox, wanting to show support and comfort him. Fox had led them on an ill-advised campaign, and they were horrified by its outcome. But they were also cognizant that Fox had paid a terrible price for his folly. And it appeared Kaw was gone, too. Fox was morose and mostly silent for our journey homeward. He was stoically dry-eyed, his face devoid of emotion, and he did chores around our camps without being asked. Inasmuch as I had previously bemoaned his disobedience and mischievous nature, I was saddened to see his spirit so completely shattered.

* * *

When we neared home, Puh whistled loudly to let everyone know we were returning. The residents of the compound turned out to welcome us, Morning Star at the lead. She ran up to us, throwing her arms around Fox and me.

"I am so glad you are home!" Morning Star cried out joyously, with tears of happiness and relief in her eyes. She kissed me quickly, but then covered Fox's face in kisses. "Oh, Fox!" she went on, "how could you worry us like this?"

Fox hung his head gravely.

"I am ashamed of what I have done," Fox replied soberly. "I am very sorry. I hope you all will forgive my reckless and thoughtless behavior."

And with that, Fox walked glumly away and ducked into the open entryway of our home.

Morning Star looked at me quizzically for an explanation.

"He has learned a hard lesson," I told her. "And on top of that, Fox is heartbroken. His long-held dream of returning home was crushed and Ena was killed during his misadventure."

"Oh," Morning Star said thoughtfully. "I suppose they are lessons he would have to confront at some point before he becomes a man."

"I believe you are right," I agreed.

 **Chapter Four** 

*The sun shines down upon us from a cloud-studded blue sky as we ascend the foothills. As if caught up in the bright and happy mood of the day, everyone is smiling and tackling the steep slope with good humor.*

I was so pleased to wake up from a pleasant Dream for a change. Often my Dreams seemed dark and mysterious, as though to offer a warning. In this Dream, however, it seemed as though a number of our compound's residents were on a journey. My entire family was present, and I also saw Puh and Black Wolf among us. Perhaps there would be others, as well. We seemed to be going to the cavernous mountain home of Black Wolf's cousin, Gray Elk, whom we had not visited since Raena had last delivered a litter of pups. It was usual for us to bring any unclaimed puppies to Gray Elk, who, as a dog breeder and trader, could then either use them as breeding stock or offer them in trade for goods.

Gray Elk, if he was still alive, would be quite elderly by now – perhaps close to sixty winters old. He had looked well when we last saw him; I hoped it would still be so. As we began our day, I contemplated speaking of my Dream to Morning Star. My thought was that Fox would be heartened to think we might bring home a new dog. He had lost Kaw and Ena, and while I disliked the idea of rewarding bad behavior, he had been extremely downcast since our return home. Fox did his assigned tasks mechanically, showing no enthusiasm for anything whatsoever. Most concerning of all, even food no longer interested him. He was no match for his mother's determination, however. Morning Star gently badgered him into eating, but he did so only to please her. I decided I would wait until we were out of earshot of the older children before speaking to Morning Star so as not to get their hopes up in case she thought my idea to be imprudent.

I was still mulling this over when Binty poked his head into our doorway. Binty was the adopted son of my younger brother Ty and his mate, Aessa. Binty was twenty-two or -three winters old at this time, but he still lived with his family, despite his being paired with one of Black Wolf's daughters, a young woman named Sky. Binty did not hunt because of his lack of hearing, but he worked alongside Ty processing firewood and creating useful items from wood, bone, rope and twine. Binty waved hallo to us and then he pointed at me.

"*Tis cawm,*" he said. Binty was not able to verbalize many words or speak clearly, but he had learned to make sounds by imitating the shapes our mouths made when we spoke and, by trial and error, he had begun to speak after a fashion. Binty motioned for me to come with him, and then he made his fingers move like walking legs. I nodded and leaned down to kiss Morning Star.

"It appears I am being summoned," I said to her with a smile.

Morning Star smiled, too, and she returned Binty's wave.

"I will see you later on, and then you can tell me all about it," she said.

It was not often that I was asked to go to my brother's home. In fact, I could not remember the last time I had been there. Ty and I had never been close, but nor was there any animosity between us. I had assumed that the lack of closeness was simply because our lives kept us at a distance. When our brother Dak was killed, Ty became the Second Son, whose duties were to take care of those at home, whereas mine usually kept me afield.

Ty was standing outside their dwelling, with a large bow in hand. He looked up as he heard our approach.

"Pleasant day to you, Tris," Ty greeted me. "Many thanks for coming."

"Pleasant day to you," I replied. "I am happy to help whenever I can."

Ty nodded solemnly and then he thrust the bow at me.

"I have been working on this bow. It is the heaviest one I have yet constructed. I strung the bowstring just this morning and I had hoped you would try it out for me — that is, if you would not mind," Ty said, explaining his reasons for requesting my presence.

"I see," I replied, giving the bowstring an experimental half-draw pull. "You know I am not good with bows," I reminded him.

Ty laughed. It was good to see him smile.

"You may not be good with bow, but you have the strongest draw of anyone here," he said. "Bror is the only one who comes anywhere near your strength, but he cannot draw back as far as you can. I need to see how robust this bow is, to find out if this combination of wood and bowstring is reliable, and also powerful enough to bring down big animals."

Earlier versions of these big bows had not been successful over the long term. They broke either at the first full draw or after a few uses; therefore, they were not dependable weapons. I still preferred my spears. They did not have the range of a bow and arrow, but they were the best weapon we had and, when used with skill, were quite deadly.

I stood back and cautiously gave the bowstring a somewhat longer draw. I had had too many bows splinter apart in my hands to not be wary of this happening once again. The wood creaked ominously. Ty and I exchanged glances.

"Full draw, if you please," he said.

I drew back once more, this time to the full extent of my reach. The bow complained even louder this time, but it held together. I maintained the draw until my arms started to tire, and then I slowly eased back on the bowstring.

"Would you like me to try again with an arrow?" I asked.

"I have not yet made any long enough for a full draw with this bow," Ty told me. "But when I do, I would appreciate if you would try it again. Would you give it a few more draws without an arrow?"

"I will," I said.

I pulled back on the bowstring several times. Each draw made the bow creak in protest, but it did not break. Ty took the bow from me and examined its back for signs of fractured fibers or cracks in the wood. He nodded with satisfaction that all seemed well.

"Many thanks," Ty said, voicing his appreciation. But then he looked at me more closely. "I do not see much of you, but when I do, I am reminded of how much everyone on this compound counts on you and the other hunters to bring in what we need to survive."

I was surprised at his remark. He had never expressed anything like this to me before now. I also thought it ironic, since Ty's labors also did much to contribute to our welfare.

"But your work . . ." I started.

"My work is nothing compared to what you do," Ty interrupted. "What you do gives you status within the community; not just here among our own people, but in the world at large. You attend The People's Gatherings; when Karno of the Wolfmen visits, he seeks out you, Puh, and Black Wolf. I do not think if he has ever so much as acknowledged my existence."

"I am not sure I would worry much about Karno's lack of civility," I broke in. "I like Karno, and I feel he has many fine qualities, but he is not what I would call a model of courtesy."

"Still, he would be more solicitous of me if I were a hunter," Ty pressed on. "I admit I have envied you your position as First Son. You had Puh's attention and tutoring, and you have excelled at all he taught you. It has enabled you to make a pairing that none of us could hope to attain. You have even been confidant to The People's Head Elder – that is, until she died. It makes me feel very small."

At that moment it dawned on me that this was likely the reason Ty did not seek out my company more frequently.

"It was never my intention to make you feel that way," I said, my heart heavy to hear his words. "I do agree that I benefit from the gift of being First Son, and I am grateful for that. But I have never felt that you were any less a man than I, or that your work is any less valuable than mine. I have nothing like your talent with wood and bone. Do you recall the first time I tried to build a travois sled? We ended up using it as a smoking rack."

Ty seemed earnestly touched to know his work was appreciated too.

"I enjoy working with wood," he said. "I think about new ways to do things all the time. I am experimenting with some smaller travois sleds to try on Black Wolf's dogs this winter. They are old and not strong enough to pull a regular sled very far. I think a lighter sled would be easier for them . . . ." For a moment, Ty had seemed excited to talk about his proposed projects. "But, of course, it is boring compared to hunting. Stories are told about hunting; no one tells stories about building sleds."

"Ty, I have been hunting with you; you are a fine hunter," I said firmly. "And if it is any consolation to you, I have always thought that you were the more intelligent of the two of us. In many ways, you resemble Muh; you have her dark red hair. But Puh is a thinker, and you have his deep, subtle way of thinking."

Ty gave me a wry but sad grin.

"Many thanks. I do not think anyone else has ever noticed," he said. "You are the kind of big brother every boy has ever wanted and wanted to be like. But then, I have always felt I was being compared to you and always coming up lacking. It has been hard. It is hard for Fox, too. He knows he is expected to be like you. To be measured against you."

I was stunned by this news. Especially his mention of Fox. It had never occurred to me that Fox might be comparing his own accomplishments to that of a grown man. Ty's expression softened as he must have noted the look of shock on my visage.

"I did not know . . .," I responded.

"Do not take my words to heart," Ty said. "I do not know why I am bringing all this up. I have no right to complain. You have earned your place in life. Every time I look at you – your great scarred physique – I know we all must honor you and the other hunters. You take care of us at the expense of your own well-being."

"We take care of one another," I corrected, but I had to acknowledge to myself that his body was relatively unscathed when compared with mine. However, I did not waste much time pondering the differences in our lives.

My role had been laid out before me from birth.  Besides, I wanted very much to lighten his mood.

"I have thought about making a trip to see Gray Elk; why do you not come with us?" I suggested. "Puh has talked about using a specialized sled to maneuver through the mountain trails. Perhaps you could speak to him about it."

Ty brightened at this.

"Would you take Morning Star and the children, as you did last time?" he asked. "I would like to bring Aessa and at least some of our children. If Aessa is reluctant to bring the entire family, Binty and Sky could look after anyone who stays behind."

"I am going to talk with Morning Star about it later today," I said. "I suspect she will welcome the idea. She has spoken of wanting to make a journey."

"Well, that is certainly a long trek," Ty concurred. "You have lost Raena, and Puh has lost his dog, Auchs. Black Wolf likely wishes to replace some of the dogs he has lost, as well. I think the time is ripe for us to make an excursion up the mountainside."

"I agree," I said, pleased that he was receptive to the idea. "I will speak with Morning Star first, but perhaps we can bring up the subject at this evening's sup."

"Yes," Ty said, nodding with enthusiasm. "And then we can make plans. I will need to ask Puh about the kind of sled he wants to use. The mountain trails will be narrow and rocky. Like the dog sleds I have been thinking about, they must be light, but sturdy enough to stand up to the rigors of the landscape."

I left Ty to return to my own family. I was still somewhat dismayed to know how he had felt about me for all these years, but now that I knew, I hoped I could in some way make amends. I also mused about Fox. Did he, as Ty had said, feel pressured to be like me? I thought about my own boyhood; I had aspired to be like my Puh, and to this day, I knew I was not his equal, but I looked at him as someone to emulate. I did not feel the need to be just like him; I simply hoped to keep learning, even if I would never be as skilled or as wise as my Puh. I also speculated that I may have been mistaken in assuming that the very astute must be a happier people, by virtue of being secure in their knowledge that they had a keen intellect. Ty had one of the finest minds I had ever known, but he was not inclined to be content. My thought processes might be comparatively simple, but I believed I was better off for it. I had my share of concerns, but I had nothing like the worries that seemed to plague Ty.

When I found Morning Star, she was mending a basket. Daisy sat by Morning Star's side on a wisent hide that looked rather like my cloak, doing her best to entertain her baby brother while her mother was busy. Morning Star smiled when she looked up and saw that I had returned. She gave the repaired basket handle an experimental tug and then, satisfied that it would hold, she put the vessel aside.

"Hallo, Tris," Morning Star said. "You appear cheerful. Was Ty not his usual dour self?"

"Yes and no," I replied.

"Ah, well, that sounds like an odd reply," Morning Star responded. "How so?"

"Ty was in an unusually talkative mood. I tried a new bow for him, but then he divulged some things he has never brought up before. He believes he does not have as much relevance within the clan as he could have. I hope I have tempered that notion, at least to some degree. I wish I had known how he felt before now," I admitted. "But it was good to speak with him."

"That is well. I am sure he feels better for it, too." Morning Star rose to her feet and lifted Owl off the wisent hide. "Come, Daisy. We must find your siblings; they are helping your grandmother again. Oh, and Tris, you may want to pick up your cloak. Daisy brought it out to sit on. Then we can go see Mama."

"I am glad they are so attentive to your mother," I said, bending to pick up my cloak and shake out the bits of grass and dirt.

"Yes, even Fox is over there; he is splitting tinder for Mama," Morning Star told me.

"While the older children are not here I would like to bring up a notion I have been thinking on," I began. "I thought we might go to see Cousin Gray Elk. I think Fox's grief might be at least somewhat eased if we brought home a puppy. He was crestfallen when Kaw did not appear at the old compound, and then what happened to Ena . . . ."

Morning Star winced at the thought of what had befallen Fox's unfortunate pet. I had given her the full story of what occurred the previous night, after the children had gone to bed.

"I did not like that animal," Morning Star said. She paused as she shuddered at the thought of Ena's gruesome ending. "But I did not wish her to meet a horrible death. Poor Fox. He feels these things so terribly. Yes, I think you have a good plan. I have felt Raena's loss; I would like another dog as well. And I have missed our cousins on the mountain."

"I had hoped you would be open to the idea," I said. Then I noted that Daisy had come to stand beside me. She lifted up her arms in a wordless request to be picked up. "Hallo, my little Daisy. What do you think about getting a puppy?"

"*Puppy!*" Daisy repeated enthusiastically. Then a new thought seemed to cross her mind. "Not stinky puppy like Ena?"

"No," Morning Star said, shaking her head. "No more stinky puppies."

Morning Star and I toted our youngest children across the compound to the home of her parents, where Morning Star and the little ones went in to retrieve our girls, while I went to the wood cache. There I found Fox, Mror, and Oak hard at work. Fox had worked to create a pile of finely split wood while the other boys labored to hack logs into firewood-sized chunks.

"Pleasant day to you all," I greeted them.

"Pleasant day," the boys answered in unison.

The boys wore just their loincloths and sheens of sweat. They were all encrusted with bits of wood fibers and bark, but Oak and Mror were grinning, nonetheless. Fox was still somber, as he had been since leaving the old homestead.

"Fox, would you come with me?" I asked.

Fox nodded, setting down his axe and wiping his forehead with a gritty forearm. I led the way as Fox silently followed. We went but a short distance, just far enough away from the others to allow us to speak in private. I gazed thoughtfully at my son, taking in his untamed mass of long curly hair, which he was so eager to have bound, well-littered as it was with bits of wood debris; his flushed skin, as yet unmarred, and his tall and well-muscled frame. I smiled at him, but Fox just looked at me wearily.

"I have spoken to your mother about going to Gray Elk's," I announced. And then I waited for Fox's reaction.

Fox's eyes flew open wide.

"To get a dog?" he questioned, at last breaking out of his melancholy.

"That is the idea," I said. "Your mother thinks we should go."

Fox drew in his breath.

"I would like that," he responded, seeming surprised at this news. "When will we go?"

"We will speak of it at the evening meal," I told him. "But it would have to be before too long. We must come and go before the autumn hunts."

Fox did indeed seem very pleased, but he just nodded again.

"Fox," I said, causing him to look up at me sharply. "If I have not mentioned this lately, I want to tell you I am proud of you and I love you."

Fox suddenly turned and put his arms around me. Even considering how dirty and sweaty he was, I cherished that moment.

"Oh, Puh-Puh," he said. "I love you. And I will never stop being sorry for leaving as I did – especially when I think of the look on Muh-Muh's face when we came back. I never meant to cause such pain. And I also regret persuading Mror and Oak to go with me. They did not really want to go, but they would not let me go alone, even if Ena was with me." Fox's voice broke as he spoke Ena's name.

I patted his back.

"I know losing Ena was hard," I said, "but she was a wild thing, and you would have eventually lost her, anyway. Like Kaw, the day would have come when Ena would want to leave. All creatures must live their lives in the way they are meant to. A hyena is not meant to live with a family of humans. They need their own families."

"Now that I hear your words, I realize that you are right," Fox said slowly. "I am still sorry, however – more so than ever, when I think that Ena did not have to die, nor the lioness. She was only trying to protect her babies. There were so many cubs hiding in there, and they will die without their mother."

"It is very possible that a number of lionesses were using the site," I said, trying to console Fox. "Lionesses, often sisters, or mothers and daughters, will stay together. We can hope that another lioness adopted the orphaned cubs."

I gave Fox's shoulder one last pat and let him go. Fox was quiet for a moment.

"Mror, Oak, and I might have been killed had you not found us in time, too," Fox said, his chin trembling and moisture glinting at the corners of his eyes. "We would have arrived at the old compound and been set upon by lions. I know that an angry mother is a force to be reckoned with; it was unlikely we would have survived. Not all of us, anyway. And all those who came after us in pursuit – I put your lives in danger as well." Fox paused. "Puh-Puh," he went on. "You have not rebuked me for leaving as I did."

"Would it have helped anything if I did?" I asked. "Would it have changed your mind and made you want to return with us?"

Fox seemed to consider this. He shook his head.

"I suppose not," he finally said. "But many thanks for not yelling at me. When Grandpa Black Wolf shouted at Oak he was quite fierce. It is a good thing Oak is so calm; he took it well, but I would not like to be shouted at like that. I am glad that you are my Puh-Puh."

I smiled to hear that Fox was grateful for his parentage, and I ruffled his hair affectionately, eliciting an answering grin from Fox. Then I thought back on all The People's Gatherings I had attended. Shouting was a normal part of the proceedings. Most of the Gathering's attendees were not often in the company of so many people at once, and thus, they were not accustomed to being subjected to so many different opinions and personalities. In their attempts to share their own strongly-felt ideas and be heard over the din, they raised their voices accordingly.

Sometimes they rose to their feet as they railed against whatever had piqued their ire, reminding me of an angry bear demonstrating a territorial display to an unwelcome intruder. Unlike an angry bear, however, once the fit of temper was expended the individual usually calmed quickly. Oak had been present at every Gathering held since his birth, so I was sure that Oak did not take much notice of forcefully conveyed vocalizations. That being said, I was also sure that Oak did not like to displease his father. He had been very contrite from the moment we had caught up with our missing sons.

"Let us take our leave of Oak and Mror, deliver the tinder to your grandmother, and get you cleaned up," I said, changing the topic. "I do not know about you, but I am hungry."

Fox's eyes lit up.

"I am hungry, too, Puh-Puh," he agreed.

I felt relief. Fox's appetite had returned. All was well.

* * *

As night fell, kith and kin assembled at the large central hearth in the middle of our compound. The giant deer buck we had killed almost half a moon ago was still the mainstay of our evening meals. Much of his meat had been smoked, and by now it was becoming tough and dry, but it was still good when served with fresh greens and roasted tubers, onions, and mushrooms. The labors of many, including Morning Star and our older daughters, had gone into creating this meal. After we had left the home of Little Fawn and Black Wolf, Fox and I had noshed on a few handfuls of berries, which were plentiful at this time of year, and part of a roasted rabbit left over from the midday meal.  Nonetheless, we were already feeling the rumblings of our stomachs when we gathered. I edged closer to the hearth to gauge the readiness of our sup.  My sister Ru noted my avid interest in the ongoing food preparations.

"It will not be long, Tris," she assured me. "But this is the last of that deer.  Bror has spoken of the need to hunt once again." Bror was her mate.

We had plenty of dried and smoked stores, but we did not like to consume them for our nightly sup unless nothing else was available.  Those stores offered sustenance during winter and other times when the weather was not conducive for hunting fresh meat.

"Then it is likely we will hunt on the morrow," I responded.  I noted to myself that we must speak on many things that night – organizing a hunt too, now, as well as discussing a trek to Gray Elk's home.  Then a flurry of activity around the entrance to Black Wolf's domicile caught my attention.

"Hold open the door flap!" Black Wolf's deep bass roared from across the compound.

I looked to see him awkwardly carrying Little Fawn out the small doorway, struggling to get her untangled from the flap of hide that covered their entryway.  Their daughter Petal hastily came to their rescue and held the door flap aside for her parents.

"Thank you, Petal," Black Wolf said, gazing at her fondly.

Petal smiled and nodded in response.

"Sit down, you two. I will get your food," she offered, leaving Black Wolf and Little Fawn to settle themselves on matting near the hearth.

Little Fawn had been unable to walk more than a few steps for several years now. She was an exceedingly tall woman. In her youth she had been robust in build, but years of toil had taken their toll and eventually crippled her. Black Wolf was also very tall, and while he was somewhat lame of foot himself, he was still quite strong and other than trying to wrangle his mate's lanky physique out a doorway that was decidedly under-sized for a smooth exit in this fashion, he had little trouble with the task.

I, too, seated myself, and Daisy joined me, sitting on my lap. Her thumb was in her mouth, but she popped it out to speak.

"Puh-Puh," she began. "Why Grandma not walk? Grandma not learn to walk yet?"

While I pondered how best to reply, Morning Star spoke up.

"Sometimes when people get older their bodies do not work as well as they used to," she explained. "Grandma has trouble with her back and her legs now."

Daisy thought on her mother's words. She seemed perplexed.

"We are carried when we are little, and sometimes we are carried when we grow old," I said, hoping that clarified the concept for her.

"Carry us when our legs not work?" Daisy finally seemed to grasp the idea.

"Yes," I told her, "that is right."

Black Wolf had been following our conversation.

"It is about taking care of your family," he stated. "No matter what, we always take care of one another."

Black Wolf and Little Fawn had not enjoyed a congenial pairing during most of their relationship, but when you are paired, it is understood that you will take care of your mate. He may not have always been a faithful partner to Little Fawn, but he had always made sure his family had everything they needed.

Daisy seemed satisfied with his answer and did not probe further. Then our daughters Pony and Raven approached us carrying trays of cooked food.

"Many thanks," I said to Pony as she stood before me offering food to each of us, one at a time. Pony smiled and nodded in return.

Daisy took a choice piece of meat and a roasted onion and left my lap to trot over to Little Fawn and Black Wolf. She gave the onion to Black Wolf and the meat to Little Fawn.

"Why, thank you, my little flower," Black Wolf said with a laugh, "I do believe this is the first time I have been gifted with an onion. I am indeed honored."

Black Wolf then pulled Daisy onto his lap and gave her a morsel from his dinner.

"I am not a flower," Daisy said indignantly.

"She tends to take things rather literally, Da," Morning Star told her father.

"But your name is Daisy," Black Wolf said lightly. "Is that not a flower?"

"I am a little girl," Daisy said pointedly, looking at her grandfather as though he ought to know better.

"That is so," Black Wolf replied good-naturedly. "But we are not always exactly the same as our names would indicate." Daisy now looked at him blankly, so Black Wolf went on. "I am certainly not a black wolf. But I was partially named for my grandfather, who was Black Elk. My cousin Gray Elk was also named for him."

Daisy thought this an interesting concept.

"Grandma, who are you named for?" Daisy asked.

"I was not named for anyone," Little Fawn said. "I was told that when I was born, I came early and I was very small, but I had long legs like a fawn. So I was called Little Fawn."

The conversation abated as everyone started to eat. When the food was mostly consumed, I broached the subject of embarking on a trip to Gray Elk's home.

"I have been speaking with my family about getting a dog," I announced. "Of course, that would mean a journey to Gray Elk's. What say you, would some of you like to accompany us to the mountains?"

"I have been thinking on that as well," Puh chimed in.

"And I am down to two old dogs," Black Wolf added. Black Wolf usually had at least four or five dogs at a time, which he used for sometimes used for hunting boars and for pulling sleds; but like our canines, many of his dogs had become aged and had died.

"I would like to go, too," Ty piped up eagerly. "We would need a few sleds to bring enough gear and stores for the trip; I could make them in a day or two."

Puh looked at Ty thoughtfully.

"I think you are due an opportunity to leave the compound for a while," Puh said. "You have unselfishly served us with your unremitting labors. You must be yearning to see new sights and visit with new people. Will you bring your entire family?"

"No," Ty shook his head. "I have queried Aessa about making the trip. She is not interested in going. She does not care to travel. Fortunately, Binty is willing to take on my chores while I am away."

I was sorry to hear that Aessa did not want to join us, but I could readily understand why. This was not an easy trek; it would take us about five days to reach Gray Elk's, and much of the fifth day would be spent clambering up a very steep, rough trail. It was more of a surprise to me that Morning Star did want to go. However, she was very attached to her cousins, and it had been some years since her last venture there. No doubt she hoped to see them once again before she, like her mother, might become too frail to travel. Morning Star was fortunate to be in good health, but she did have eight children to tend. And especially now that Daisy was weaned, leaving only Owl still nursing, there was the potential that she could fall pregnant again at any time.

"We will need to hunt before we take an extended trip," I said.

"That is true," Black Wolf agreed. "I think my feet have recovered enough to go out on the morrow. Perhaps we could bring in a boar? That would be a nice change from venison."

"So the treatments are helping, Da?" Morning Star asked.

Gray Owl, our healer, had tried to persuade Black Wolf to submit to various remedies to ease the pain in his feet, but Black Wolf had stubbornly resisted. The latest outing to recover our sons had finally driven Black Wolf to seek out Gray Owl's help. Since our return, Gray Owl had been subjecting Black Wolf to a regimen of potions, oils, heated wraps, and foot massages. Gray Owl also entreated Black Wolf to stay off his feet whenever possible and not to run unless it was necessary. On this last point, Black Wolf was glad to accommodate Gray Owl. He vigorously disliked running and did so only when there was no alternative and it was absolutely required by the situation.

## Chapter Five

*Ominous gray clouds hang low in the sky, as though the rain within is weighing them down. Gusts of wind begin to whip through the forest, causing the trees to sway as though engaging in a synchronized dance.*

The next morning found me awake well before sunrise and ready to venture out for our boar hunt. Morning Star prepared a quick breakfast and helped me assemble my gear.

"I can feel a cold draft coming in from around the door flaps," she said as she secured my knife's sheath to my belt. "Will you wear a tunic today?"

I had been pondering this myself. The weather could be tricky at this time of year, and the previous night's Dream had done nothing to inspire confidence in the day's conditions. Mornings were often chilly, but by midday it could be downright hot. A long-sleeved tunic would keep me comfortable during the early part of the day, but then it would be burdensome once the heat settled over the landscape. Nevertheless, we could not be sure how long we would be gone. If we had to stay out longer than a day, I would need to don more clothing at night.

"Yes, I will," I replied.

Morning Star located one of my tunics and held it up for inspection by the light of a small lamp, this one being made from an upturned animal skull filled with fat and fitted with a braided fiber wick. Even in the dim conditions, it was obvious my clothing had endured a lot of hard use. Morning Star regularly checked each article for wear and needed repairs.

"This one is ready to be cut up into nappies," Morning Star announced, shaking her head at the condition of that particular item. "I will find another."

Morning Star took the lamp into one of our storage rooms, soon returning with a newly constructed tunic.

"I was holding this aside until winter, but I can see that if you need to push through a lot of brush, you will need something that will protect you from the thorns and all," Morning Star said. She knew that we hoped to bring back a boar or two, and that usually involved a lot of tracking the animals through densely wooded areas.

"Many thanks, my sweet." I paused to pull her to me and gave her a kiss before tugging the heavy garment over my head. It was still a little stiff and smelled of freshly smoked hides.

Morning Star left me once more to enter another of the storage rooms, where I could hear her movements as she placed various foods into little sacks. I busied myself with filling a small water bag from the large household bag. I would be carrying a pack that would contain just enough supplies to keep me fed and watered for a few days, plus a hatchet, rope, strands of sinew, pieces of flint and iron pyrite, and other necessary gear.

Fox was still sleeping peacefully. I went to his sleeping chamber and smiled to see him curled up so that he could fit within the space. It was time to enlarge his chamber – past time, actually. Fox had grown so much in the past few years that I wondered when he would stop. I was tall for a man of the Old Ones, but I supposed that it was probable he might surpass me and grow to a great height, like that of his grandfather Black Wolf.

"Fox," I said quietly, so as not to disturb his siblings. "We must go soon."

Fox cracked open an eye.

"Yes, Puh-Puh," he responded sleepily.

Fox dressed and ate at the same time, continuing to shove food into his mouth while he too filled a small water bag and loaded his pack with bags of dried foods and whatever additional equipment he chose to carry. He knew what to bring and stowed each item with care.

Pony awakened just as Fox and I were preparing to duck out the doorway.

"Wait! I want to say goodbye," Pony called to us.

Pony was still tugging her clothing into place as she appeared before us. She gave her brother a hug and then threw her arms around me.

"Farewell, my pretty one," I said to her, kissing her forehead.

"Farewell, Puh-Puh," Pony answered. "Stay safe and come home soon."

"We will return as quickly as we can," I told Pony, and then I released her so I could take leave of my mate. I embraced Morning Star for a long moment and kissed her for what I hoped was sufficient duration to reinforce the depth of my love for her. "Until our return," I said, looking into Morning Star's eyes.

"Yes, until your return," she replied.

Fox was already exiting the doorway, so I gathered up my spear and quickly followed, pausing for one last glimpse Morning Star and Pony as they stood side by side. I smiled at the sight. Like Morning Star, Pony would be a beauty. Of all our girls, Pony was the one who most closely resembled her. Pony was already taller than her petite mother, but she shared her slender, fine-boned physique. They returned my smile and waved.

* * *

When I emerged into the cool air, I was glad for choosing to wear a tunic over my loincloth, leggings, and boots. All but the brightest stars had been extinguished by the coming dawn. There was just enough light to see dark forms milling around the compound's central hearth, where a small fire had been brought to life. Puh and Mror crouched by the flames, warming their hands. As Fox and I joined them, Black Wolf and Oak also approached, and lastly, Bewok entered the circle of light around the fire.

"Are we ready to leave?" Black Wolf asked.

"I believe so," Puh replied.

Every passing moment the sun rose higher, giving the eastern sky a rosy glow and bathing the landscape in a soft light. We started down the trailhead, talking amicably and not bothering to hide our presence. The branches of the trees and brush were alive with birds. The tiny feathered creatures sang loudly, making us raise our voices to be heard over their song.

What we needed to do just now was to cover a lot of distance in the shortest period of time, and our noisy procession would warn animals of our approach. Many predators were still on the prowl at this time of day, and while they would not be apt to attack a group of this size, they also did not care to be surprised and we did not want them to react violently to our intrusion. However, if alerted to our proximity, they most often would move off without revealing their presence, and without choosing to engage in an attack that would be needlessly risky for both sides.

If luck was with us, we would be able to locate areas where the boars had been foraging the previous night and track them to wherever they had chosen to bed down for the day. But first, we had to find their patches of furrowed ground. Boars use their tusks to plow the earth in order to find tubers, roots, worms, and other small prey, but they will consume almost anything they can digest. They have been known to kill and eat animals as large as deer. Boars are intelligent, powerful animals, with keen a sense of smell and acute hearing. Their eyesight is not as good as some beasts', so that, and their habit of sleeping during the day, gave us a slight advantage. And, fortunately for us, boars are generally plentiful; they did much to provide welcome variety to our meals.

As usual, the three boys walked together, chatting and pointing out things of interest to one another. Fox was still more subdued than normal, but I was pleased to see that he was no longer as morose as he had been after his disastrous excursion to the old compound. Right now, he seemed especially alert. Nothing escaped his sharp senses. I liked to think that we were all aware of our surroundings, but at the moment, we were just in traveling mode. Hunting mode would not be needed for some time.

We hiked for a while without seeing any fresh furrows. The sun rose higher and higher, causing the day's warmth to be clearly felt by all of us. We removed our tunics as we walked, tying them around our hips or, for those wearing a newly made rather stiff tunic like mine, tucking our sleeves into our belts.

Eventually we reached a place where the furrows had been recently excavated. We paused as we looked over the site.

"A sounder," Puh said, referring to the group of sows, half-grown youngsters, and shoats. Indeed, the hoof prints indicated animals of all sizes. Puh pulled out his water bag for a swig. I thought it a good time to slake my thirst and did the same. The others quickly decided to have a drink as well.

"Yes," Black Wolf agreed, taking a long draught from his water bag and wiping his mouth. "A large sounder, by the looks of it. They certainly have dug up a lot of ground."

"Ho!" A voice called out from somewhere close by.

"That sounds like Karno," Bewok said, his face lighting up with pleasure, presumably at thought of seeing his old friend. Karno was the leader of the Wolfmen, and Bewok's friend since childhood. Bewok had left the company of his comrades to become paired with my sister

Twie, and while he seemed happy in his new home I suspected he missed his friends.

"I believe you are right," I concurred.

"Ho!" Bewok shouted in reply – and he received a bark and a short howl in response.

Moments later, Karno and a few of his fellow Wolfmen emerged from forest. They were dressed in the traditional garb of the People of the Wolves. Like us, they wore loincloths and leggings, and their tunics were secured around their hips by the sleeves, but they also wore cloaks made of wolfskins, complete with the wolf's head still attached and worn atop their own skulls. Unlike us, they wore their shiny black hair cropped very short; the Wolfmen's dusky skin was adorned with animal tattoos, and they sported many necklaces and bracelets.

"Ho," Karno said again in greeting as he saw us. "Karno hear voices. Karno hope it be you. Travel many day, look for you. Ah, Bewok. Old friend! Karno so happy to see you!" Karno and Bewok embraced.

"I am pleased to see you, too, Karno," Bewok told him. "I am glad you found us."

"Looking for us?" I repeated. "Why?"

"We hunt deer, but then see woolly rhino battle," Karno began. "It happen very quick. One win, he move off. One wounded, he run away. We want find wounded rhino!"

"Even an injured rhino can still put up a fight," Black Wolf said skeptically, no doubt recalling our previous woolly rhino hunt with the Wolfmen. It had occurred many years ago, but the memory of it was still clear in my mind. The creature had put up a strenuous defense; it had been surprisingly nimble for an animal of that size. It was only due to our numbers and Karno's daring that we had been able to bring it down. This time, we had far fewer hunters: the seven of us – and three of those still boys – plus Karno and his two companions.

"It *wounded*," Karno said with emphasis, as though Black Wolf were not very bright. "We find rhino and stick him good. It be hurt. It be tired."

"It be in a really bad mood," Black Wolf said, mimicking Karno sourly. "If it is still alive, it may not be as easy as you think."

Karno waved Black Wolf's remark aside.

"*Gah!*" He said dismissively. "Remember wounded mammoths? Did we not kill them?"

"They were not so much wounded as impeded by virtue of having their tusks tangled together and exhausted by the mating season, plus several days of pushing one another about," Black Wolf pointed out. "Just now we are looking for boars."

"All these fresh furrows may mean they have bedded down somewhere not too far from here," Oak added. "That is, if all our conversation has not awakened them and scared them away. If so, we will have to track them down."

Karno looked down at the clumps of turned-up earth.

"Little tracks, lots of babies," he commented, unimpressed. "Karno cannot go home with . . . with . . . *babies!*"

It was true that he had come a long way and he would need a sizable animal to make the journey worthwhile.

Puh had been silent, and he appeared to be deep in thought.

"We are seeking to bring down a sow or two," Puh said. "We are hoping to make a trek to Gray Elk's soon after our return home, so we had not planned to be away for very long."

"Gray Elk?" Karno echoed, his eyes lighting up. "You go for dog?"

The Wolfmen loved dogs, Karno most especially.

"Yes," Puh answered.

Karno sighed and pushed back the hood of his wolfskin cloak. The wolf's forelimbs were tied loosely at the base of his throat, causing the wolf with its gaping grin to peer over his shoulder as though it were enjoying a piggyback ride. It was a rather rank, tattered garment, and Karno must have been hot under the thick pelt. He ran his hands through his black spiky hair, now lightly sprinkled with strands of white. His two companions stood by impassively, perspiration beading up on their faces, but they steadfastly kept their cloaks in place.

"Karno love dog," Karno stated. He was not someone I thought to be overly sentimental, but his eyes softened as he spoke the words. "Karno want dog more than rhino. Well, maybe not more than rhino today."

"How far away was the rhino when you last saw him?" I asked Karno.

"Few day walk," Karno replied. "Karno know we cannot take him down, but we could if your clan help. He leave good blood trail. We find him, sure."

Requests for assistance were turned away only with the deepest reluctance. I could see by the looks on my companions' faces that no one wanted to disappoint Karno. Even Black Wolf seemed unhappy, despite his reservations about the proposed hunt.

"Let us continue to follow the sounder's tracks," Puh suggested. "Perhaps if we find our quarry and make a kill, we can take it home and then set off with Karno to look for the rhino. After all, we will be heading in that direction when we go to Gray Elk's. We will have our families with us, but we will also have more men."

"Yes, with luck, we can accomplish both missions," Bewok agreed, pleased that we might have found a resolution to our quandary.

"Karno think that good plan," Karno said, nodding his head. He looked to his comrades for confirmation. They nodded as well.

As we moved forward it went unspoken that stealth was now required. There was no more conversation. All communication was done by hand signals. We were careful to step on the newly churned-up ground to silence our footfalls on the soft earthen lumps. Then the forest opened up to a field of tall golden grasses. The furrows seemed to stop here, but the height of the ripened grasses with their full seedheads waving in the wind made it difficult to tell where the animals had proceeded from here. We could see that there were many trails through the grasses, but we could not ascertain which ones the boars might have used.

We all instinctively looked to Black Wolf, since he was by far the tallest of us, in hopes he could see what was ahead. Black Wolf stretched himself up on his toes and craned his neck for a better view. Mror was the smallest of our group, as a wiry thirteen-winters-old boy. He touched Black Wolf's arm to gain his attention, and then motioned to place him on his shoulders, and thus attain an even higher perspective. Black Wolf nodded and ducked down so Mror could clamber up. Mror climbed on, and Black Wolf slowly stood upright.

It was a novel sight to observe the spritely Mror, with his freckled face and mane of flowing bright red curls, poised atop the dark and solemn figure of Black Wolf. Black Wolf, however, did not appear to share our amusement as Mror gazed around him for several moments, and he started to become impatient to know what Mror could see. All at once, Mror's eyes widened and his mouth dropped open.

"What . . .," Black Wolf uttered in a hushed voice, but as the word escaped his lips, a chorus of grunts and squeals could be heard, and suddenly the tall grasses parted in numerous places as torrents of furry bodies charged toward us.

There was nothing we could do but meet them with our spears. Mror clung to Black Wolf as best he could as Black Wolf lunged toward the nearest boar, lancing it handily. Although it was modest in size, this was no mean feat, what with a solidly built lad perched atop his shoulders.

The boars were not about to give us a pleasant welcome. They harried us as we positioned ourselves in a defensive circle. As the boars made their passes, they tossed their heads to slash at us with their sharp tusks as they went by. We were able to sidestep their assaults and fend them off with our spears, but not without injury.

One particularly large sow had already run at us, but then she decided to come back for a second try, as though she were quite determined to show us her displeasure at having her sleep disrupted. This time, she dashed straight into our midst, refusing to be discouraged by our thrusting spears. Bewok and Puh hit her on each side as she broke through our grouping. When I heard Bewok cry out, I knew that she had managed to wound him.

The great beast went down and at once, all the other boars disappeared into the tall grass. The giant sow was still alive, but she would never again arise. Another boar also lay on the ground, and Black Wolf's boar dragged itself about feebly, its hind end now paralyzed.

We gathered around Bewok, who groaned as he grasped his leg just above the right knee, dark blood gushing around his fingers. Puh removed his tunic from where it was tied around his hips and quickly sliced off a strip of hide, which he hastily tied tightly around Bewok's leg, a little higher than the gash. As Puh did this, I dug through my pack for a bag of dried foods, the contents of which I promptly dumped into the pack, then placing the now-empty beg over Bewok's wound and lashing it down snugly with a length of rope.

"The bleeding seems contained," Black Wolf noted, helping Mror climb down off his back. "But we need to bring Bewok home as soon as possible. Gray Owl will know how best to treat him."

"Yes, Gray Owl fix Bewok," Karno agreed. "Tris, you and Karno leave now. Take Bewok to your home. Rest can follow with boar."

"That would be best," Puh concurred.

I nodded.

"Fox will come with us, too," I said. "Fox and I can carry Bewok." This made sense, because Fox and I were similar in height, making it easier to carry a load. Karno would then provide protection for us while we were thus encumbered.

"I am sorry," Bewok apologized. He seemed abashed at the turn of events.

"There is no reason to be sorry," Black Wolf told him. "We all need assistance now and then. Gray Owl will take care of you, just as he did last time. If he could mend you after that lion got hold of you, he can easily handle this."

Bewok nodded grimly.

"Come, friend," Karno said to Bewok. "We use cloak, make litter, you lay on it."

Karno and his companions had already cut down and de-limbed two long saplings. They fastened their wolfskin cloaks to them with rope, tying the wolfskin legs to the poles.

"Fox, take that end," I instructed Fox, handing my spear to Karno as I lifted one end of the litter. Fox also passed his spear to Karno and picked up the other end. We sidled up to Bewok and motioned for him to lie down. He gingerly lay down, placing his head at my end and feet by Fox. Bewok held his pack to his stomach and appeared pained. "Does it feel secure to lie on?" I asked Bewok.

"Yes," Bewok replied, trying to work up a reassuring smile. It appeared to me his skin had lost some of its color. Even considering his dark complexion and all his tattoos, he seemed wan indeed.

"Let us go, then," I urged.

"Wait, take the tourniquet off before you leave," Puh said as he stepped forward, reaching for Bewok. Puh carefully loosened the tourniquet and watched the bandage to see if the wound began to bleed through the wrappings. There was no obvious change. We traded glances. "Watch to see if the bleeding worsens," Puh advised. "Bewok, keep pressure on the bandage if you can."

Bewok nodded grimly. He would have to bend the injured leg to reach the wrappings over his wound. Puh then dug into his pack to retrieve his food sack, which he placed under Bewok's raised knee, to support its weight. Fox gave me a worried look. He too had recognized his grandfather's food bag that was now situated under Bewok's leg, but Fox said nothing. I knew Puh would be fine without it. Even if they did not return until tomorrow, the others would make sure he would not go hungry. And they certainly had plenty of fresh meat on hand. That being said, I expected they would make it home before nightfall. They just needed to dispatch the wounded boars, gut them, and tie them by their hooved feet to poles so the creatures could be transported back to the compound.

"Go quickly," Puh said to us. "But try not to jostle him if you can help it. We will see you soon."

"Yes, Puh," I replied. Fox and Karno nodded to Puh in response.

We took our leave of the others in our hunting party and set off down the trail at a fast walk.

"*Gah!*" Karno said as we strode along. "*Back Woof* say rhino dangerous!" Karno never could pronounce Black Wolf's name. "Karno say boar dangerous!"

As I noted Bewok silently wincing with pain and Karno's serious demeanor, I harkened back to the jovial and fun-loving young men I had met many years ago, when the Wolfmen first came into our lives. Of course, we were all older now, but it seemed as though so much had changed with the passing of time.

While we trekked, Fox and I concentrated on our footing and keeping our patient level on the gurney, and Karno walked alongside, vigilantly keeping watch of our surroundings for any potential threats. I was deeply concerned for Bewok, but I comforted myself that he had survived far worse injuries from the lion attack.

"Bewok," I said to rouse him from his silent suffering. "We will arrive at the compound before too long."

"I look forward to it," Bewok said between clenched jaws.

"Hang on my friend," Karno uttered to Bewok. "We go fast. Gray Owl fix you."

Bewok simply nodded and he closed his eyes.

"Are you feeling faint?" I asked.

"No," Bewok replied, shaking his head. "I am nauseated. I am not used to traveling like this, and it is making my stomach uneasy. Closing my eyes seems to allay the sensation."

I had never been carried horizontally – at least not as an adult – so I did not realize that it might make one ill.

The sun had reached its apex and was now making its descent in the western sky. Fox and I were sweating with effort; Bewok was not as tall as were we, but he was a well-filled-out man, and my hands and the muscles in my upper body were protesting at this unusual usage. If Bewok was unused to riding on a litter for any length of time, we were unused to carrying a litter for any distance. Game was carried on poles that rested on our shoulders, but Bewok could not be toted in such a fashion, so we grasped the poles with our hands at about hip height. If my hands were aching, I knew Fox's hands had to be hurting as well, but he did not complain or ask to rest.

Sunlight filtered down from the tree canopy overhead, and the breeze-tossed branches created changing patterns on the forest floor. Birds sang and all seemed peaceful. A few grazing deer started at our presence. We came upon a large bear with her three cubs; she snapped her jaws at us and gave us several soft woofs before she and her little ones vacated the area. Many sows might have put up a surly defense of her cubs, but I imagined that Fox and I presented something of a puzzlement to any animal that laid eyes on us, appearing as we did – like a huge ungainly creature with a lurching gait, with four legs and a head at each end. At one point we heard the sounds of a powerful beast crashing through the brush. So strong was the urge to poise a spear to fend off whatever might be coming our way that I almost dropped my end of the gurney. But I had no spear; Karno was holding it, along with Fox's weapon.

We halted, and Karno took a position between us and the sounds that drew ever closer. Moments later, a massive bull elk crossed the path in front of us, never pausing or slowing his mad dash.

We breathed a collective sigh of relief.

"That bull have cow in mind," Karno guessed.

"He is definitely onto something," I concurred.

I was relieved to smell the fires of home. We were nearly there. Fox knew it as well.

"Karno smell smoke," Karno informed us. "Be there soon, Bewok."

Bewok's eyes were still closed, but he managed a brief smile, and he grunted a little. By now, his skin was waxy and almost gray. Bewok no longer had the strength to keep pressure on his wound. Blood had seeped around the edges of his bandage and pooled under Puh's food bag.

"Stay with us, Bewok." I said to him. "Twie and your children are waiting for you."

Bewok stirred slightly.

"Twie will be preparing the evening sup," I went on, renewing my grip on the gurney. "She will be awaiting your return," I said again, trying to keep his mind engaged.

Bewok moved his head feebly from side to side.

"Twie," he spoke barely audibly. "Twie."

Karno looked down at his friend and then his eyes met mine.

"Walk faster," Karno urged.

We hastened our progress toward home, finally arriving as the sun was almost halfway through its journey to the horizon. Someone must have noted that we were approaching carrying a man on a litter and gone to summon Gray Owl, because he met us as we entered the compound.

"A laceration," Gray Owl said gravely as he peered at Bewok's apparent condition. "You found the boars?" he surmised.

"We did indeed," I answered. "One of them caught Bewok just above his knee."

Twie must have been sent for as well. She came to us at a quick trot, carrying an infant on her hip, with her older children trailing behind.

"Oh!" Twie cried out when she saw her mate. "Oh, Bewok!" Then to us she said, "Fish Hawk told me you were coming! Please bring Bewok home."

"I will meet you there," Gray Owl told us, turning to leave. "I will need to gather up a few things, but I will be only a moment."

"Many thanks, Gray Owl," Twie called after him.

Twie led the way toward their dwelling as many curious faces looked up from their work or peered from an entryway as we passed by. A group began to assemble and followed us, alarmed at Bewok's state and surprised to see Karno accompanying us. When we entered Twie and Bewok's home, Twie then instructed us go into their bedchamber and to set Bewok down on their bedding.

Fox and I gently lowered the gurney to the floor matting. There, Fox paused, unmoving.

"Puh-Puh," Fox began. "I cannot let go."

My hands, too, were locked around the litter's poles. I slid my hands free and, seeing this, Fox did the same. My fingers still did not want to flex, so I knocked them against my thighs to loosen the joints and finally managed to make them at least marginally functional. My fingers still stiff, I reached for Fox's hands and massaged them clumsily for a moment.

"You take his feet and I will lift him from under his shoulders," I said to Fox.

"Yes, Puh-Puh," Fox replied.

Bewok groaned as we placed him on the bedding just as Gray Oak came in the doorway.

"Did you have far to come?" Twie queried.

"Walk since about midday," Karno answered. "Walk fast."

More of our neighbors began to crowd into the little abode.

"I will need more light, if you please," Gray Owl requested.

My brother Ty was amongst the arrivals.

"I will bring lamps," Ty volunteered.

"I will take the children to my home," Ty's mate, Aessa, said.

"Many thanks, Aessa," Twie said. Aessa reached for Twie's baby, who willingly went to her. She was very familiar with Aessa and the children who resided in her household, and she seemed pleased to go to her. "Many thanks," Twie repeated as Aessa ushered the gaggle of little ones away.

Ty returned with as many lamps as he could carry. He tied the home's door flap open to also let in more sunlight, but only a little of that light shone in the bedchamber.

"I will need room to work," Gray Owl stated.

"I will leave you, but I will be close by if you need me," I said.  Fox and I started to walk away, still massaging our hands.

"Will you bring water?" Gray Owl asked.

"The water bag is near the hearth," Twie said, walking with Fox and me to the fireplace.

As we passed the bloody gurney, she looked down at it.  Twie suddenly bent and retrieved Puh's food bag.

"It is covered with blood," she said, appearing ashen. "What is it?"

"It is Puh's," I responded. "He propped up Bewok's leg with it."

"It is his food bag," Fox informed her.

I unhooked the water bag to carry it to the other room, but Twie stood there, staring at the article in her hands.

"Puh's?" she said, scarcely speaking above a whisper. Suddenly, she seemed to gather her wits. "I must thank Puh when he comes home. I will make Puh another food bag."

I nodded and followed her into the bedchamber, still carrying the water bag.

Gray Owl had removed the bandage and was examining the wound.  Karno still knelt soberly at the side of his friend.

"It is deep, but it will heal," Gray Owl pronounced. "Bewok must rest. He must stay still and eat plenty of food. I will clean away the blood, anoint the wound with a salve, and re-bandage his leg." Gray Owl paused and looked up at Twie. "We must keep the wound clean, but he should be fine. He is strong, and he is young." He smiled at Twie to help instill confidence in his assessment. Twie smiled weakly in return.

"Many thanks, Gray Owl," she said quietly, stroking Bewok's long black curls away from his face.

"We will take the litter out of here," I told Twie.

"Tris." Twie stopped me, touching my hand. "I am deeply grateful to you and Fox for carrying him home, and to you, Karno, for making sure he made it here safely."

"Bewok my friend," Karno said matter-of-factly. "Bewok would do same for Karno."

"Exactly," I added. "Bewok has been a good friend, and we all know he would do the same for any of us." I patted Twie's shoulder. "Just let me know if you need anything."

"I will," Twie responded.

Then, I leaned around Twie speak to her mate.

"Bewok, I will check on you later today," I told him.

Bewok worked up a smile.

"Thank you, Tris and Fox," he said. "I will see you when you return."

"Yes, we will talk then," I replied.

Fox and I had no sooner collected our spears from Karno and poked our heads out of Twie and Bewok's entryway when we were met by Morning Star and the rest of our family, Puh's mate, Ria, and other extended kin.

"Pleasant day to you all . . .," I said, but my words were quickly drowned out by a barrage of questions.

"Tris, what has happened?" Morning Star asked anxiously. "Where are the others?"

"Where are Tor and Mror?" Ria joined in. "What happened to Bewok? Was that Karno who came in with you?"

"Where is Da?" Black Wolf's daughter Petal joined in.

"The others are fine," I informed them. "Bewok was cut by a boar and thus he was unable to make the walk back home. We had run into Karno and several of his companions. They were with us when we found the boars. Karno came with Fox and me to bring Bewok here while Puh, Mror, Black Wolf, Oak, and the remaining Wolfmen dealt with the fallen boars. They should be here well before nightfall."

Our audience seemed to visibly relax at this news.

"Muh-Muh, I am hungry," Fox announced to Morning Star.

"Then come with me; I will feed you," Morning Star said, tip-toeing to buss his cheek.

"Many thanks, Muh-Muh," Fox eagerly replied.

Morning Star beamed at Fox; she was clearly proud of him for assisting in bringing Bewok home, and Fox happily basked in his mother's approval. Then Morning Star turned to me and pulled me down for a kiss, as well.

"You must be hungry, too," she said.

"I am indeed," I responded. "First, we must break up this litter and burn it." Bewok's blood had soaked into the grain of the wood. Then I considered the Wolfmen's cloaks. "Do you think we can get the blood out of these pelts?" I was sure the Wolfmen would be pained to lose these treasured items.

Morning Star looked at the Wolfmen's cloaks, the sad wolf heads with their empty eyes staring up from amid the bloody fur.

"I think so. We can try," she said, smiling as she accompanied us to the compound's large central hearth. There Fox and I slipped the litter's pole ropes apart.

We placed the poles in the fire as it was being built up to cook our nightly sup. I thought the rope was salvageable, so I carried the rope and cloaks.

"My sister Petal is better at working with pelts and hides than I," Morning Star added thoughtfully. "I will ask for her advice on cleaning the Wolfmen's cloaks. I know how much they value them."

* * *

Our nightly sup was still roasting over coals when Black Wolf, Oak, Puh, Mror, and the Wolfmen arrived at the compound, toting the three boars between them. The large sow that had injured Bewok required four men to carry it. The beasts were suspended from trees to complete the bleeding-out process, and then the weary men settled themselves near the hearth.

Black Wolf groaned as he lowered himself to the ground.

"I do not mind admitting that I am glad to take some rest," he said.

"I am glad to rest as well," Oak agreed, taking a seat next to his father.

Most of our combined families had now assembled by the fireplace to hear about the day's hunt. Fox and I had at least temporarily sated our appetites, but we still maintained our places at the hearth. Morning Star had inspected our sore and blistered hands and given us a soothing salve to rub into the already thoroughly callused skin.

We were eager to follow her instructions to continually work the ointment into the skin on the palms of our hands, lest the blisters worsen and burst. Between the greasy salve and the massaging, my hands were already markedly improved, but also rather slick with oil. I was tasked with holding our very cheerful and active baby while Morning Star and our three oldest daughters worked on our upcoming meal. Owl wanted very much to stand and, it would seem, break away from the confines of my lap to go exploring. He was bright-eyed and bouncing and also drooling copiously. I took care not to let little Owl wriggle or slide out of my greasy grasp, bringing to mind the long-forgotten memories of holding onto the slippery frogs I used to catch when I was a boy.

Karno appeared to be nearly as restless as Owl. No doubt he was frustrated at the delay to pursue the woolly rhino, but unless he and his men wanted to set out on their own, they had no choice but to wait for us to be ready to accompany them.

As Karno and his comrades joined us around the hearth, they seemed oddly naked without their ever-present wolfskin cloaks. However, those garments would need a thorough cleaning before they were ready to once again be donned. Yet another delay.

# Chapter Six

On the morning of the third day after the boar hunt, we embarked on another journey. This one was to be far more lengthy and ambitious than our last. Our group was strung out for some distance down the trails. Karno and the other Wolfmen were at the lead. Black Wolf and Oak followed, pulling one of Ty's new sleds. Morning Star and our younger children, my sister Mi, and Ria came next, and they were flanked by Mror and Fox. Then came Puh and me, pulling another new sled, and Ty brought up the rear. This arrangement protected the most vulnerable of our party by keeping them at the center of the procession.

The Wolfmen's wolfskin cloaks now looked much better than they had since they were last worn by their original canine owners. Morning Star and her sister Petal had done wonders with the skins, giving them a good cleaning and fluffing. Morning Star had divulged to me that the vile liquid that ran off the filthy cloaks had contained much more than just Bewok's blood. My mind wandered back to our first meeting of the Wolfmen and how startling the smell had been. They claimed their cloaks were an asset when hunting, but I thought they were more apt to broadcast the news of the Wolfmen's proximity to any nose that was downwind. I shrugged off this notion. The Wolfmen were skilled hunters, so who was I to criticize their methods?

Morning Star was not pleased to know we would be attempting to track the rhino on our way to Gray Elk's mountainside home. Enough time had elapsed since the creature had last been spotted that I had my doubts whether or not it was still alive, and, if so, if it had remained in the area. Unless it had been badly gored by its opponent, it had most likely ambled off to some remote location in which to heal its wounds. Nonetheless, Morning Star took little comfort from my speculations. Over the years we had been together, she and Gray Owl had mended my battered body after many a hunt, and she was painfully aware that it was a dangerous business.

I was not devoting much thought to the rhino. It was a fine summer's day. The travois sleds Ty had constructed specially for navigating the steep, rocky mountain trails we would encounter on the way to Gray Elk's were proving to be a vast improvement over our traditional sleds. These sleds did not have the capacity to carry large loads, but they were far better than packing everything on our backs or doing without the gear and supplies they transported.

Karno set a brisk pace. He said they had been walking for two days at the time they had found us, and we were setting out a half-day's walk from our meeting place. He was eager to make up the time we had lost in the interim and most anxious to pick up the beast's trail from where he had last seen it.

Our steady march did not stop Black Wolf from serenading the countryside with song. He often favored The Mighty Hunter tune, and this was no exception. Black Wolf enjoyed changing the words with each rendition, as his mood dictated. His resounding bass floated on the air back to Puh and me as we trudged along.

*The Mighty Hunter is wily and clever*

*He follows the sun and watches the weather*

*If it is cold, the Mighty Hunter wears a warm cloak*

*If it is hot, he might find a lake and take a long soak*

*The Mighty Hunter eats fishes, fowl, and meat*

*If he is lucky, at night he comes home to a woman that is . . .*

Black Wolf faltered for a moment as he remembered Morning Star's admonishments the last time he had made insinuations along these lines in the presence of the younger family members now accompanying us. Then he continued in the same lung-bursting volume.

*. . . that is neat!*

Morning Star giggled.

"*Neat?*" she repeated. "Oh, Da!" Morning Star looked to the rear of the procession with a mischievous smile and said to me, "I hope I am sufficiently *neat*."

"As neat as anyone could wish for," I assured her, doing my best to maintain a deadpan expression and fight back the dopey grin that wanted to form on my lips.

"*Back Woof,*" Karno started, "someday you sing about Karno, yes?"

"Possibly," Black Wolf replied. I thought it more probable Karno might garner a song about himself if he would learn to correctly pronounce the singer's name. Black Wolf's voice once again rang out.

*The Mighty Hunter has senses that are keen . . .*

"And at home, his mate always keeps things clean!" Morning Star sang.

"Do not interrupt," Black Wolf said indignantly.

"Well, Da, I was just staying in the *neat* theme," Morning Star teased.

Black Wolf went on.

*And sometimes the Mighty Hunter suffers jibes that are mean*

*The Mighty Hunter travels over terrain that has hills high and low*

*Where he hopes to find the predators blind and deer that are slow . . .*

* * *

We picked up the woolly rhino's trail exactly where Karno said it would be. It was midday when we made the discovery, so we found a shady place to break from our trek and take some food and drink. The sun was hot, and the air was still. The signs of the rhino's presence were several days old by now, but the bloodstains dotting the earth were unmistakable.

"There is not much blood," Puh pointed out. "But that might indicate that he did not linger here for very long."

"Yes," Black Wolf agreed. "He may have gone some distance from here by now. Do we really want to search for this beast?"

Karno seemed disappointed at the direction the discussion was taking.

"We go look," Karno insisted. "Just few day. If not see, then go to Gray Elk."

The decision weighed heavily upon us. We looked to one another, hoping someone would say something that would sway us one way or another. It would mean leaving the trail and venturing into the forest with our families.

"We will bring down much meat," Karno persisted. "Rhino be sore with wound."

Fox, Oak, and Mror seemed intrigued at the idea of going after a woolly rhinoceros. We did not often see these animals, and when we did, we did our best to avoid these ill-tempered brutes. A rhino might ignore you and simply saunter off, or it might suddenly charge for no reason at all.

I then noticed that Puh was scanning the skies overhead.

"What is it, Puh?" I queried.

"I felt a breeze, and then I saw that the wind is steadily increasing," Puh began. "If you look between the tree branches – over there – you can see clouds building."

Black Wolf took note of our remarks, and he too peered up past the tree canopy.

"Thunderheads!" he said. "And they are getting taller by the moment."

"We must find shelter," Ria stated. "We passed a rock shelter earlier. I think we should go there with all haste."

"Yes," Puh nodded, still staring skyward. "I am sorry, Karno, but I believe we should take shelter. Those clouds indicate a potentially substantial storm."

Karno did not speak for a time. His shoulders slumped as he took a long look at the thunderheads. Finally, Karno shook his head.

"You right," Karno admitted. "Cloud get big. Wind up. Sky grow dark. Time to find place of rock."

A distant rumble of thunder rolled ominously across the landscape.

"Let us go," Black Wolf said as he and Oak turned their sled around.

Puh and I also dragged our sled to face the opposite direction, and we all set out at a quick pace, determined to reach the rock shelter as quickly as possible. The wind began to whistle harshly through the trees. Flurries of leaves, ripped from the twigs on which they had sprouted in spring, flew through the air. Increasing in force, the gale caused the branches to sway and clash against one another, finally tearing free from the trees. The air was filled with the aromas cast by their splintering flesh and fine droplets of sap. When some of the larger branches could not take the thrashing and came crashing to the ground, we were forced to dodge them as best we could. This spurred us to walk even faster. The smallest children were carried to speed our progress. Then the pelting rain began to fall. We covered the littlest ones with our cloaks to help keep them dry and protect them from flying debris.

It was not long before the violent movement of trees produced a profoundly disturbing effect on the trees' root systems. The trees creaked and groaned as they heaved to and fro. The violence of this action caused the ground beneath them to undulate with the rising and falling of the trees' ponderous underground foundations.  It looked as though the trees were as anxious as were we to escape the oncoming storm and were struggling to break free from their earthly bonds.

When we reached the rock shelter, we were startled to find it already occupied by a large, very old boar bear. He carried the scars he had accumulated over his many years, and he was missing patches of fur.  The bear was slumbering despite the raging storm, and when our visit disturbed his nap, he gave every evidence of being as surprised as we were.  His eyes popped open in alarm and he sprang to his feet.  He snapped his jaws at us to show his displeasure, and then he woofed.  The old boar made a quick departure, despite an obvious limp, and he disappeared into the rain-shrouded forest, leaving the rock shelter conveniently vacant.

"Poor old bear," Fox said with sympathy, as we squeezed into the confines of the space.

"He has a thick fur coat to protect him and plenty of fat to keep him warm," Black Wolf pointed out.  "And you have neither of those things."

The small enclosure appeared to have been used by people at least occasionally.  It consisted of a large slab of rock that jutted out of a hillside, which was walled in on two sides by smaller stones, with the gaps between the stones filled with mud and an assortment of sticks, dried grasses, and other bits of miscellaneous matter.  The front was open to the weather, where a large fireplace occupied a prominent spot just under the ledge.

This shelter was not ideal, in that wind and rain still blew in from time to time, but it was a big improvement over the conditions outside. The thunder and lightning continued to battle it out overhead, making the ground tremble. The rain fell in sheets and the wind moaned like a living thing. Someone had left an armload of wood within the structure, but we knew we would need more than that to keep a fire lighted for any length of time.

"We will probably have to stay here through the night," I said. "I will dash out and pick up some wood."

"I will go with you," Ty volunteered.

We were joined by Fox, Oak, and Mror, while Puh set about striking up a fire with flint and pyrite over a bit of tinder, and the others worked to make our accommodations more comfortable. It took only a few moments of scouring the vicinity for any fallen deadwood and we returned, our arms loaded with wood. Morning Star was waiting for me.

"Oh, Tris! You are soaked," she said, reaching up to dry my face with a scrap of hide.

"I was already wet; I do not think I could have become any wetter," I replied, squeezing the water from my thick length of bound hair.

Morning Star now moved to stand behind me so she could attempt to dry my back. I did not think the little scrap of hide was going to absorb enough to make much of a difference, but I appreciated her care of me.

While some of us were collecting firewood, the Wolfmen had harvested a number of large branches off nearby fir trees, from which they created windscreens to help enclose the front of the rock shelter. A space was left open to allow the fire's smoke to escape, even if the wind did occasionally blow the smoke back into our faces.

While these screens were not weathertight, they did help cut down on the general draftiness of the dwelling.

The storm-darkened sky meant that there was little light, other than what the fire provided and the brief blinding flashes of lightning, so we huddled around the flames and gnawed on dried stores, talking quietly amongst ourselves. The children had endured our flight from the storm and subsequent crowding into the rock shelter without complaint. They had appeared to be uneasy at the situation, but still, I was proud of them. Even little Owl had not fussed at our dash through the elements.

Daisy now sat on my rather soggy lap, thumb in her mouth and clutching a doll that Pony had made for her shortly before our departure from home. This cherished toy now accompanied Daisy everywhere. It was made of a small chunk of de-barked wood that sported knots resembling eyes and an outcropping that might look like a nose. The doll's tree-knot eyes were oddly configured; causing the doll to look as though it were trying to stare at its nose. Pony had added a mouth, carving a smile into its face. She had made "hair" by cutting a small piece from my wisent skin cloak, asking me to glue it on the doll's head. As of now, the doll was tucked in a rabbit skin blanket, and all I could see of the beloved item was its face, frozen in a perpetual cross-eyed gaze, and the wild mane of thick wavy hair sticking out at all angles.

"Did you have enough to eat?" I asked Daisy as I pulled her closer.

"Yes, Puh-Puh," Daisy said as she removed her thumb from her mouth. "We see puppies tomorrow?"

"Not for a few more days," Black Wolf told her. "If this storm blows out overnight, we can recommence our hike tomorrow. Then it will not be long."

"Rhino be gone," Karno said sadly. "Need another after leave Gray Elk."

"I do not know who will be in residence when we get there," Puh started, "but we can ask them what animals have been seen in the area."

"That is true," Black Wolf concurred. "When we arrive, we often find that Gray Elk's hunters are in the field at that time, but even if they are, someone ought to be able to tell us what is around. There are always ibex, sheep, and the like, but I suspect you want something bigger to feed your clan."

Karno nodded.

"Much bigger," Karno said. "Rhino or mammoth best."

I wanted to ask Karno how many people were in his clan now. However, I knew he struggled with numbers, especially when speaking in a language that was not his native tongue, and I did not want to cause him embarrassment. Black Wolf either forgot about Karno's difficulties or did not mind causing Karno potential discomfort.

"Like most clans, your clan must be growing," Black Wolf noted. "How many do you have to feed these days?"

Karno seemed to consider this. Then he held up his hands, palms facing us, and fingers splayed, and he quickly opened and closed his hands several times. Black Wolf blinked and a puzzled look appeared on his face. Karno, realizing that Black Wolf did not grasp his meaning, held up both hands again, and very slowly and deliberately ticked off each finger. The last hand he showed only had three fingers raised.

"One, one, one, one, one, one . . ." Karno said *one* each time he touched a finger until he had said one thirty-three times.

I smiled at Karno's clever response.

"Jura add one more soon," Karno said of his mate. She already had a small boy when they became paired, the child of Karno's deceased friend Mino. "We wait long time for baby," Karno added. "Karno want boy this time. Last time Jura grow huge. Karno hope for large son. Instead, Jura have girl and girl. *Gah!* They getting big. Time for son."

"If it is not a boy this time, it will be another time," Morning Star assured Karno. She passed a bag of berries to Karno. "Have some of these; we must eat them before they go bad."

The fire made the shelter pleasantly warm, even if the smoke and heat from the flames made various insects suddenly fall from the rock ceiling and into our midst. My young daughters exclaimed softly and jumped at each unexpected visitor. Spiders, crickets, and other tiny creatures were a part of daily life, but they did not usually fling themselves at us with such frequency. Given that these insects were dispersing themselves amongst us while lightning flashed and thunder crashed outside our shelter, I could hardly blame them for being jumpy.

"They are just tiny beings, they cannot do you much harm," Black Wolf assured his granddaughters, appearing amused at their startled squeaks. In spite of all his bravado, when an especially violent crack of thunder and lightning rent the sky just overhead, Black Wolf cried out and ducked his head, just the same as the children.

"That close," Karno stated. "Smell light bolt on air!"

The storm went on unabated as total darkness set in. Finally, it sounded as though the rumbles of thunder were coming from farther away, and the lightning was only evidenced as occasional distant illuminations in the clouds. I could still hear the steady patter of rain falling outside our enclosure, but the wind had let up. We kept the fire burning brightly. I was weary, but I was too uncomfortable to sleep very much. There was not enough room for any of us to lie down, so we sat up all night, napping now and then when exhaustion overtook us. Only the children managed to get a good night's rest.

* * *

The rising sun brought light to a forest still dripping after the previous night's storm. The morning mists captured the golden sunlight, shrouding the woodlands in a hazy glow. We had let the fire die down to coals and a few weak flames, which were extinguished when stirred and thus smothered with a thick layer of wood ashes. It did not take long for us to repack the sleds, breaking our fast as we worked, and we set out down the trail once more.

The foggy conditions did nothing to improve on my foggy sleep-deprived brain. The children seemed almost exasperatingly chipper, but I was glad to know they had been able to get sufficient rest during the night. Daisy skipped lightheartedly alongside Fox, her new doll clasped to her chest with one arm.

"Fox, when we get to Gray Elk's may I help you pick out a puppy?" Daisy asked her big brother, looking up at him with open admiration.

"Of course you may," Fox replied. "But your doll is slipping out of her blanket; be careful you do not lose it."

Daisy glanced down at her doll, and true enough, the roughly cylindrical chunk of wood was sliding out of the rabbit skin wrapping. Daisy fumbled with the doll to amend the situation.

"I will fix it," Fox volunteered, holding his hand out for the doll.

Daisy gratefully passed it to Fox, who – being hampered by carrying his long spear in one hand – cradled the bundle against his chest with his forearm, bit down on an end of the rabbit skin, and used his free hand to adroitly swathe the doll with the blanket. Fox then returned the doll to Daisy, brushing bits of loose rabbit fur from his lips.

"Many thanks, Fox," Daisy said, beaming at him.

"Just keep a tight hold on it," Fox advised.

I marveled at this exchange. It was not too long ago when Fox would have been more impatient with Daisy. Morning Star must have taken notice as well, because she turned to look at me and we exchanged smiles and knowing looks.

The mists soon evaporated as the heat of the day grew stronger. When the sun reached its apex, we halted for a brief but welcome break. As we often did, we chose a spot where potable water was available so we could top off our water bags after we slaked our thirst. The small stream bubbled and burbled over a stony bed. This was good. Fast-running water is most often clean water. The refreshing liquid and light breeze made for a pleasant stop indeed.

We had just finished eating when Morning Star saw a change in Owl's expression. He grimaced and his complexion reddened as he grunted. Morning Star immediately stood up and walked with Owl a few steps from our group. I too rose to my feet and joined her, spear in hand. We had seen signs of various animals accessing this water source and I did not want my mate and infant to be exposed to potential danger.

Most times, Owl wore a nappy only at night to protect his bedclothes from being soiled; during the day, Owl was watched carefully for signs that he need to relieve himself or pass stool, which was usually not long after he was fed. After Owl had completed these bodily functions, I again accompanied them as Morning Star carried him to the downstream end of our break site, where she washed his bottom.

Owl was not an irritable baby, but he did not enjoy the cold water on his backside. He did not cry, but his visage took on the appearance of one thinking *not this again!*

It was then that a shriek met my ears. The all-too-familiar voice and the terror it contained made my heart feel as though it had momentarily stopped. Morning Star and I both spun around to see that everyone had risen to their feet, blocking our view of what was beyond.

"What is it?" Morning Star called out as we rushed toward them.

I looked wildly around us as we walked, and slowly the situation began to formulate in my mind. Flashes of rust-colored fur caught my eyes as the beasts dashed between trees and bushes, and then a few low chortles and an unpleasantly familiar odor confirmed my suspicion. Hyenas.

We had gone only six or seven steps from the others to wash Owl's bottom, so we were back amongst our companions in a moment, but my mouth dropped open as I saw what had brought everyone to their feet. A pack of hyenas had found the gumption to engage a relatively large number of humans. We had found that hyenas almost never attacked people unless they vastly outnumbered them, and I now wondered how many of those creatures were hidden by the brush, just out of view. If they were this brazen, they must have confidence in their numbers. I also had to admit to myself that it was possible that they were attracted to this site by my younger children's piping chatter. To a predator, such voices sounded like prey.

Morning Star gasped as she came to the same realization. But then a determined look came over her face. Still carrying Owl, she picked up a length of fallen branch, and held it before her, ready to do battle. The children instinctively clustered near the center of the group – all but Daisy, who stood by her big brother, seemingly unfazed by the intruders. After all, Fox had kept a hyena as a pet. Did she see them as doggies looking for a family to adopt them?

"Get back, Daisy," Fox said to her.

Daisy opened her mouth to protest when one of the hyenas darted toward her, and in an instant, its jaws closed on my precious child. Daisy screamed. I sprang forward with my spear, but Fox had already lanced the beast. The hyena promptly went down, mortally injured, but then another hyena ran in for another attempt, only to be driven off by the spiky reception of several spearheads.

A few more hyenas made tepid charges, but the sight of their fallen comrade seemed to act as a deterrent. Hyenas are opportunistic hunters, and they are intelligent enough to know when the risks outweigh the benefits of a rash attack. When the animals dispersed, we crowded around Daisy, who was sobbing in Fox's embrace.

Morning Star passed Owl to me, who looked upon the scene with avid interest, and then Morning Star took Daisy from Fox.

"There, there, my little one," Morning Star said to Daisy, inspecting her for injury. The only blood Daisy appeared to wear must have come from the hyena. She was completely unharmed. "You are not hurt, but that must have been so frightening." Morning Star said, hugging and kissing Daisy to console her.

I was greatly relieved, but also perplexed. It had looked as though the hyena had not just bitten Daisy, but chomped down on her belly. The horror of it kept replaying itself in my mind, but miraculously, she did not have a scratch on her.

"I am so glad you are not injured," I told Daisy, kissing her tear-dampened cheek.

Daisy was weeping so wholeheartedly that when she now spoke, she was difficult to understand. Morning Star was usually able to discern the speech of small children better than I, but even she struggled to interpret was Daisy was saying. I then noticed that her doll was not in her arms. I looked about us and then saw the rabbit pelt lying on the ground by the now-dead hyena. I approached, Fox joining me to also look at the fallen beast.

Fox seemed grim as he looked down on the hyena.

"It reminds me of Ena," Fox said quietly.

"You did a very brave thing," I responded, placing a hand on his shoulder. "You have probably saved your sister's life. I know it must have been hard."

"It was not hard to do," Fox said with a shrug. "I did not even think about Ena at the time. Daisy was in trouble. It was just lucky the hyena bit down on her doll and not her."

"I am grateful to you, Fox," I told him, giving his shoulders a squeeze before turning to pick up Daisy's doll.

I examined its wooden form. There I discovered, just as Fox had said, were the teeth marks where the hyena had bitten down on the doll. I rewrapped the doll in its blanket and returned to Morning Star and Daisy. Daisy stopped crying the moment she saw her doll and she held out her arms for it.

"You found her!" Daisy exclaimed, holding the doll tightly to her cheek. "Many thanks, Puh-Puh."

"You must also thank your big brother," I said.

Daisy nodded, now beginning to smile.

"Yes. Fox kill bad doggy!" Daisy stated firmly. "Bad doggy bite my doll! *Bad, bad doggy!*" Daisy looked over her mother's shoulder toward Fox. "Many thanks, Fox!" she called out. "Many thanks!"

"My silly Daisy," Morning Star began. "Do you mean to say that all those tears were over your doll?" Morning Star snuggled Daisy closer. "You are a funny girl."

"I am not funny," Daisy insisted. "My poor doll." Daisy then addressed her toy in the same tone her mother had used with her. "There, there. You must have been so frightened. But not to worry. I will take care of you."

"Congratulations on making your first kill, Fox," Puh said to him, patting his back.

Fox's face suddenly brightened.

"I have made my first kill," Fox concurred, seeming surprised, as though it had not occurred to him that not only had he saved his sister, he had just joined the ranks of manhood.

"I will bind your hair tonight," Morning Star said. "You should be very proud."

Fox only nodded and smiled a bit in reply.

"Let us leave this place," Black Wolf suggested. "The smell of blood and in the near future, the added odor of decay, will attract more predators – at least the ones that do not have discriminating tastes."

We all agreed that we should leave as soon as possible. We threw the hyena's carcass into the forest, where it would not contaminate the water source, and then we hastily finished consuming our midday meal as we refilled our water bags and repacked the foodstuffs.

"Would anyone like more dried venison before I put this away?" Morning Star asked, holding up the sack of dried meat.

"I have had enough," I assured her.

The others turned her down as well, except for Fox and Oak, who each helped themselves to one last stick of venison.

"Berries?" Morning Star now offered. "They are going soft and must be eaten soon."

Again, the boys each took a handful. Morning Star looked to the rest of us, so I felt obliged to help dispose of the fruit.

"Not me," Karno waved her away. "If Karno have more, Karno spend rest of day in bush."

"Well, we cannot have that," Morning Star said, stowing the small basket of berries on the sled.

We trekked steadily until evening came, and then we set up camp in the dying light. It had been a long day, and I was glad when our shelters were erected and a fire was lighted. The air cooled as night set in, and after our evening sup, it was finally time to bind Fox's hair.

Brilliant stars shown in the night sky. When a series of stars streaked through the sparkling firmament, it seemed appropriately auspicious as a commemoration of Fox's first hair binding. The fire was built up to create more light in which Morning Star could begin the task.

Puh donated a long leather thong, which would be used to keep Fox's hair bound into a thick rope, just the same as ours was. Our daughters giggled as their mother laboriously untangled Fox's great mass of thick curly hair and then divided it into sections that were twisted into cords. Lastly, the cords were gathered into one bundle, which was lashed at the nape of the neck and then wrapped in a tight crisscrossing of the leather thong down to almost the end of the cords.  Fox's hair, when bound in this fashion, fell almost to his waist.

"Your hair is much longer now that it is not in loose curls," Morning Star informed Fox. "And you look so much older. More mature."

Fox seemed very pleased at this.

"Many thanks, Muh-Muh, for binding my hair," Fox said, and he impulsively gave his mother a hug.

Morning Star gladly returned his hug, but I saw that moisture glinted in the corners of her eyes.  She hastily wiped away a few tears.

"My son is a man now," Morning Star declared softly.

"Oh, Muh-Muh, do not cry," Fox pleaded.

I rose to embrace Morning.  She seemed grateful to receive my comfort and she smiled through her tears.

"These are happy tears," Morning Star responded. "It is just that I did not think this day would come so soon."

# Chapter Seven

*The beast meanders slowly and painfully through a field of summer flowers. From my vantage point, I can see only its shaggy backside and flickering tail. There are no water sources in this area; the creature must slake its thirst very soon.*

I was awakened by the sharp cries of a fox. A quick peek out of our lean-to showed that the sun was just rising. Fox was awake, sitting by the fire and nibbling on dried stores. He looked thoughtful. The fox barked again, causing Fox to glance up.

"You have arisen early," I whispered to him, so as not to awaken the others.

"I did not sleep well last night," Fox admitted. "I have been sitting here, tending the fire and listening to the vixen. I think she is just over there." Fox pointed into the forest. "When I hear or see a fox, I feel almost as though it is a kindred spirit."

"I have felt that, as well," I told him. "They share our red hair."

"And our protruding nose," Fox said, smiling ruefully. "At least, I am told I have a large nose." Fox put a hand to his face to gauge the length and breadth of his proboscis. "We are a family of large-nosed people, are we not?"

"We are indeed," I assured him. "But our noses are smaller than that of a fox and many other creatures, besides."

Since Fox seemed dismayed at the size of his nose, I hoped this notion would comfort him. Not only were we of the Old Ones well known for this characteristic, but also, much to his mother's consternation, Black Wolf had passed along a prominent nose to a few of his offspring, as well. To my knowledge, Morning Star had seen her reflection only once, fifteen years earlier, when she gazed down into a spring. The sight of her nose must have stayed with her, because she still complained of it now and then.

"Puh-Puh," Fox began and then he paused. "How did you ask for Muh-Muh?"

I was startled by this question. I had known that one day Fox would seek a mate, but I had not expected him to speak of it just yet. I was also abashed to recall my awkward conversation with Black Wolf.

"Rather poorly. Perhaps I am not the best person to advise you on such things," I said.

Fox stared at me with surprise. The fox called out again. My son did not respond for a moment. He appeared troubled.

"However, do not feel you cannot speak with me about this," I added hastily. "It is probably better to prepare oneself. I had known for many years that I wanted to ask for your mother, but I had no notion of what to say. I was clumsy. I asked to give my attentions to her. Your grandfather Black Wolf was taken aback. He said *do you not want to be paired with her?* It was only much later, when I heard Puh ask for Ria, and he talked of love and caring, that I came to realize how I should have spoken."

Fox appeared thoughtful.

"You may have wondered why I have been so eager to go to Gray Elk's to get a puppy," Fox said. "It is not only because I would really like to have a dog. I have longed to see Misty again. Although it has been several years, she is never far from my thoughts."

Misty was Gray Elk's granddaughter, and she had numerous siblings and cousins who all resided with their families at Gray Elk's home. Her full name was Misty Morn, and I remembered her mostly because she had a twin sister named Sunny Morn, and twins were not common. Karno and Jura's twin daughters were the only other living twins of which I knew. Like our infant Eagle Owl, both Misty and Sunny were called by only one of their names. Misty and Fox had been playmates as children, but as he had just stated, he had not seen her in some years now.

It was quite possible she might be promised to another already, given the steady stream of people who came and went from Gray Elk's cave. That being said, The People tended to become paired a few years later than did most Old Ones. Additionally, it crossed my mind that while Gray Elk had never shown any misgivings against pairings between Old Ones and The People, it was possible Misty and her parents did not feel the same way. I still did not really understand this concept, but there was no arguing that for some, this was their mindset. Nevertheless, we Old Ones had only ever been treated with the utmost courtesy when we visited at Gray Elk's; I could not imagine that anyone dwelling there would harbor ill feelings toward us.

"Have you ever broached the subject with Misty?" I asked.

Fox shook his head.

"You two are up with the sun," Morning Star said sleepily, raising her head just enough to view us. "How nice to see that you have revived the fire!"

Fox did not pick up the thread of our conversation again, but just the same, I was pleased that he had chosen to confide in me. I had been saddened and confused by his growing remoteness as he grew older; I – who had always been so close to my Puh – could not understand why Fox shunned me. This morning I felt a profound relief that he had opted to open himself to me once more.

* * *

My happiness at the conversation with Fox buoyed me throughout the day. Even while dragging a heavy sled with Puh and staying alert to all the perils we might meet along the trail, my heart was full and my thoughts were light. I only hoped that Fox's desire for a life with Misty would not be dashed after our arrival at Gray Elk's. I knew what it was to desperately love someone, with no idea as to whether one's feelings would ever be returned. I considered myself to be infinitely fortunate to have made a pairing with the one woman who had ever owned my heart.

A little after midday, we were just about to cross a broad expanse of meadow when sounds heralding the approach of a large herd of mammoths met our ears. Any time I viewed mammoths, bittersweet memories came to mind of the cow mammoth I had once known. She had saved my life twice, and yet when she was in peril I had been unable to save her. Even after all these years, the thought of her still pained me.

We had already paused for our midday meal, but there was nothing to do except wait while the hairy beasts lumbered along. We retreated some distance back up the trail and settled ourselves in the shade of the trees. It was a good place from which to watch the procession pass. The animals varied in age from massive matriarchs to the littlest infants. The youngest of them struggled to keep up with their elders, sometimes losing their footing and stumbling, or trotting off in some wayward direction, only to be rounded up and returned to the correct path by their attentive mothers.

The mammoths maintained a determined pace, ignoring all the flowers and verdant grasses that might have filled their stomachs, no doubt in hopes of reaching their destination in good time. If they noticed our presence from where we observed their passing by the edge of the forest, they gave no indication of it. Karno watched the mammoths with particular interest.

"Much big mammoth," Karno said. "But big herd – not good hunt."

We nodded. Even Karno had to acknowledge that it was not prudent to take on a herd of these creatures. These groups were made up of mothers, grandmothers, aunts, sisters, and all their collective offspring. The bulls were allowed to stay with the herd only until they reached maturity, and then they had to find their own way in the world. However, until that point, all those that were part of the group benefited from the protection of their fellows. There was no singling out an animal to be taken down; you threaten one and you must face them all.

Our mammoth hunts typically targeted the bulls, which were often loners. If you were lucky, you might find a young, inexperienced bull that could be lured into a location where you could use the landscape to prevent him from using his incredible size and strength against you. Even so, confronting a mammoth – even a young adult – was fraught with extreme danger and not entered into without having a large hunting party and a good strategy in place.

Eventually the mammoths moved on and we recommenced our journey. The largely open grassland also contained a multitude of animal species. Among those we saw a herd of horses in the distance. The cries of two stallions caught our attention as they fought each other with tooth and hoof. Even from far off, we could see that each strike brought forth a cloud of dust from the coats of the horses.

"Does this bring back memories, Tris?" Black Wolf called over his shoulder.

It took a moment before I realized to what he was referring. Like the two stallions fighting over mating rights, I also had to fight to win my mate.

"Now that you mention it, I guess it does," I replied. "I must say, I am glad I did not have to fend off sharp hooves and large teeth."

Morning Star's step did not falter, but she turned to meet my gaze for an instant.

"Do not speak of it," she said. "Every time I think back on that day I feel sick. It was the most awful thing I have ever witnessed."

"We will speak of it no more," I assured her.

"Speak of what?" six-winters-old Willow asked.

"Hush," her mother responded sternly.

"There are wisents, I think," Oak announced, pointing toward a far-off rise.

"I think you are correct," Black Wolf told him, shielding his eyes as he also looked at the dark mob of beasts. "They have quite a few calves. If we could bring down a youngster or two, we would have fresh meat for tonight's sup."

"Karno say good plan," Karno concurred.

I scanned the landscape for a place where our families could wait out the hunt. There was not much protection for them on this broad expanse of meadow. Puh, too, looked about us.

"We are upwind," Puh said. "We must cut through the lea. When we reach the forest again, we will be more or less downwind, or crosswind, at least. Perhaps there we can find a spot where our families can safely wait for our return. If not, I think we should push on."

I nodded in agreement.

"Yes, Puh, I believe you are right," I said.

As we continued our trek, the wisents also continued theirs, taking them farther and farther away from us. When we at last came to the tree line, we looked back and by then, the wisents were gone from sight.

"*Gah*," Karno exclaimed, "great beasts are gone!"

"They are indeed," Black Wolf said resignedly. "And I was looking forward to a tasty meal, too."

Puh suddenly held up a hand to quiet us. I listened. Everyone else stood absolutely still, his or her head cocked. Even little Owl appeared to be alert. It then occurred to me that when we reentered the forest, the ground beneath my feet had felt somehow different. There was a light, crunchy texture that was beyond what we might expect to find in a piney wood such as this. I ventured a quick look down the path and saw the large quantity of very dry grouse droppings that dotted the ground behind us. As we moved ahead, the droppings we encountered appeared to be more recently deposited. It was then that I heard the faint sounds of fowl foraging on the pine needle- and cone-littered woodland floor. We seemed to have blundered into a flock of grouse, and by the looks of it, these birds had been in this area for some time.

Ria seemed to have come to the same conclusion. She quickly strung her bow and grasped a handful of arrows, skillfully arraying each one between her fingers. We had yet to see any of the grouse, but their sounds indicated that they were a short distance in front of us.

Puh slowly stepped out of the sled's harness and went to Ria's side. They exchanged nods and then Puh turned to us and once more held up a hand. Ria, armed with her little bow and Puh with his spear, left us, carefully placing their feet on the soft pine needle-covered earth as they soundlessly weaved their way through the trees.

We waited nearby, choosing a place where the grouse had not yet deposited their droppings. As warm summer air wafted through the fragrant forest, we listened to the sounds of the woodland creatures: the now distant shuffling-scratching of the grouse as they searched for insects, the songs of birds, the cries of squirrels as they scolded us from the safety of lofty branches, the buzzing flies and mosquitoes. A hawk screamed from a nearby treetop. I looked up at the sun to judge the passing of time and reminded myself to be patient.

At last, Puh and Ria returned. They were grinning and each toted several limp hens.

"Are we to assume that Ria's arrows made the kills?" Ty asked.

"Yes," Puh replied proudly, leaning closer to Ria to give her a kiss. Small game was most easily brought down with snares, throwing sticks, or arrows. Puh had only gone along to provide protection for Ria, lest some creature choose to make a meal of her.

"It not wisent, but it fresh," Karno said approvingly.

The sun was now well into its decline. We quickly cleaned the birds of most of their feathers hand organs and set out once more. As we made our way down the trail we began to keep watch for a place where we might set up camp for the night.

* * *

The following day brought fine weather.  The grouse had been consumed the previous evening, the only visible remnants of them being their charred bones within the now-dying fire.  After breaking our fast with a meal of dried meats, chewed laboriously as we broke up camp, we struck out down the path just as the sun fully cleared the horizon.

We had not gone far when Black Wolf called for us to halt.  He waved for Puh and me to join him and the other men at the head of our procession.  There, he motioned toward a large bear wallow.

"It is rather unnerving to think we were sleeping just a short distance from where a beast big enough to make this wallow has obviously enjoyed much leisure time," Black Wolf stated.

"Perhaps the bear caught sight or scent of us and did not care for the idea of sharing this locale with us, and has left the vicinity," Puh countered lightly.

Puh was not just speaking in jest.  It was true that oftentimes bears avoided people if they could.

"Let us move on," Puh suggested. "I think we will reach the foothills soon after the sun climbs to its apex."

We trekked until midday, when we halted to rest and take sustenance.  It was warm if you were subjected to the sun's full glare, perhaps a bit too warm, but I did not mind.  Most times, there were enough trees to shade us, and we had plenty of water to keep our thirst at bay.  Sometimes we found patches of berries of various kinds, and if they were an edible variety, we would stop briefly to harvest some of these delectable fruits.  By now, we had collected more than we could eat, but any excess could be gifted to Gray Elk's household. As always, we brought presents of dried meats, smoked fish, pots of fats, and tools such as spear and axe heads. Additionally, we packed a number of cured beaver, otter, fox, and lynx pelts, which we hoped to trade for puppies.

"Do you think we will arrive at Gray Elk's tomorrow?" I asked Puh.

"Yes," Puh replied, nodding. "If the weather stays fair and we don't have to hunker down through a storm." Puh then paused as he looked at Fox. "What have you there, Fox?"

Fox seemed to be lost in thought, and he jumped a little when Puh addressed him.

"I saved two of the grouse wings," Fox said. "I am trying to make them into a fan for – um – Misty." Fox blushed. "I thought she might use it to fan tinder that is slow to light and to help direct smoke away from her face."

"Misty?" Ria repeated. "She is one of Gray's Elk's granddaughters?"

"Yes, she is one of the twin granddaughters," Black Wolf responded. "She was born to Sky Fire and Sweet Rain, I believe. She would be a young woman now." Black Wolf looked at Fox more closely. "Do you have an understanding with her?"

"No, Grandpa," Fox replied, "not a formal understanding."

Fox seemed pained at the public discussion of something so close to his heart.

"Speaking of Sky Fire, I hope to see him and his brother Running Buck while we are there," I said, changing the topic and earning a grateful glance from Fox. "I have not seen them in many years."

"I hope to, as well," Black Wolf chimed in. "Sky Fire had made a remarkable recovery since the bear attack. He has been out hunting every time we have visited of late, so I consider that to be a good sign that he is well enough to do vigorous work."

"I would expect it is an indication that he is fit," Puh remarked.

"I wonder if he still barks," Black Wolf mused aloud.

Morning Star laughed at this.

"Oh, I should not laugh," she admitted. "Poor Sky Fire; how terrible to be attacked by a bear and receive such awful head injuries, and then to lose his speech for a time."

"He barked?" Oak said, his tone betraying puzzlement.

"At the beginning, he did," Black Wolf informed his son. "Seeing as he was raised amongst all those dogs, it should not have been a surprise – but it was, nonetheless."

* * *

As Puh had guessed, we found the mountain's lower slopes not long after the sun had begun to sink to the west. As the bird flew, we did not have that much distance to cover, but the winding trails and the strenuous climb meant it would take us the rest of today and part of tomorrow to reach Gray Elk's home.

Fox had finished his work on Misty's fan during our breaks from the trail, and I thought he had done a rather nice job. He did not use the whole wings, but just the final segments with the longer feathers. Fox crafted a handle from several supple twigs, which he bent into oblong loops, with the ends sticking out like fishtails. The fanned feathers were placed between the two fishtail-shaped parts of the handle and lashed securely. Fox borrowed a bone needle from his mother and used some of the twine he carried in his pack to sew the wings to the handle. His careful stitches made quite a nice pattern against the feathers. It would be an impressive gift for a young girl to receive. It was the sort of thing one might expect to be given as a pairing offering.

The last day and the final leg of our ascent was the most trying. None of us were accustomed to this type of terrain; we could hike all day for days on end without becoming unduly weary, but this would test the strongest man's stamina. Ty had never been to the mountains before, so he was excited to finally see the much-acclaimed landscape he had often heard about. For one who did not have many opportunities to venture out to novel places, he did not seem to mind some discomfort. Karno, on the other hand, was not impressed. If he took note of the beautiful scenery, the lovely flowers scattered on the rocky soil, the occasional tiny rivulets and waterfalls that bounced down the mountainside, colorful rainbows floating in the air on their mists, he did not choose to comment on it.

"*Gah!*" Karno cried out. "Leg on fire! Leg need rest!"

"We will rest soon," Black Wolf assured him. "There is a place just up ahead where the trail widens a bit. There we can stop for a bit."

"We will have a good view of the valley," Puh added. "I had hoped we might meet up with friends or family on our way through the mountains. This trail has an offshoot that leads to the pass to the valley on the far side of the mountains where many go to hunt."

When we broke from the trail, the spectacular view of the valley we had crossed the day before revealed a number of ibex and sheep, and a single eagle riding on the wind, but no additional travelers. And no one appeared at the trailhead that led to the pass between the mountains. When we packed up to make our final leg of the journey, I saw that Puh was still peering down the valley and the trailhead, hoping for a glimpse of those we had not seen in a very long time.

"Were you hoping to see Lor or Dor?" I inquired. They were my cousins, the sons of his late older brother, Mror, for whom Puh's youngest child was named. We had last met with those cousins about seven years before, near this very spot.

"Yes," Puh said. "I thought the chances were few; it is too late in the season for them to be coming after the migrating reindeer as they do every spring, but you never know."

"Yes, you never know," I concurred.

The sun was more than halfway to the horizon when we reached the mouth of Gray Elk's cave. As always, we were greeted by a throng of barking dogs, their shaggy bodies blocking our entry, so we had to push through, shouting to announce our presence to be heard over the din. This was the first time that Gray Elk had not been there to welcome us.

The dogs usually dwelt near the entryway where they kept watch for visitors. When their barks alerted Gray Elk to the arrival of guests, he had always been on hand to give us a warm reception. I felt a pang in my chest. Had he passed since our last visit? It would not be unlikely, considering his age, but still, I could not imagine this place without him. I was stricken with feelings of dreadful anticipation as we entered the long passageway that led to the main chamber.

"Halloo!" Black Wolf shouted. "Halloo! Gray Elk? Halloo!"

Lamps lighted the long hallway to the main chamber, their acrid smoke hanging in the thick air as they illuminated the many skulls and antlers of the giant deer, red deer, and elk that lined the tall rock ledges overhead. Our footsteps, voices, and the scraping of our sleds along the floor drowned out any responses that Black Wolf's calls may have elicited, so we were relieved to finally reach the huge main room with its cheerful fire ablaze within the hearth.

The room's occupants seemed to be absorbed in some game that had them on their feet, leaping and darting about while simultaneously looking upward toward the cavernous ceiling.

"Halloo!" Black Wolf called out once more, bringing the cave's residents to a momentary standstill. Then they turned to face us.

"Halloo?" Gray Elk's voice replied, but I could not see him.

I was glad to hear that Gray Elk sounded strong, but I was mystified as to his location. Everyone in attendance before us was quite young.  Where was Gray Elk?  His mate Buttercup? His adult children?

"Gray Elk?" Black Wolf said tentatively. "Where are you?"

Black Wolf craned his neck from his great height to look over the heads of the young people, and then divesting himself of his sled harness, he waded into the group.

Suddenly, it became apparent what had caused all the commotion at the time of our arrival.  A bird flew from its perch on a ledge, high up the face of the chamber's rock wall, and lit out across the room, settling on another ledge.

"It flew in by accident and we are trying to catch it!" one of the girls told us. "But it will not come down where we can reach it."

As the youngsters dashed to follow the bird, the vacancy around the hearth now allowed us to at last see where Gray Elk was lounging.  He was lying on a pallet that had been placed up against a pelt-covered wall.  Gray Elk was dressed in fine garments and wrapped in a cloak made of snow leopard skins.   Even his boots were skillfully made, although when he slowly swung his legs around to sit up, I noted that the soles of his footwear showed little signs of use.

Black Wolf quickly crossed the floor to meet him.

"Help me up, Cousin," Gray Elk said to Black Wolf, holding up a hand to him.

Black Wolf eagerly obliged and they embraced as soon as Gray Elk was standing erect.

"Gray Elk, it is so good to see you," Black Wolf gushed, brushing away emotional tears from the corners of his eyes. I wondered if his tears were not just those of happiness, but also sorrow to witness the sad decline of his cousin's health.

"It is good to see you as well," Gray Elk responded. He had been a tall man when he was in his prime, but he seemed shrunken now. "Let me down again, if you please."

Black Wolf gently lowered Gray Elk onto his pallet again and adjusted the man's cloak to better cover him. Black Wolf was seldom at a loss for words, but now he seemed speechless.

"How is it with you, Gray Elk?" Puh inquired, coming forward to take Gray Elk by the hand. Ria and Mror advanced with him.

"Tor!" Gray Elk said, greeting Puh heartily. "And Ria and Mror! I am so pleased you are here! Forgive an old man for not being able to greet you properly. It has been a long time ... too long! Many people come and go from this place to trade for dogs, but I have not seen many familiar faces lately. I did, however, see your two nephews Dor and Lor last moon. They brought much cured reindeer meat and took four dogs. It was a good visit. We talked of the old days ... of their father, your brother Mror. He was a fine man. How I miss his stories."

"I miss him, too," Puh said, still clinging to Gray Elk's hand. "But Dor and Lor? They are well? Their families are well?"

"They seemed to be thriving," Gray Elk began. "They were accompanied by a few companions, but they were men from another clan and I did not know them. They had never seen dogs before, and they did not really understand why your nephews wanted to bring a few of them home. They did say that their mother and her new mate, Sere, had passed. I was sad to hear it, but then, they were old," Gray Elk said with a shrug. "But then, I am old too. It is more of a surprise that I am still here than that they are not."

"And Buttercup?" Morning Star asked hesitantly, as though afraid to hear the answer.

Gray Elk did not reply right away. The look on his face said what his mouth struggled to articulate. Gray Elk visibly swallowed.

"I cannot speak of it without losing my composure," he admitted. "I will let you make of it what you will."

"I am truly sorry," Puh said to Gray Elk, looking into Gray Elk's face earnestly. "I know what it is to grieve a mate," Puh added quietly, speaking hardly more than a whisper.

Gray Elk nodded, but then he seemed to gather himself together, and he gazed up at the rest of us, waving us to come closer. Morning Star was there in an instant, Owl still in her arms as she knelt by Gray Elk's pallet. She placed her arms around his neck and hugged him, as best she could with Owl between them.

Gray Elk smiled at this.

"Morning Star! Still as lovely as ever, and you have a new little one!" Gray Elk said, returning her hug. "Is he not an armful? What a lively little lad!"

"He is indeed an armful!" Morning Star agreed. "This is Eagle Owl, named for your cousin, of course."

"Eagle Owl," Gray Elk repeated. "That is a name I have not heard in some while. He was a good man to be named for." Gray Elk chucked Owl under his drool-covered chin. "And let me see the rest of your family . . . Tris, my how the years tell on you!"

I smiled at this and reached out to grasp Gray Owl's free hand.

"I have heard that much of late," I said. "I cannot deny that it is true. These are our daughters; you may remember Pony, Raven, and Lily, but we now have Willow, Fawn, and Daisy, too. And, of course, you know Fox, our eldest son."

"Like me, you are fortunate to have a bevy of beauties in your household," Gray Elk said with a laugh. But then he settled his gaze on Fox and his eyes widened. "This must be Fox! Let me look at you!" Gray Elk let go of Morning Star and me, and reached out to Fox, who took his hands. "How you have changed since your last stop here. Your hair is bound, and you have the beginnings of a beard. You are grown now. If I did not know better, I would think I was looking at your father when he was a young man."

Fox smiled shyly.

"I hope to be the man my father is," Fox said humbly. "I have not seen Misty since our arrival. Is she here?"

"Oh, yes," Gray Elk replied. "Misty is my little bird-catcher. Birds sometime fly into the cave and she is usually the one to trap them, but this one has proved elusive. I sent her and her twin Sunny to fetch a cast net from one of our storage rooms. They will never catch that bird by chasing after it. They must net it. That is, if the poor thing does not perish from fright after being harassed by all those who want to snatch it from the air."

Just then, the lookalike twins appeared at the entrance to one of the many tunnels that branched off the main chamber, netting in hand. I could not ascertain which sister was which, and I had a moment to wonder if Fox could tell them apart. Both girls appeared astonished to see that a number of guests had arrived during the brief interval since they had left the room. I recognized Misty and Sunny from our last visit, but like my children, they had matured considerably. Both girls were slender and comely, their long, braided hair shining in the lamp and firelight.

One of the two recovered from her surprise and approached us with a broad smile.

"Morning Star!" the girl exclaimed, throwing her arms around her. "It is I, Misty! What a wonderfully unexpected pleasure to see you!"

Morning Star hugged Misty too.

"And I am so pleased to see you," Morning Star responded. "I am so glad to have an opportunity to catch up on everyone's news. I suspect your father and uncles are hunting, but where are your mother and your aunts?"

Misty did not answer right away.

"There is too much to tell. Let us speak of it later," Misty said, releasing Morning Star and turning to Black Wolf to embrace him. Black Wolf's height obliged him to crouch down to meet her hug and kiss her cheek.

"Hallo, Misty," Black Wolf said, but in an instant, she had moved off to welcome the next-closest person.

Now that Misty had set an example, the other young people came forward to greet us as well. Many I knew, but there were others – smaller children – I did not know, and I thought they must have been born since our last stop here. Even the Wolfmen received a warm welcome. Karno, as the leader of his people, was a bit stiff, but his two companions, who had been largely silent and somber throughout our time together, seemed delighted to become acquainted with this lively group.

When Misty drew opposite Fox, I watched their encounter, hopeful for Fox's sake that she would show some sign of reciprocating his interest. Like the rest of us, she gave him a hug and she smiled at him, but unlike the rest of us it seemed to me she took a moment to gaze at him, clearly impressed at the changes she saw. He was no longer the rambunctious little boy, so full of mischief. Not that those days were very far behind him, but I felt sure they were now behind him for all time.

Fox and Misty did not say much to one another, nor did Fox present the fan he had made for her. However, Misty did point out the bird to Fox, and she made a motion with the net to demonstrate her intention. Fox removed his pack and took the cast net from Misty. Fox had often used a cast net while fishing in the lake at home, but that meant throwing the net downward. This prey was most decidedly not going to come down amongst all the anxiously staring faces anytime soon.

Fox opened the cast net to gauge its size and weight, and then gathered it up in his hands again. Peering up at the bird, he studied it briefly and then, as we all watched in silence, he tossed the net into the air with a skilled snap of his wrists that caused the net to spin open as it flew. The net smacked the rock wall, capturing the bird within its folds, and it fell to the cave's floor in a heap.

Misty quickly collected the net and its fluttering catch, gave Fox a triumphant grin and then started down the long corridor that led outdoors. Fox, not one to let such an opportune occasion slip by, hurried to join her.

* * *

Over the evening sup, the long tale of what had transpired since we had last visited was told. Not only had the family lost Buttercup, but also Misty's mother, Sweet Rain, had passed during childbirth. One of Gray Elk's daughters had lost her mate when he was killed on a hunt, but she had since become paired with another man. It was sad to hear of so much death. Nevertheless, in spite of all the tragedy, the family seemed to be doing fairly well. Just now, Gray Elk was the only adult left at home, as the others had left on a midsummer hunting and foraging campaign. This was the height of the season, and food had to be harvested not only for immediate consumption, but also to store away for winter.

Gray Elk was delighted with all we had brought to add to their stores, but he shook his head when we said we hoped to trade for puppies.

"I have no pups that are weaned," Gray Elk said. "Tor, your nephews Dor and Lor took the last ones I had: four very nice half-grown pups. But I have a few litters that will be weaned in a half-moon or so, if you can linger here for a while."

We exchanged glances. A half-moon was longer than we had planned on staying. But we had traveled all this way. Ty seemed particularly downcast.

"It does not make sense to leave when the dogs will be ready to leave in a half-moon, but that will mean we will be away from home for an entire moon, if not longer," Ty pointed out.

"You are afraid your families will worry?" Gray Elk questioned.

"Yes," Ty replied. "I am sure they will be concerned when we do not return on time."

Yes, they will worry, I thought, but it seemed to me we seldom returned exactly when we hoped. That said, I knew that Ty was not accustomed to being away from home. Nor was his mate, Aessa, used to being without him. This was no small matter. Even though Morning Star had learned to cope during my long absences early on in our relationship, this did not mean it was easy for her. It helped that many of our children were now old enough to lend a hand with the daily chores; but Morning Star was also forced to rely upon our neighboring family and friends for occasional assistance while I was gone. I could understand why Ty was eager not to be away for too long.

"Well, the only consolation I can offer is that you will be more likely to have a chance to see those of us who are currently afield," Gray Elk said. "I expect them to come home any day now. And you will have more time to look over and select the best pups."

Ty nodded.

"Aessa will worry, but she has Binty and his mate there to help her." Ty paused, but then he went on,

"Perhaps if someone stops in here who will later pass close to our compound, they would be willing to carry a message to our families."

"That is a distinct possibility," Gray Elk said. "For a remote location, we do get visitors fairly frequently. More and more each year, it seems."

"The more people hear about your dogs, the more will come," Black Wolf predicted.

"That is true," Gray Elk agreed. "I do not know how word is spread so far and wide, but I never seem to have enough pups these days." He turned to Ty. "With luck we will succeed in getting word to your loved ones before they become too concerned at your lateness."

"Many thanks, that would ease my mind," Ty responded.

As I looked at the sea of faces that surrounded the hearth, I noted that Fox had seated himself by Misty. He was not speaking with her much, but Misty definitely held his attention. I wondered when he would bring out the grouse-wing fan he had made for her.

I shared Ty's frustration at extending our time away from home; it was not only the fact that our families would wonder at our absence, but the thought of the accumulating work that would await us upon our return. That aside, I was glad that Fox would have more time to woo Misty – assuming she was not already spoken for.

Just then Morning Star nudged me. She, too, was watching Fox, smiling as though she were very pleased.

"I asked Sunny if Misty was promised yet," Morning Star said in whisper. "Sunny says she is not, but she admires a young man who visits annually with his father and uncles."

"Oh?" I replied, feeling my heart sink, perplexed at Morning Star's presently blithe spirit.

"But Misty looks at Fox very sweetly," Morning Star pointed out, as though we should take it as a positive sign. "After all, a young girl's heart can be as changeable as the weather."

 **Chapter Eight** 

*The ceiling becomes so low that I must crawl in the semidarkness on my hands and knees. I take in dust with every breath, causing me to cough and my eyes to fill with grit. Then I come upon a large chunk of rock that blocks most of the tunnel. Still scrabbling on all fours, I squeeze past the obstruction and finally I am able to walk upright once again. I peer ahead into the murky beam of light illuminating the passageway and I wonder how much farther it will be until I reach the end. And perhaps most importantly, what will I find there?*

I awoke in darkness. My mind had been so completely absorbed in the Dream that it took me a moment to remember where I was. Morning Star and I had bedded down in one of Gray Elk's spare chambers, and the lamp had by now burned out. Our older children had asked to spend the night in the sleeping chambers belonging to the offspring of our hosts, so Morning Star and I were alone, except for Owl. Our littlest one was sound asleep on a nest of bedding in one of the alcoves off our room. We had made good use of this time to ourselves, and we had not slept until we were overtaken be exhaustion. I was quite comfortable in my slumbering mate's embrace and in no hurry to get up, except for the persistent nagging of my full bladder.

I did not know if it was morning or still night. I slipped from Morning Star's arms and felt around in the blackness for my loincloth, which I quickly donned, and then I cautiously proceeded toward what I hoped was the opening that led to the main chamber. As I passed by Owl, I was reassured to hear his soft breaths.

It was the slight movement of air on my skin that alerted me to the passage's entryway, and there, I saw a dim light at the end, indicating the entrance to the main room. My spear still leaned against the wall, along with the spears belonging to the rest of my group. So I chose mine from the collection of weapons, and from there, I traversed the long passageway to the cave's entrance, where a cool breeze whistled though the opening. There, Gray Elk's dogs napped, their bodies curled up and pressed against one another, unperturbed by the wind.

Some of the dogs awoke and rose to their feet when they sensed my presence. Their tails wagged in recognition. Some woofed quietly in greeting. I patted a few furry heads as I went by, and several accompanied me outdoors, where we each found a place to relieve ourselves. The moon had set, but the stars still shone brightly from a dark sky. There was no indication that the sun would be rising anytime soon. It was good to know that I would have time to sleep a little more. Shivering, but feeling much better, I retraced my steps back to the bedchamber I shared with Morning Star, picking up a lighted lamp along the way. The cave was still silent, except for the soft crackles from the low fire within the hearth.

Once I had returned to our room, I peered at Owl by the light of the lamp. He lay on his back, unmoving except for the rising and falling of his chest. Morning Star had not awakened whilst I was away, so I undressed and lay back down with her again. Morning Star stirred sleepily.

"Your skin feels cool," she said. "Did you go outside? And did you check Owl while you were up?"

"Yes," I answered. "And yes. Owl is fine. Sound asleep."

"I am glad Owl has not awakened yet. But I do not understand why you will not use the indoor receptacles," Morning Star told me. "You do not need to go out just to urinate."

"Somehow it just seems cleaner to go outside," I said. "And I do not like to urinate in anything that then must be emptied outdoors. It just adds an extra step."

"I suppose that is true." Morning Star then giggled. "I hope you put on clothing, lest you frighten anyone you might have met up with."

"I dressed in my loincloth," I replied. "Even that would have been frightening enough to behold. But the only beings I encountered were the dogs, and they did not seem unduly put off."

"I am glad you have brought in a lamp so I may see you," Morning Star said. "Even after all this time, I still love to gaze upon you."

I raised myself up on one elbow and returned her gaze.

"You are still the one my eyes seek out, as well." As I spoke, I touched her long black hair. Morning Star had loosened it the night before and it was now arrayed all around her face, the shining black tresses spilling across our bedding. I then bent forward to kiss her lips. "I love you. I will always love you."

"As I will always love you," Morning Star said, kissing me, too.

I never ceased to feel wonder at my good fortune to have this woman in my life. Perhaps it was our time apart that made us genuinely appreciate one another, but I would like to think that we would be just as content if we were able to spend all our time together. My plans to go back to sleep soon vanished.

Some while later, we lay still entwined, and I was once again contemplating going back to sleep.

"Tris," Morning Star said softly in my ear.

"Yes?" was my mumbling response.

"I was thinking . . ." Morning Star trailed off.

"Oh?" My eyes had been closed in hopes of drifting off to sleep, but now they opened. "What are you thinking?"

"I am so sad about Buttercup," Morning Star told me. "She was always so wonderful to me and my family. So gracious. I will miss her."

"I will, as well," I agreed. "She has always been very kind to me."

"I was thinking – if we have another girl, I would like to name her after Buttercup."

I smiled at the thought.

"I like your idea," I said. "Perhaps we just made another girl."

Morning Star laughed lightly.

"Perhaps."

* * *

When we finally arose, the household was bustling with activity. The fireplace in the main room now boasted a roaring blaze, which lent a wonderful warmth to the chamber. Torches and lamps were lighted, food was offered aplenty, and everyone seemed in a festive mood. Black Wolf, Puh, Ty, Karno, and the other Wolfmen were gathered around Gray Elk as he reclined on his pallet, so I left Morning Star's side to join them.

"We have a lot of meat at this time, so there is no hurry to procure more," Gray Elk assured the other men. He seemed eager that they should stay. No doubt he was enjoying their company and did not want them to leave so soon, even if it was just for a hunt.

"Karno need find wounded rhino," Karno pressed. "Must find him."

Gray Elk seemed thoughtful.

"I hesitate to say for fear of offending you, Karno, but I will say it anyway," Gray Elk said. "For as long as I have food, no friend of mine will ever go hungry. Remember that."

Karno was silent a moment. He ran a hand through his close-cropped black hair and then rubbed his bearded face. I attempted to read his features to guess whether he had been offended or not, but Karno's visage betrayed no anger, just a mixture of frustration and surprise.

"Karno think much of Gray Elk," Karno said. "Gray Elk good to us. And Karno tell you same thing, for as long as Karno have something to share, Karno will share it. Just now, Karno want to go after rhino, and maybe have something to share. And something to trade for dog. Karno want to trade for dog – this many." Karno held up four fingers.

Gray Elk nodded, looking up at Karno from the pallet. Gray Elk smiled at Karno.

"We will trade," Gray Elk answered. "But wait a few days before you embark on a hunt. The men should be back by then. They will bring news of game you might pursue."

"Karno want to look today," Karno persisted. "Even if only to scout."

"I think that is a good plan," Black Wolf concurred. "We have a good view of the valley from up here. We can venture down a few trails and see what is nearby."

I happened to glance toward Fox and saw that he looked somewhat disappointed at this. I knew he hoped to stay close to Misty during this visit. He had spent the previous night in a chamber with Oak, Mror, and some of the other boys and had returned to Misty's company only a little while ago. Recollecting how I felt about Morning Star before we were paired, I could appreciate his conflicting emotions: the desire to spend time with the girl he loved versus the desire to explore more of the mountainside and possibly find prey.

"Let us leave after we have broken our fast," Black Wolf suggested.

There was a collective nod of agreement, and then I left the group to find my mate and daughters, who were comfortably seated by the hearth. Daisy immediately came to me, arms out, so I lifted her off her feet. As always, her doll was in her grasp, staring at me with its peculiar wooden gaze from within its rabbit skin blanket. In Daisy's other hand she held a bone that had been nearly picked clean.

"Hello, my Daisy!" I greeted her. "What are you eating?"

"Muh-Muh says it was an animal. An eye-buck," Daisy said.

"Ibex?" I guessed.

Daisy shrugged.

"It was good!" Daisy stated happily, nibbling at the little bits of meat still clinging to the bone. "We need eye-bucks at home!"

"They do not live where we live," I said to Daisy. "We can only eat them when we visit the mountains."

Daisy shrugged again.

"I like eye-bucks, Puh-Puh."

"I like eye-bucks, too," Fox said with a grin as he came to join us. "I was hoping we would have time to look over the puppies today."

"They are still very young, yet, but perhaps we can see them after we return from our scouting expedition," I remarked, settling down on a mat next to Morning Star,

Daisy still in my arms. "I do not think we will be gone long."

"Misty said it is raining this morning," Fox informed me. "When she took food to the dogs, she said it was drizzling steadily at that time."

I was surprised to hear this, since I had seen a star-filled sky when I had arisen earlier in the day.  It seemed clouds must have blown in since then.

"Perhaps that will cool Karno's enthusiasm for the rhino," Morning Star commented.

"Perhaps, but I doubt it," I replied. "But I think he will feel better if he is doing something to bring him closer to an actual hunt. He is clearly anxious."

"I cannot say as I blame him," Morning Star said. "Jura will be giving birth soon. He is not only eager to feed his clan, but to go home and see if he finally has his long-awaited son."

"I suppose that is true," I remarked. "And to make sure Jura and the new baby are well."

We did not linger long after breaking our fast. Gray Elk had imparted what information he had of game animals recently seen in the area.  As the snows had melted and lower slopes of the mountainside had become carpeted in grass and dotted with flowers, many creatures that retreated to the lowlands over the winter now ventured up the mountain to graze on the new growth. This included ibex, sheep, chamois, and even some species of deer.  There were many other beasts, as well – some more worrisome than others.  Snow leopards were stealthy enough to remain unseen, but their footprints provided ample proof of their presence.  Wolves did not often come up this high, but bears and lions sometimes made the climb.

Morning Star, my sister Mi, and my seven youngest children stayed behind with Gray Elk and his extended family, but the rest of us stepped out of the cave into a cool, damp day. The wind had died down and the rain had ended except for the occasional drop, and a heavy fog now hung over the land. Droplets of mist caught on our clothing and in our hair, giving our party's appearance a surreal, almost ethereal quality.

"This fog is not going to help us find game," Black Wolf noted.

Karno sniffed.

"Smell, *Back Woof!*" Karno said. "We smell animal."

Black Wolf appeared somewhat miffed at Karno's words.

"Some of us more than others!" Black Wolf grumbled irritably.

At first Karno appeared confused, but after a moment he realized that Black Wolf had misunderstood his meaning.

"No, *Back Woof*, Karno not say we smell like animal," Karno explained, and then he made a show of sniffing the air. "Karno mean we smell for animal."

"The animals are more likely to catch our odors long before we might catch theirs," Black Wolf stated discouragingly.

Karno gazed into the fog and sniffed a little more. Then, apparently deciding that he had picked up a promising scent, he pointed eastward.

"We go that way," Karno directed, still gesturing.

There was no point in any discussion, since none of us had anything worthwhile to suggest as an alternative, so we followed Karno along the mountain trail, listening carefully for sounds of animals, whether predator or prey, moving nearby.

As the morning wore on the sun gradually dissipated the fog, and a bright world came to light. The dampness was still prevalent, but it was just enough to make the rock surfaces glisten and to freshen the summer foliage. We crossed a few small rivulets as they bounced and bounded down the stony slopes. Many birds were taking advantage of the temporary abundance of water as they cheerfully chirped and bathed in the sparkling waters. We spied a few well-grazed areas where the plants had been nibbled down almost to the ground, and some tufts of an animal's woolly undercoat stuck to the wet path, but the only creatures we saw besides the birds were a number of chamois that watched us suspiciously from across a ravine. There was no sense in pursuing them, since they were more than capable of evading us. They could easily leap the many crevasses and be far, far away before we could come within striking distance.

Just as the sun was nearing its apex we arrived at a spot where the slope leveled out onto a plateau. The morning's rain had produced numerous small waterfalls that cascaded down the mountain here and there, and this particular place featured a very pleasant cataract. It had a long vertical drop that was perfect for drinking, refilling our water bags, and – now that the sun had come out – washing the sweat from our faces and bodies, as well. It was wonderfully refreshing.

We enjoyed this stop so much we decided to break from the trail and consume some of the dried stores we carried in our packs.

"Droppings," Ria said, motioning toward a scattering of small dark fecal matter. "These are too large for chamois, but too small for a beast of any significant size."

Puh looked, too.

"Ibex, perhaps," Puh hazarded a guess.

"I am sure many creatures have come here to drink their fill after all that rain," Ty speculated. "This must be a dry place for most of the year."

"The rock holds the water, at least for now, that is," Oak said, peering at a large puddle that had collected at the base of the stone wall near where the cataract had formed. "Father, look at this!" Oak cried out suddenly.

"What is it?" Black Wolf asked, hastening to Oak's side. Oak, as usual, was seated with Mror and Fox, and all three were staring into the puddle.

"I see images in the water!" Mror said in amazement. "Puh-Puh, Muh-Muh! Come see!"

"Those are reflections," Black Wolf informed the boys, edging closer so he might view the reflections, too. "It is not often one can see oneself clearly in water. I have not seen my own reflection, at least not a good one, in many years."

The boys marveled at the sight, touching their faces in wonder as if to confirm that what they were seeing really were their own visages. Black Wolf seemed uncertain as to whether or not he wanted to see himself, but when he did look, he smiled.

"Well, it is not as bad as I feared," Black Wolf said with a broad smile. "Not bad for a man who will be forty-nine winters old next season. I am still handsome," he added, without a trace of conceit, as though he were simply stating a fact.

I was not sure I cared to look, either. The boys and Black Wolf moved aside so others could experience this novel phenomenon. Karno was quite keen to view himself, and he spent several long moments studying his reflection. Like the boys, he touched his face, and he turned his head from side to side as though to see himself from as many angles as possible.

"Karno look like mighty hunter," Karno pronounced with great satisfaction.

The other Wolfmen gazed into the puddle, too. They smiled at what they saw.

"I see my father in the reflection," one of the Wolfmen said. "I did not realize that I resembled him so closely."

"You do," his friend assured him. "And that is well. Better you should look like your own father than someone else's." Both men laughed at the joke.

I had always been told I took after my Puh, and like Black Wolf, I had not seen my reflection in a very long time; not since before Fox was born. At that time, Puh and I had peered into a spring together and I had been struck by how much I looked like a younger, larger version of him. Puh and Ria were now at the puddle.

"Oh, Tor," Ria said mournfully. "How good of you to stand by me for all this time. I look wretched. My hair, my wrinkles, *oh*!"

Puh gathered her into his arms comfortingly.

"You are beautiful to me," Puh uttered softly. "When I see you, I see the woman I love."

I collected my courage and knelt by the small pool, next to Puh. Fox joined me. Even though I knew I was looking down at us, it took me a moment to reconcile my image of myself to the stranger in the water who stared back at me. If Puh and Fox had not been at my sides, I would not have believed it was truly my own reflection.

My physique still had the same basic outline. People had always remarked that I was big, especially for a man of the Old Ones, but there was no denying that I was a tall, strongly built man. Strands of white glinted from my red hair and beard. My face was marked with deep lines — both from scars and exposure to the weather as well as the rigors of thirty-two years of life. When had all these changes come about? It then occurred to me that I recalled when my Puh was the same age as I was this day, my teenage self thought he looked quite old. Gazing at my reflection, I had to admit that it was likely Fox now thought the same thing about me.

"What are you all looking at?" A voice called.

We all turned in unison to see a group of people walking toward us. On closer inspection, I saw that it was Gray Elk's itinerant family, and they were loaded down with heavy packs. They smiled as they recognized us.

"Black Wolf! Tris! Tor!" Running Buck cried out. "Are you visiting with our father?"

"We are," Black Wolf replied, stepping forward to embrace his cousin. "We hoped to trade for pups, but your father tells us it will be a while before they will be ready to leave their mothers."

Sky Fire, brother to Running Buck, eagerly embraced Black Wolf, too. I noted the vivid scar on Sky Fire's scalp was still evident, in spite of his long, braided hair. The sight of it reminded me of his lengthy recovery from the bear attack and longer-still recovery of his words. The last I had seen him, he was able to speak haltingly and I wondered if his words came more easily now.

As the greeting process proceeded, Sky Fire eventually came to me, also hugging me warmly.

"Hallo, Sky Fire," I said to him. "This is my eldest son, Fox. He was only little last time we saw each other."

"Hallo," Fox said to Sky Fire.

Sky Fire smiled brightly, and he too wrapped his arms around Fox.

"I remember you," Sky Fire spoke at last. "The boy has grown to man."

Fox seemed pleased that Sky Fire had noticed his maturity.

Sky Fire patted his shoulder and moved on to Oak and Mror. Mror was also only a tot the last time they had met, but these members of Gray Elk's family had never met Oak. If they had attended the annual fall Gatherings they would have seen him there, but no one representing Gray Elk's family had gone in many years. It was a very distant place to travel, and the needs of the family and the dogs took up all their time and attention.

Sometimes I wondered why they stayed on this remote mountainside, where all their supplies had to be hauled up steep slopes and twisting pathways. Perhaps it was because a cave as huge as Gray Elk's was not commonplace. The cave was cool inside, but it was mostly dry and the main chamber featured a natural chimney hole. The cave's many rooms offered accommodations large enough to house several families and store enough goods to keep them comfortable for years.

"What were you all looking at?" Running Buck asked again, pointing toward the puddle that had so fascinated everyone.

"Look," Black Wolf gestured downward. "Look, and you will see."

Running Buck and the others peered into the puddle.

"Reflections!" Running Buck exclaimed. "I have not seen my reflection in a long time! This pool of still water in the shadow of the rock face captures our images perfectly!"

After a period of gazing into the puddle, sometimes mugging comically for assorted effects, we returned to our conversation.

"We hope to bring in our harvest as soon as possible," Running Buck told us. "Are you headed that way, too? Will you come with us?"

Those of us in my party looked to one another for their reactions.

"Could we go with them, Puh-Puh?" Fox asked me.

I suddenly realized why he hoped to join them. Sky Fire was Misty's father. No doubt he wished to make a good impression on his beloved's parent.

"We may as well go, too," Black Wolf responded. "What say the rest of you?"

"It would be productive to speak on hunting as we walk," Puh answered.

Karno only grudgingly agreed.

"You tell us where you see game?" Karno said to Running Buck. "You see rhino?"

"Oh, there is lots of game to be seen," Running Buck replied, starting to walk down the trail again. "We were out to harvest herbs, tubers, berries, onions, and greens. We have meat from the spring hunts and from making trades for dogs, but we needed to find vegetable matter while summer is upon us."

"But we saw plenty of game," Sky Fire added. "That always seems to be the way. When we are not hunting or if we are too pressed for time to take down animals, we are practically tripping over them. We did take a small deer while we were out, but we ate it at our camp."

"What kind game?" Karno questioned, walking in step with Running Buck.

"The kind you would expect," Running Buck shrugged. "We spent most of our excursion in the forest, but we also ventured into the valley between the mountains, where there is a pond with lots of cattails and water lilies. There we saw many wisents, assorted deer – all come up to escape the heat of the lowlands – and off in the distance there was a herd of aurochs, but they were moving away. We even saw woolly rhino tracks. We could see where one of them had bedded down one night. It must have been injured, because it left bloodstains where it had lain."

Karno's eyes widened.

"That rhino Karno look for," he said. "How far to bed spot?"

"A day's walk," Running Buck informed him. "But that rhino could be anywhere by now. The wisents are numerous enough to almost fill the valley, and they have many calves. They would be easier targets than a wounded rhino."

I thought this was true, but Karno could not be dissuaded.

"Karno want rhino," Karno said. "Karno need big rhino."

"Wisents are big, and they have a lot of meat, too," Sky Fire pointed out.

Karno muttered a response that was unintelligible to my ears, but I could guess at the gist. He seemed to have anticipated much more enthusiasm for his mission. Within his own clan, as leader, his word was obeyed without discussion or question. Karno did not always have a well-thought-out plan, or any plan at all. However, his results were generally successful – whether because of good luck or skill, or some combination of both.

The noise of our large procession, what with all our chatter, was enough to scatter the many animals we saw grazing on the slopes. It was a wonder to me that the plant life managed to survive on this rocky terrain, between the hostile growing conditions and the constant nibbling by various creatures that depended on them for sustenance. Nevertheless, the profusion of flowers seemed to thrive, abuzz with bees, butterflies, and other insects that were also eager to take advantage of this brief verdant season.

Our eyes constantly scanned our surroundings as we trekked, also taking care to look down occasionally, lest we stumble over an unfortunately placed stone on the pathway. Ria strung her little bow as we walked.

"If we can surprise an ibex or a chamois, I might be able to hit it," Ria said.

"Tris and I can accompany you to the front of the procession," Puh began, "and if we can walk far enough ahead of the others, we may be able to get within range of your arrows."

Puh turned to me, and I nodded. He and I would provide protection for Ria, who was small enough to be tempting prey for any large predators that might be lurking about. We could not hope to strike these agile animals with our spears. Ibex and chamois will graze placidly while letting hunters come tantalizingly close, but not near enough to lance with our spears before they bounded off. Ria's arrows, on the other hand, substantially improved our chances of bringing down an animal.

Our companions, having overheard our plan, stepped to the side of the narrow trail to let us pass by. It went unspoken that our sons would stay behind with the group. When pursuing flighty prey, fewer hunters meant a quieter approach. I could see that most of the others were dismayed not to be included, but they understood the wisdom of being left behind.

"We will wait here for a few moments before following," Running Buck said. "To allow you to get ahead of us."

"Many thanks," Puh answered.

I was pleased to be actively hunting.  It was gratifying to feel as though I was doing something productive.  We moved quickly and stealthily, Ria positioned between Puh and me.  When we came to a bend in the trail where the path skirted a large rocky projection, Puh held up a hand.  We stopped to exchange glances.  Puh motioned to the rock, and we knew without speaking that he wanted us to now advance at a creeping pace until we could peer around the rock to see what was ahead.

When we reached the stone outcropping, we could hear the animals that were feeding or lounging on the far side.  We listened to the sounds of their peaceful grazing, occasional hoof clatters against the stone, and their softly uttered rumbles and baas.  Ria turned to us and silently mouthed one word. *Many.*  She slipped three arrows from her quiver, and still holding them in her fingers, she notched an arrow and then leaned around the rock.  Her bowstring twanged three times in quick succession, as the sounds of scrambling hooves and surprised bleats met our ears.  Ria grabbed another handful of arrows and shot them off just as quickly.  Her archery skills never failed to amaze me.  I could never notch an arrow and fire it as swiftly, and still manage to hit my target.

We dashed from cover just in time to see a snow leopard close its jaws around one of the fallen animals. Ria was not about to let the beast take her kill, unchallenged.  She ran forward, simultaneously reaching for the last few arrows rattling around in her quiver, but when she attempted to launch them, her bowstring broke. Undaunted, Ria charged the snow leopard, swinging her bow in wide arcs while yelling at the creature.

"Get away," Ria shouted, "get away."

Puh and I ran along with her, careful to avoid her flailing bow, spears poised to strike the snow leopard and thus recover our stolen prey. But it stared at us balefully for just an instant, growling even with the limp chamois still dangling in its jaws. The snow leopard did not relinquish the chamois; instead, it turned away from us to hastily escape with its prize before it met the same fate as the fallen chamois.

"The leopard must have been hunting the animals at the same time as were we," Puh said.

"It took my arrow, too," Ria noted unhappily. "But at least we still have these two beasts to bring home."

Ria had managed to take down three chamois in all before the herd vacated the area, and despite losing one of them to the snow leopard, I thought she had done well. Ria recovered the arrows that had missed their marks while Puh and I began to gut her victims.

After a short time, the rest of our party caught up with us. We planned to lash the chamois to a spear by their hooves so they could be carried back to the cave, but we dared not do that and thus lose the use of one of our spears until the others had made their way up the trail to meet us.

When they arrived, they also bore two chamois with them. As soon as I saw the beasts, I realized what must have happened. The fleeing chamois must have bolted in the direction of our companions as they hiked up the trail, and they then had made the most of this unexpected boon.

"Thank you for sharing the chamois with us," Black Wolf called out. "We tried to stop as many as we could when they blundered into us, but could lance only these few."

"They came bounding over the rocks at the side of the trail," Running Buck said. "We had only an instant to react. The creatures tried to leap to the rocks on the far side of the path, but as they took to the air, Ty sprang into action and speared one of them in the chest as it passed overhead. Black Wolf struck the second one."

Ty was glowing with pride at his success. He did not often have much opportunity to hunt, so this was an important day for him. I was very happy for him. We each smiled when our eyes met. When our chamois were lashed to our spears, we set out once more, cheered by our good fortune. Our scouting mission had been more fruitful than we had hoped.

* * *

I had never witnessed how kills were processed at the cave, so I was interested to see that they had a butchering site a short distance from the entrance. There were no trees here from which the carcasses could be suspended, so wooden frames were erected. A small shelter of sorts was also built by stacking loose stones until they formed a semicircle. This structure was currently open at the front and on top, but it would not take much to add a roof. A fire pit was situated near the shelter. I guessed this was a place to smoke foods and animal hides, and although the shelter was not more than a windbreak, it still offered a little protection from the mountain's sometimes fierce weather.

Fox, Oak, and Mror asked to do the butchering, and the rest of us were more than happy to grant their request. We had carved up enough animals that the novelty had worn off a long time ago. Puh, Ria, Black Wolf, and I stayed to oversee them, but the others continued their trip back to the cave. Gray Elk's kin were understandably eager to get home, and Karno had lost all enthusiasm for this outing, so he too was ready to be done with it.

"Karno go back and look at pup," Karno announced as he took his leave of us.

"Dogs are nice, but the young women lodging at the cave are far nicer," one of Karno's companions said.

Karno smiled. He had not been overly merry of late, so I was glad to see it.

"Yes, women nice," Karno concurred. "I know you hope to find nice woman. Speak with Gray Elk about this. I take home dog after we get rhino. Maybe you take home woman."

"I like the little bird-catcher," the same companion said.

Fox's head jerked around as he heard this, and he stared at the two Wolfmen. Fox frowned. He was the one who had actually caught the bird, but there was no doubt as to whom they were referring. The *little bird-catcher,* as she was fondly dubbed by her grandfather, could only be Misty. I could see that Fox was debating with himself as to how or even whether he should respond. But the men walked away before he had made up his mind.

Fox appeared unsettled. We could not help but notice the abrupt change in Fox's demeanor, and each of us knew why.  I wanted to say something that would soothe him, but I also did not want to embarrass him.  I went to stand by Fox as though to watch him work, but I placed a comforting hand on his shoulder for a moment.  A year ago Fox would have shrugged off my hand, but he looked up to meet my eyes.  Fox appeared troubled, but he gave me a small smile to acknowledge the gesture.  My silent message – *I understand; I am here for you* – had been received.

 **Chapter Nine** 

*The charred stick's harsh scratching against the stone's rough surface produces echoes that linger in my ears. It leaves a black line on the rock wall. And another black line. Yet another line, but this one curves.*

I was relieved not to revisit the Dream of the dark and endless tunnel. Was this Dream telling me to make an image, like those on the Talking Stones? The Talking Stones adorned one of the walls in the chamber Morning Star and I currently inhabited. This was a room in which we had stayed as a family in years past. The room was completely dark except where lamp light illuminated it, so I sometimes forgot the Talking Stones were there until I happened past them with a lamp in hand. When the children were younger they had liked to sleep by the Talking Stones, usually requesting a lamp so they could gaze at them until they fell asleep. This time all but Owl were sleeping elsewhere, so I had not had their keen interest to remind me to look upon these wonderful pictures.

Soon, many of us would leave for the valley Running Buck had spoken of, in pursuit of Karno's rhino – or maybe just a wisent or aurochs or two. In the midst of our preparations to embark on this extended hunt, I borrowed two lamps and several charred sticks and took them to our bedchamber.

I set down the lamps on rock ledges near the Talking Stones. Suddenly, the images came to life. The rampaging bull mammoths drawn as though they were in full battle, wolves running, their legs extended front and back as they dashed toward their intended victim, a giant deer. There were many other animals displayed across the face of the Talking Stones. They were exquisite in their detail and finely portrayed in their various activities. Underneath these drawings were the more primitive sketches that had been made many years before by Fox and Pony.

I was hesitant to add my own attempt. What could I contribute to the Talking Stones? I was afraid I could offer nothing worthy of this magnificent collection of drawings. What could be as awe-inspiring as these images? Even Pony's and Fox's renditions of a boy and a crow were elegant in their simplicity.

All at once, I knew what I would do. I had never drawn anything before, except to etch a map in the dirt to instruct on how to get from one place to another. But as my hand directed the charred sticks, the black lines began to form a face: an oval face with flowing black hair that encircled the head, the way my mate's did when we lay in bed together.  I drew a soft smile, the familiar eyes, the graceful neck . . .

"Tris, what are you doing?" Morning Star had come up behind me.

She, too, carried a lamp, which she held up before her as she studied my work.

"I Dreamt I was making a Talking Stone," I told her. "I wanted to try."

"What is it?" Morning Star asked.

I was disappointed she did not recognize herself, but then she had not been with us at the puddle where we had peered down at our reflections, and perhaps she did not remember how she looked.  It was also possible the likeness was not as accurate as I imagined.

"It is the dearest thing to my heart," I replied, hoping she would at least appreciate the loving spirit in which it had been rendered.

Morning Star gazed at me blankly for a moment, and then she went nearer the drawing for a closer look. Morning Star began to laugh.

"Oh, my! Is it me?" she said, still tittering.

"In my mind, it is," I answered, somewhat abashed at the reception my Talking Stone had garnered.

Morning Star wrapped her arms around me in a tight hug and then she tiptoed up to kiss my lips.

"I am honored," Morning Star said, kissing me again. "I never thought to appear on Gray Elk's Talking Stones. I am pleased to be represented here amongst all these grand pictures."

"I am glad," I said, returning her kisses.

"I came looking for you because I hoped we might talk while we are alone," Morning Star said, becoming serious. "Fox has seemed rather subdued since coming back from your outing. Did something happen?"

"Well, he was disappointed to learn that one of the Wolfmen has also taken notice of Misty," I said.

Morning Star seemed surprised.

"That worries him?" she asked in disbelief. "They are at least ten years older than Misty. She is much more apt to be interested in someone who is closer to her own age."

"He may be thinking of my sisters Twie and Saree, who each became paired with much older men," I pointed out.

"Maybe," Morning Star considered for a moment, "but Twie was born old, and Saree . . . well, Saree is Saree. She has a mind of her own. Speaking of your sisters, I am surprised your youngest sister Mi has not found a suitor. She reminds me so much of your mother, with her pretty face and dark red hair. She and Misty are about the same age."

"Perhaps she is too shy," I speculated.

"She is very quiet," Morning Star noted. "She does not like to draw attention to herself. Although it seemed to me that Sky Fire was looking at her very closely. I wonder if she might prefer older men, since her sisters seem to? Or at least be willing to consider an older man?"

"Muh-Muh!" Pony's voice echoed across the chamber as she entered the room. "Muh-Muh! Owl wants you! I do believe he is hungry!"

Pony approached with Owl perched on her hip. He was not a fussy baby, but he was looking rather mournful, and he was drooling, as was often the case.  He began to whine piteously as soon as he saw his mother.

"Thank you, Pony; I will take him." Morning Star left me and took Owl from Pony.

Pony seemed grateful to be released from the care of her baby brother.

"I will rejoin the others in the main room," Pony announced. "Karno is telling us how they will kill the woolly rhino. Why does Karno call himself *Karno*? Why does he not say *I* or *me*, like everyone else?"

"Karno's thought processes are a little different from everyone else's," Morning Star responded.  I thought it a rather astute answer.  Karno was not stupid, but he was certainly singular in his mental faculties.  Morning Star then added, "Be sure to keep an eye on your younger siblings. Is Daisy behaving well?"

"She fell asleep in Fox's lap," Pony answered. "I think the excitement of playing with so many other children has tired her. But she has been happy, just the same."

"That is well," Morning Star said.

Pony then left us, and Morning Star sat down with Owl on a bedding platform and began to nurse him.  He quieted immediately.  I could hear his suckling from where I stood as I looked upon my drawing.  It was true that my portrayal of Morning Star needed work.  I decided I would attempt to improve it before we made our eventual departure.

Morning Star suddenly flinched.

"What is it?" I asked.

"I predict that Owl will soon have a few teeth," she replied.

"Owl, you must be nice to your mother," I chided him gently.

"It is not too bad," Morning Star assured me. "Nothing I have not gone through with all of our previous children, and nothing that will not happen with any future children."

"Sometimes I think women are tougher than are men," I mused. "The first time I was bitten by one of our infant offspring, I marveled that you were willing to put any part of your anatomy in that mouth. Even without teeth, their bite commands a good deal of respect."

Morning Star laughed lightly.

"After going through childbirth, nursing a baby is the easy part," she said.

I had been present for only a few of the births of our children, but even so, I could appreciate that this was profoundly true. The birth itself was incredible to behold, but witnessing the grueling process of getting to that point was grim indeed. She had borne the painful and exhausting process mostly in silence. This was the closest Morning Star had ever come to complaining about the experience. I took comfort in this and the fact that she generally reveled in motherhood. Some moments were less enthralling than others, but Morning Star earnestly seemed to take joy in her care of her children.

"I am sure that is true," I said, bending down to kiss her forehead. "I am going to the main chamber. I want to hear what plans are being made for our hunt. Will you come out, too?"

"I think Owl may doze off," Morning Star started, "and if he does, I may opt to take a nap, too. Either way, we will soon join you."

I kissed her one last time and caressed Owl's cheek before leaving. I ventured a glance back at them to view my lovely mate and our little son, enveloped by the soft glow from the lamps. Morning Star was gazing toward my portrait of her, appearing somewhat disconcerted. I resolved to work on making refinements to the drawing later that day.

* * *

The large central chamber seemed bright and very warm compared with our lodgings. The room was filled with happy chatter from the several groups that congregated in various clusters. Most of the people were busily occupied with work, readying weapons and gear for the morrow's venture, preparing food, sewing hides; Gray Elk himself was constructing something that looked as though it might be the frame for a backpack.

Many of the men were gathered by Gray Elk. Karno must have had his say, because now he was just listening to the conversation. I found an open space by Fox and sat at his side.

"We will need to travel light, so we can transport the meat home," Running Buck said.

"Will there be trees from which we can make sleds?" Ty asked. "We have brought our sleds, but they will not be enough to carry all the meat from a woolly rhino."

Running Buck shook his head.

"There are very few trees in the valley, and what trees there are, are not very big," he said. "We will need to bring as many people as we can — anyone who can tote a load."

"Are there no rivers in the valley?" Black Wolf queried.

Again, Running Buck shook his head.

"There is a stream, but no river. Why?" he asked.

Black Wolf chuckled.

"I suppose it was too much to hope for," he said. "I was thinking of when we floated the meat from two mammoths home. It was not easy, but it did allow us to carry a tremendous load."

"That . . . that must have been an unusual sight," Sky Fire said, laughing, too. "How does one float a woolly mammoth? Did you kill the beasts in the water and then ride on their backs as they floated downriver?"

"Nothing so simple," Black Wolf replied. "They were in shallow water when they were taken down, but it was not until after we skinned them that Tris thought to make rafts from their hides and then use the rafts to bring the fruits of our hunt upriver."

"Upriver? Ugh. That must have been quite a slog," Running Buck said with sympathy.

"A heavy, wet, smelly slog," Black Wolf agreed. "But it worked."

"Given the day's heat, you will have to smoke the meat on site before it spoils and then pack it out," Gray Elk stated. "That is why I am working on making packs. We have a number of them, but you will need more. Have you thought about who will go with you to help carry?"

"Anyone who can be spared and who is strong enough to handle a load over the distance," Running Buck replied.

I looked to Karno, to see how he was taking in this discussion. Karno was uncharacteristically quiet, but then Pony had said he had already talked about his ideas. Karno seemed pensive. Was he thinking about the hunt? Was he concerned that the rhino would have left the valley for distant lands? Was he thinking of his family at home, his pregnant mate, his clan? As always, the other Wolfmen sat at his side, flanking him. If they had any worries, one could not tell. They appeared relaxed and ready to take on the next adventure, whatever it might be and wherever it might take them.

Some of the men left the group, now that the subject had been exhausted. Fox, too, got up, and I smiled to see him seek out Misty. I was pleased to see her motion to Fox to settle next to her. Soon, Misty was chatting animatedly with him as he listened, responding with an occasional nod.

I then noted that Gray Elk was struggling to bend a piece of wood into shape. I quickly stepped forward to assist him.

"Thank you, Tris," Gray Elk said. "I have grown so old I can no longer do the things I used to do with ease. My muscles do not obey me, my stomach rebels at certain foods, and my hearing is slowly going dim."

"I am older as well," I admitted.

"You are mature," Gray Elk corrected. "But you are still a powerful man. Your skin may be lined and your hair and whiskers may be frosted with white; you may be scarred and rough and callused and . . ."

"Your eyesight is still sharp," I interrupted with a grin.

Gray Elk laughed, his eyes almost disappearing into the deep creases on his face.

"I am glad you have a sense of humor, Tris," he said, still chortling. "I hope you do not take my remarks to heart. I was just trying to say that you are still a formidable man; I meant no offense. Besides, only a fool would seek to ignite your wrath. I hope to still have my wits about me for a while yet. Should I one day become foolish with age, please promise to be patient with an old man."

"Should that day come, I will," I vowed, patting his hand as though to seal the promise.

"I wonder," Gray Elk continued. "Do you think you will find Karno's rhino? I do not hold out much hope. We humor him, of course. He is a guest here, and I would not wish to insult him or his companions. I suspect the hunting party will return with loaded packs and sleds, but not loaded with rhino meat."

"I suspect you are right," I concurred. "I do not claim to understand his purpose – why the rhino is so important. He could have brought home a lot of game by now, if he were not so determined to kill the rhino."

"He wants a big animal," Gray Elk reminded me.

"Many animals are big," I pointed out. "He could have slain a wisent or an aurochs . . . several of them, in fact, since he left his clan. However, I am sure Karno must have some goal in mind."

"He is growing older, as well," Gray Elk said. "Karno is a proud man. The rhino is an impressive and notoriously aggressive animal. It has great horns that make spectacular trophies. Killing one of those beasts may inspire stories of daring feats and songs of brave men. That is what Karno seeks. To make his mark while he still can, to prove himself a young and vital man."

I nodded as I absorbed these thoughts.

"I thought he might want to bring his mate a special gift," I mused to Gray Elk. "She will soon bear him a child, and I thought he might like to bring the horns home to her. I had even pondered the notion that the rhino or its horns might have significance for the Wolfmen. Perhaps I will ask him." Gray Elk struggled with the pack frame again, so I reached out to lend a hand once more. Then I went on, "Gray Elk, I want to tell you while it is on my mind: I recall that you once gave us permission to draw on your Talking Stones, but I want to let you know nonetheless that I have begun a Talking Stone of my own. I will not disturb the images that are already present."

"I see," Gray Elk acknowledged. "What is it you are drawing?"

"I am attempting to capture Morning Star's likeness on the stone," I said, shaking my head. "It is not as easy as I would have supposed. My eyes see her face and my hand tries to replicate it with a charred stick, but it is not going quite the way I would have hoped."

"Take some white ash from the hearth," Gray Elk advised. "And maybe some chunks of ochre. A little color may help."

"Many thanks, Gray Elk," I told him. "Those are good ideas."

Gray Elk advised me on where to look for the pieces of ochre, and I did locate a few chunks in shades of yellowy-orange and red. I also carefully scooped up a handful of cooled ash from the hearth. These items were then brought to the wall of Talking Stones, and, holding up a lamp to the drawing with one hand, I dabbed on color with the other. The ash I used for the whites of her eyes and to highlight her forehead and the ridge of her nose. I used the orange and red to color the tones of her skin. I then used more orange to mark the stone around Morning Star's image, to contrast against the black of her hair. I stood back to assess these additions. I thought they were an improvement. I had accidentally smeared some of the black charcoal lines, so I did my best to repair them. I still had more work to do, but I hoped Morning Star would approve of the finished portrait.

* * *

We were away early the next morning, embarking as the sun was still cresting the horizon. The mountain air was cool; cold even. I was glad I had dressed warmly, even though I would probably have to shed layers as the day went on. Puh and I were pulling our sled, and Black Wolf and Oak pulled another. Running Buck and Sky Fire had yet another. Gray Elk's daughters' mates had not returned from their hunting expedition before our departure, so we planned to leave without them, although it would have been nice to have a few more seasoned hunters with us. Everyone else bore a backpack, some hastily assembled for this excursion. We hunters were accompanied by many of the residents from Gray Elk's home. His daughters had opted to stay home to keep the household going, as did Morning Star, who did not relish the idea of taking our smaller children on a potentially long hunt. Running Buck's mate and all of the children who were strong enough – including my Fox, Pony, Raven, and Lily – would come along to help bring home whatever was harvested.

I hoped that we would not be gone too long, nor have to travel too far. My daughters were eager to accompany us, but I did not like to expose them to anything too arduous. I knew that life would not always be kind to them and that they would face much hard labor in the years to come. They were maturing quickly; after all, Pony would be old enough to find a mate before long. Just now, though, it seemed all too soon. I mused that Puh probably felt the same way about Mi, his youngest daughter, who was only a few years older than Pony.

I kept a close eye on my girls, who hiked steadily in front of Puh and me, ringed by Ty, Mi, Fox, Ria, and Mror. Black Wolf and Oak pulled their sled behind us. Gray Elk's sons pulled their sled at the lead, seeing as they knew where we were going. The Wolfmen were close on their heels. I was sure Karno wanted to be as near to the front of the procession as possible, so as not to miss anything. Gray Elk's other kin were positioned just behind the head of our party. I noted that our group of twenty-four individuals was much larger than most of our hunting parties, but it was made up of as many young packers as experienced hunters. I could not help but worry that all these young people would be too distracting for those of us who would need to keep a vigilant watch on our surroundings.

The first day of our trek took us across the face of the mountain, back down the trail from which we had recently returned with the chamois. The many little waterfalls that had appeared after the rain had run their course, so water was not so plentiful at this time. We came across one sparkling stream as it bounded its way down the rocky slope. Our group stopped to top off our water bags, eat, and rest for a few moments but soon continued on. We wanted to cover as much ground as possible before sunset. There was little on the landscape that offered shelter here, so we would be forced to use our mostly empty sleds to erect lean-tos for the night. We had brought a small amount of firewood with us, since we would be venturing out on a countryside with scant offerings for fuel, but that wood was not lengthy enough to use in constructing a frame of any size. Nevertheless, our tarpaulins strung over the upturned sleds should provide sufficient shelter to preserve our body heat through the cold nights.

We had progressed a good distance into the valley by sunset. Mountains loomed heavily on either side of the valley, casting evening shadows across the vast grassy expanse that ran between the two summits. The air was cooling quickly.

"We must find a place to set up camp," Black Wolf called out.

"I see a large boulder up ahead," Puh said. "Perhaps we could set up camp there."

I thought this was a good plan. The boulder was about twice as tall as a man, and it would offer some protection from the wind. Also, a fire near its base would heat the stone, which would then not only gradually release the heat even after the fire had burned down, but would reflect the heat, too.

"That is where I had hoped we would spend the night," Running Buck yelled back to us from his place at the front of the procession. "We have camped there many times in the past."

When we reached the boulder, I could see that the grass was worn away in spots, and a well-used hearth awaited us. Misty immediately began to collect tinder. Pony stepped forward to help her. They soon had arranged a small mound of dried grasses topped by more dried grass, tied into knots. The tinder would not burn long, but it would help catch the sparks from the flint and iron pyrite when they were struck together. Birch bark was something that was carried in almost every pack, so bits of crumpled-up bark were added to the pile as well.

In the meantime, those of us with sleds had emptied them of their meager contents: mostly our extra spears, axes, our cloaks, empty sacks, tarpaulins, rope, and a small quantity of firewood. We hoped that by the time we were ready to return home we would have burned through the wood and thus have more room to load the meat, hides, and other harvested materials.

The empty sleds were then turned on their sides and lashed together into a frame. Once the tarpaulins were secured over the frame, our lodgings would be complete. It would be a very crowded shelter, but we would need our neighbors' warmth to comfortably get through the night, anyway.

Fox began to rifle through the items we had taken off our sled. These things were being spread around; the empty sacks were placed on the floor of our shelter, our rolled-up cloaks were also deposited along the outer walls, and our extra spears laid down in places where they could be accessed at a moment's notice, so at first I took no notice of Fox's actions. Then I saw him draw out the fan he had made for Misty from where he had stashed it between some of the empty bags. Fan in hand, he approached Misty as she tried to breathe life into the tenuous flames within the hearth.

"Try this," Fox said to Misty, holding out the fan.

Misty looked up at him from where she kneeled on the ground, surprise evident on her face. She soon smiled and reached out for the fan.

"Thank you for letting me borrow this," Misty said as she gently waved the fan at the fire. "How clever to make a fan. I have never seen anything like this!"

"It is a gift," Fox replied. "I made it for you."

Again, Misty appeared astonished.

"But it is beautiful. It is special," she responded. "You must not give it away."

Fox seemed pained that so many were present to hear this exchange. He appeared to consider his answer for a moment.

"I am glad you think it is special," he said quietly. "I made it for you. It is yours."

Misty stood and gave Fox a quick hug. I noted that Karno's companions were observing this exchange closely.

I saw the realization come to them that they now had a much younger competitor for Misty's heart. There did not seem to be any resentment toward Fox, only disappointment over this development. Then one of the Wolfmen nudged his saddened friend and murmured something to him that made him smile. They both turned and pointedly looked at Misty's twin sister Sunny. Misty and Sunny shared a similar appearance, but their personalities were quite different. Misty's outgoing and lighthearted demeanor contrasted sharply with Sunny's demure and serious disposition. This did not appear to worry them, however.

"Thank you, Fox. I will always treasure this fan," she told him. "No one has ever given me anything so nice. Truly. I thank you."

Fox just grinned and nodded, apparently pleased at her reaction. I was happy on Fox's behalf. However, we did not have much time to dwell on this event. There was still a lot of work to be done before we could settle down for the evening.

When at last the fire was well established and each of us had found our spot near the hearth, we dug into our packs for the food, water, and an assortment of small items they contained. We had brought various dried meats; roasted nuts from the previous year, which by now were well past their prime; and some rather wilted greens that the young people had picked at the stream where we had broken from the trail earlier in the day. This uninspiring meal was consumed amid occasional chatter.

"We should take turns standing watch tonight," Black Wolf suggested.

There was no doubt that any number of beasts might wish to investigate our camp as we slept. The moon was in a waning cycle, just a frail crescent rising amongst a sea of stars. I did not know if I had ever seen so many stars all at once, shining so brilliantly. Fox noted my skyward gaze, and he too looked up.

"The stars are so bright, Puh-Puh," Fox observed. "I have never seen them like this."

"It is the mountain air," Sky Fire informed us. "We have seen that the stars always appear more dazzling when viewed from our homeland than they appear when viewed anywhere else."

"But we are not on the mountain now," Ty stated.

"No, but the valley is still much higher than the forest below," Running Buck said. "I think we are closer to the stars, and that is why we can see them so clearly. It almost feels as though we should be able to reach out and touch them."

"Look, a star is falling!" Mi cried, pointing toward the sky.

Falling stars were not that uncommon, but it was still fascinating to watch, in the same way that fireflies never failed to catch my fancy.

"Oh, and there's another!" Oak chimed in. "And another!"

Many stars began to take flight across the firmament, like a flock of tiny white birds startled from their roosts. We were mesmerized by the sight, and we repeatedly exclaimed at the beauty of it. The spectacle seemed to go on and on. Then Puh nudged me. I turned to him and he silently motioned toward the fire, but what he wanted me to see was beyond the flames. Numerous pairs of glowing eyes stared back.

My daughters were sitting close to me, and they saw that my attention had been diverted. They, too, observed the eyes that flashed in the firelight.

"Puh-Puh," Lily said, moving close and putting her arms around me, "what are they?"

Puh stood up and clapped his hands at the unseen creatures, which turned tail and ran away. We then had a glimpse of the furry bodies.

"They were wolves," I replied. "Do not worry. We will not let them come close."

"We are a large group of people," Puh added reassuringly. "They will be afraid to come too near, especially while the fire is lighted."

"Will we keep the fire going all night?" Pony asked.

"Yes," I answered. We had enough wood for a few nights. After that, we had to hope that we would be on our way home, or else we must find more combustibles elsewhere.

Even though we had sufficient numbers for a few to stand watch at a time so that no one had to lose much sleep, it was still a long, wakeful night. I was used to the idea that predators were bound to be lurking just beyond the glow of our campfire, but now that they had been seen in close proximity, many of our younger companions were unnerved, including my girls. Throughout the night, they vied to cling to me, their restless tossing and turning continually rousing me from what little sleep I managed to get.

Even after the sun has set, the valley was a busy place as many creatures went about their lives – and met their deaths.  The soothing chirps from crickets were frequently interrupted by piercing screams, roars, moans, groans, snorts – although it was possible and even probable that many of those sounds emanated from Black Wolf, whose hearty snores sometimes alarmed uninitiated sleepmates.

# Chapter Ten

*The rocky path before me is illuminated by a small circle of light. As the debris rolls under my feet, I lose my footing. It is as though I am falling unnaturally slowly, but at last, I have hit the tunnel's floor. The circle of light abruptly comes to rest on the skull bones and antlers of a giant deer buck. Its empty eye sockets stare back at me.*

The next morning I awoke feeling as though I had been through an ordeal, both because of the lack of quality and quantity of sleep, and what I had experienced in my Dream. The palms of my hands burned, and my knees stung as though I had actually taken a tumble. It had been so real that I involuntarily checked my hands and knees for blood, but of course, they had no fresh abrasions. This Dream was starting to annoy me. Why was I still having it after all these years? Where was I, and what did it mean?  In my many years of experiencing these visions, I had hoped that they might ultimately be for some good. The Dreams had disrupted my sleep and my peace of mind for my entire adult existence, but I thought that if I could just interpret them correctly, I could use the knowledge they were trying to impart to help me navigate through life.  However, this one did not seem useful at all. Why, then, was it so persistent?

As the Dream faded from my consciousness, I became aware of a low undercurrent of sounds.  Lifting myself up slightly, I saw distant shadowy forms in the early morning mists.  They appeared to be aurochs.  The herd must have wandered near us during the night.

Puh and Ria were outside our improvised shelter, adding fuel to the fire against the dawn's chill.  They were speaking quietly, their words coming out in foggy little clouds.

Karno roused, too.  He sleepily sat up and rubbed his face.

"*Gah*, Karno not sleep much in night," he said to me, when he saw that I too was awake. "Tris sleep well?"

"No," I shook my head.  I looked down at my slumbering offspring. "I thought I might be tired enough to get some rest, but I am not used to sleeping in such crowded conditions."

"Karno not use to, neither," Karno said, scratching his scalp and making his hair appear even more unruly than was usual.  He then peered out of the shelter, and he must have taken note of the far-off herd of aurochs, too, because he smiled broadly. "Ah! Aurochs! Much meat there. Karno think he hear beast, but he think it just *Back Woof.*" Karno grinned at his joke.

"Yes, they do represent a lot of meat," I agreed. "More meat than we could ever eat. We could bring down a few animals and be back at the cave before long."

"But not rhino," Karno insisted.

"Karno, have you thought . . ." I broke off, hesitant to press him on the matter, "have you thought of what you will do if we do not find the rhino?"

"Must find rhino," Karno answered. "It injured. It be easier to kill. We need the meat, but we also need the horn."

"I do not understand," I said, bewildered as to why the rhino's horns were so important.

Karno cast a glance around the shelter to make sure everyone around us was still asleep.

"It pairing gift," Karno whispered. "Artok and Brumo" – he motioned to his fellow Wolfmen – "they lose mate. They want new mate, so they need pairing gift. We need this many horn" – he held up two fingers – "but this many" – he held up one finger – "is good for now."

I suddenly recalled that when Karno was wooing my sister Ru, he had given her a set rhino's horns. Black Wolf had thought it a rather untoward object to give a nubile young woman, but we had assumed that it was just an impulse on Karno's part. It never occurred to me that this was a facet of the Wolfmen's culture. However, when Karno's friend Bewok had become paired with my sister, Twie, he had given her a finely crafted necklace instead. I still was not sure I understood him, or why he seemed reluctant for the others to know.

"Must they give horns?" I asked. "Bewok gave Twie a necklace."

"*Gah*!" Karno waved my remark aside. "Bewok Karno life-friend, but he is *Woofman* no more. He give gift like you. You give your mate necklace, Bewok give same. My people give necklace to friend, only." Karno fingered the many necklaces that he wore. "These gift from friend," he said. "Artok and Brumo need horn for mate." Karno again held up two fingers. I was glad to see he was clarifying that he was not meaning to say they were going to share the horn or the mate, but in fact needed two of each.

"But what if we do not find the rhino?" I persevered. Karno shrugged.

"We find him," he said as though there were no option but to locate the creature.

"Karno, do you prefer the others do not know about the real reason you want the rhino?" I inquired, wondering if I should not divulge this information to anyone else.

"*Gah*, it just that . . ." Karno hesitated. He seemed somewhat embarrassed. "Karno think other people find it silly. Not want to look foolish. Other people think we waste time."

* * *

We decided to use the shelter as our camp for the duration of our time in the valley. We would leave the youngest of our group behind while we were canvassing the area, and also a few of our less experienced hunters to guard the camp in our absence. Ty and Ria were among those who volunteered to keep watch over things; Fox,

Mror, and Oak were less happy at our request to remain with them, but I was sure that Misty's presence would be of some consolation to my son.

We skirted the herd of aurochs, which eyed us warily, keeping well away.  Even at a distance, the smell of the beasts wafted to us on the damp air.  I could hear their various moos, brays, and snuffling.  I thought it a shame to walk past so many prime animals, but at least for now, we would look for Karno's rhino.

Running Buck and Sky Fire soon found the place where the rhino had bedded down.  It was clear that this was a badly injured creature.  Dried blood still stained the ground and the flattened grasses where it had lain, even after the recent rain had washed the landscape.

We followed its faint trail.  The trampled greenery was already starting to revive, and thus it was harder to see where it had trodden.  By midday the sun had burned away the cool mists, and the temperature was quite warm. We stopped to drink and gnaw on dried stores, but only for a short time before proceeding onward.

"I smell something," Puh said, sniffing the air.

We paused to sample the wind, as well.

"Something is rotting," Black Wolf stated.

It was not unusual to hear the calls of crows and ravens amid the usual birdsong, but their raucous cries now took on new meaning.  We hastened toward the sounds, only slowing our pace as we drew closer, lest any large predators be nearby, also drawn by the pungent odor.

The hulk of the rhino's carcass lay on a broad expanse of crushed grasses, where it had attracted a great number of flies and scavenging corvids and vultures. Many of the birds took wing as we approached, but they did not go far. They settled on the ground near the rhino's remains, waiting impatiently for us to leave so they could resume feasting. Even though the rhino was almost entirely consumed at this point, it would feed scavenging creatures for days to come.

We looked upon the once-magnificent beast somberly. The rhino's large horns were still attached to its skull.

"Well, we found your rhino," Black Wolf said to Karno. "I am sorry to say it no longer offers much meat. It looks as though we will have to go back to the herd of aurochs or find something else to hunt."

"Take horns, first," Karno replied.

We were not carrying the most effective tools for removing the huge horns from the rhino's skull, but we made do with what we had. It was a laborious process, but we finally managed to remove the two horns, along with a chunk of the surrounding bone. This prize was both cumbersome and weighty, requiring both of Karno's companions to carry it back to our camp. We hoped to deposit this trophy there, and then, if the aurochs herd was still in the area, begin our hunt anew.

The large birds returned to the carcass before we had taken very many steps away. Black Wolf seemed remarkably cheerful, considering the disappointing conclusion of our quest. He cleared his throat as we trekked and began to sing in his deep bass.

*The Mighty Hunter may bring down the largest beast*
*If his arm is strong, he and his kin will feast*

*The Mighty Hunter needs luck and great skills*
*And his life will be one of plenty, with many thrills*
*The Mighty Hunter may leave the carcass for the crows*
*But if it's a rhino, they can have all but his nose . . .*

Karno looked to Black Wolf darkly, but Black Wolf just grinned. I thought we had been quite fortunate. Karno had managed to get his prize without the risks involved in taking down an ill-tempered and powerful woolly rhino. His companions certainly seemed quite happy. However, they were still short one set of horns – that is – unless they wanted to split up the rhino's two horns, and one of them would agree to take the smaller of the two.

I was pleased to see the aurochs had not moved far from where we had left them. As before, we left a lot of room between us and the herd as we went by, trying not to give the impression that we were interested in them, even though we were very eager to size up the animals in hopes of singling out one or two that might be injured or otherwise slow to bolt away from us.

When we returned to the camp, we were greeted by our waiting family members.

"Puh-Puh, you have been gone most of the day," Pony said to me, welcoming me with a hug. "Did you find the rhino?"

"Well, yes and no," I answered.

Pony, and the rest of those who had stayed behind, gave me a questioning look. Then the Wolfmen marched by with the huge horns carried between them.

"Where is the rest of it?" Ty queried.

"Where is the meat?" Ria added.

"In the bellies of a multitude of creatures," Black Wolf quipped.

"The rhino was dead when we found it," Puh told Ria. "The Wolfmen wanted the horns, so we are only here to drop them off, then we will try our luck with the aurochs."

Ria nodded.

"That is a good plan," she said. "I have been watching them from here. They seem very placid. Unusually so. Perhaps they know all the predators have eaten their fill for now and will not be harassing them until they are once again hungry."

"That is good news for us," Running Buck observed. "Let us take advantage of their tranquil mood and set out right away."

We traded looks. Those who were previously left to guard the camp and its younger inhabitants looked on anxiously; I am sure they would have liked to join us. Even so, they knew we could not leave the camp unattended, or leave the youngest members of our party vulnerable to attack by predators. The aurochs might not be too concerned at this time, but we knew it was unwise to weaken our defenses. We paused just long enough to drink and eat a little before we took our leave of our loved ones once more.

As we walked away, Puh turned to Running Back.

"How far does that ridge run?" Puh asked, indicating the ridge of land that rose up behind the large rock beside which we were camped.

"Quite a distance" Running Buck replied. "You may be thinking what I am thinking, that we should get behind the ridge and use it to cover us as we close in on the herd."

"Yes," Puh said. "We can observe them from behind the rise, as well."

I sidled up to Karno as we walked.

"Would a large aurochs's horn do?" I whispered to him.

"No," Karno shook his head. "It is not size, it is beast. Rhino, mammoth, very important to *Woofman*. Very strong. For strong pairing, gift must be strong."

Now at last the Wolfmen's mission began to make sense to me, in a convoluted sort of way. I pondered whether all Wolfmen insisted on giving their mates a love token from rhino or mammoth, or whether some lesser matches might not require such an offering. Perhaps I would ask Karno one day, but just now, he did not seem inclined toward frivolous talk.

The sun was nearing the horizon, but we were only a short distance from camp, so we did not worry about retracing our steps too soon. All at once, there was a commotion amongst the aurochs and the herd parted, each half going in a separate direction. We watched, perplexed, until the reason for their movements became apparent. A large male woolly rhino had entered their midst, and although an aurochs is a formidable animal, even they did not want to linger in the rhino's company and risk being subject to a sudden fit of wrath.

Karno immediately perked up. He nudged his companions and they grinned to one another. If this beast could be brought down, their conundrum would be solved. They briefly conversed in their native tongue. I could not understand their words, but they seemed to come to a consensus. Karno turned to the rest of the group.

"Karno, Brumo, Artok – we go down and keep rhino busy at front," Karno said, pointing to the rhino. "You all get behind, you stick him good."

I should have been surprised at his plan, but I was not. This was not something we would normally attempt with a group of hunters only eight in number, but it was exactly the kind of adventure Karno sought out and reveled in. The Wolfmen would harry the rhino head-on while the rest of us snuck up at its rear and attempted to fatally wound it before it could inflict any damage of its own. Without waiting for the consent of the others in our hunting party, Karno promptly clambered over the ridge, quickly followed by his faithful comrades.

"He is insane," Sky Fire said in disbelief. "Why would anyone do this?"

"We will do as he asks because we must," Black Wolf answered. "We must, or we will watch those men die before our eyes."

The rhino had already taken note of the little band of humans intruding on his peaceful afternoon. His head lifted and he took a few tentative steps forward, tail rising to signal his ire. The Wolfmen walked three abreast, about an arm's length apart, spears poised. They counted on their speed and agility to keep them from being gored or trampled before the rest of us could strike the beast from the rear.

We ran a short distance behind the ridge in order to approach the rhino unseen. When we gauged we had gone far enough, we crested the ridge and quickly, but stealthily, crept up on the rhino's flanks. In the meantime, the Wolfmen had come close enough to incite the animal to charge them, thus occupying its attention and allowing us to successfully come within lancing range of its unprotected rump.

A rhino has tough skin, and it takes much strength to pierce its hide deeply enough to do it a lethal injury. We would need to strike with force and then tug our spears free so we could stab the beast multiple times. This would be no easy task, since as soon as the rhino knew he was under attack from the rear, he would surely turn around and attempt to foil our efforts with every bit of his considerable brawn and weaponry. But strike, we did.

As predicted, the rhino wheeled to face us, and the Wolfmen raced to meet him once more while we also leapt and sprinted to avoid its defensive maneuvers, positioning ourselves once again at his backside. We drove our spears into his body as hard as we could, twisting the spears as we plunged them into the flesh to widen the wounds. This dance of death continued until the creature began to falter from blood loss and sank to its knees.

Now that it was off its feet, we stood by as we watched its labored breathing, our own breath coming in great gasps as well.

"That is an impressive beast," Running Buck said with admiration. "And we are close enough to camp to transport the meat there for final processing before we go home."

"We will have to work through the night to take advantage of the cool air," Puh pointed out. "Let us see if we can hasten his blood loss now that he is down."

Puh stepped forward with his spear, which was already red with the rhino's blood, and thrust it into the beast's neck, working the spear from side to side and causing a river of red to flow from the gash. The rhino thrashed a bit at this new assault but soon it let out a soft groan and rolled heavily onto its side, its still legs twitching as the last bit of life left its body.

The Wolfmen were still at the rhino's head; I thought they were happily admiring their handiwork, but when I went to join them, I saw that they were not smiling. Artok and Brumo stood by their leader, supporting him. They were speaking urgently in their own language, their eyes filled with angst. Karno was holding the long front flap of his loincloth over his stomach, but now he moved it just enough to peek underneath, revealing a wad of bloodied material he held tightly in place. It was only then I noticed that Brumo and Artok must have emptied their water bags to provide a soft, pliable stuffing to stanch the bleeding of Karno's wound, and prevent his intestines from escaping his body cavity.

"What has happened?" I asked. "Karno, are you gored?"

Karno looked up at me, and again spoke to his fellow Wolfmen in their tongue. They gingerly lay Karno on the ground. Brumo positioned himself at Karno's head, where he removed his pack and frantically began to go through its contents. Artok was also looking in his pack. He was first to find what he sought, and he retrieved a small bag that seemed to be medicinal in nature. Artok was speaking to Karno in the Wolfmen's language; he seemed to want to bind Karno's abdominal wounds, but Karno shook his head and weakly waved his hand as though to wave away his ministrations.

"Tris," Karno then spoke to me. "Sit." He motioned to a spot next to him.

I did as I was bidden, by now I was very much concerned for Karno's welfare. As if to confirm my fears, a bubble of blood appeared on Karno's mouth and a thin scarlet-hued stream ran down his bearded chin and dripped onto his chest.

"What has happened?" I asked again, even though it was apparent that Karno must have been impaled. My mind was numb with shock and I was horrified at the deep red blood that continued to burble up onto his lips and seeped around the fingers that still held the bandage in place.

Artok began to weep as he knelt by his lifelong friend. Karno touched his friend's arm to comfort him.

"Artok, Brumo, this good place. This where star fall from sky. Many, many star fall from sky," Karno said. I thought it an odd sentiment to share just then, but perhaps Karno was not thinking clearly at this time. "Tris, you good friend many year. Karno give this to you." Karno pulled one of his necklaces from over his head and he placed it in my hands. Karno groaned. "*Gah,*" he winced. "Leave me where star fall," Karno said to me. Then to Artok, "Artok, you take Jura – my family. Give Jura horn. Yes? I say this before all people, so all people know, Jura yours now, by my word." Artok nodded, still weeping and apparently unable to articulate a response. "Brumo, horn for you too now. You go home and give Yalla horn." Brumo now began to sob, too.

"Yes, Karno," he answered, his response barely comprehensible.

Karno struggled to remove his other necklaces with his free hand, giving one to Brumo and one to Artok.

"My friend," he said. His breathing was ragged. "My friend," he repeated. "Have Bewok sing . . . sing my Last Farewell . . . no one sing like Bewok . . ." Karno fumbled at his bracelets, trying to remove those as well, handing them to Black Wolf. "Give to Bewok . . ."

I was still grappling with the suddenness of it all. More blood began to spill from his mouth and nose as he struggled to breathe. I came to understand that this powerful man, this man whom I had known in friendship for many long years, was dying. Karno began to choke on his own blood. He struggled to sit up, so his companions now propped him to a semi-upright position. This did not do much to help Karno. He continued to fight for breath.

"Karno," I said, my voice cracked with grief. I wanted to tell him how much his friendship had meant to me, how much I did not want him to leave us, but I could not formulate the words.

*The Mighty Hunter leaves us today*
*He was strong and brave in every way*
*The Mighty Hunter always finds his game*
*And without him, nothing will be the same . . .*

Black Wolf normally sang at a lung-bursting volume, but this he sang quietly, almost softly. I looked to Black Wolf and saw tears streaming down his face. Black Wolf worked his mouth as though he wanted to sing another verse, but he did not.  Until that moment, I had not realized that the rest of our party had joined us.  Karno's head slowly drooped.  His eyes began to roll back.  Karno's blood now flowed freely from his mouth.  I then felt Karno relax against me.  He was gone.

# Chapter Eleven

As requested, Karno was laid to rest in the rich dark soil over which the stars had fallen. We did not have enough firewood to melt the permafrost, so we dug a shallow grave and there laid him, first wrapping him in his wolfskin cloak and including his kit and his spear. The grave was filled with the loose soil, and next we covered it with a large pile of stones to protect his body from scavenging animals.

The rhino's butchering lasted until dawn, but the chore scarcely registered in my mind, in spite of the onslaught on swarming mosquitoes that feasted on our blood. As we toiled, more stars rained from the nighttime sky. All I could think of was the loss of my friend. Memories from years ago visited my mind: our first meeting with the Wolfmen, the many hunts and adventures; our fates had been entwined from the start. Life seemed less bright now that his spirit now longer walked the earth. And poor Jura, to lose a second mate and to once again be passed to another man with no say in the subject. For that matter, Artok appeared to have no say, either. He seemed a good fellow and I hoped they would fine happiness together, but this practice was alien to my clan.

When the new day dawned, we were physically and emotionally drained. We worked near enough to the camp to be assisted by the many willing hands that had sheltered there during our hunt. They had helped to scare off any interested creatures that might wish to sample our wares, tended the torches, and brought us food and drink while we worked. They also helped to slice larger chunks of meat into thinner pieces that could be smoked or dried. Some was cooked and consumed on the spot, but we found we had little appetite. Under normal circumstances, it would have been a time to feast and celebrate our success, but there was no joy this morning.

"Puh-Puh," Fox said to me as we finally settled by a smoldering fire that was curing a large rack of the rhino's meat. "What happened . . . with Karno, that is?"

Although everyone had been present when Karno was interred, no one had spoken of the hunt, the rhino, or what had befallen Karno. In fact, there had been almost no talk at all. Gray Elk's kin did not know Karno very well, but he had been close to my clan for a long time, and we grieved him terribly. Our begrimed faces, smeared with blood and gore and blackened from the smoking processes, were all marked with pale telltale tear streaks.

"I did not see what happened," I answered. "The rhino's horn must have caught him on his stomach. I would guess that one of his lungs was also pierced."

"The Wolfmen were at the front of the rhino," Black Wolf explained to Fox. "Those of us behind the beast were so occupied with our task that we did not realize what had happened to Karno until after the creature was down."

"I am sad," Fox stated. "I have known Karno all my life. He was different, but I liked him. He was always very kind to us children."

"He gave you one of your first toys when you were a baby," I told Fox. "It was the rattle shaped like a bear cub's head. He made it himself. The handle was lost a long time ago, but I think the head is still rolling around somewhere in our household."

"I remember his singing," Ria joined in. "Although it was not really singing as we know it. More like chanting. But it was wonderful – he had such a strong voice."

"He did," Black Wolf agreed. "Bewok was the only one of them I ever heard to sing in the way we are accustomed. He asked that we have Bewok sing for him after our return home."

Fox wiped his eyes. I myself had no tears left to weep. We Old Ones may not make sounds when we cry, but even so our soundless grief was usually still accompanied by tears. Misty noticed Fox's sorrow, and she placed her hand over his. Fox raised his eyes to meet hers and she gently brushed the tears from his cheeks with her other hand.

The sight brought back a memory from long ago. When I was even younger than Fox, my family had suffered the loss of one of my little brothers. Morning Star, also a small child then, had taken my hand to console me. What with all the collective misery within our camp at that time, I was heartened to remember the sweetness of her gentle touch. Additionally, I was glad to see that Fox and Misty had formed a bond.  I could not tell if Misty had become enamored with Fox.  She was a kind girl who might have sought to comfort anyone who was mourning, but all the same, just now she was focused on Fox.

Fox took Misty's hand in his and he gave her a slight smile.

* * *

By the end of the day the smoking process was finally completed.  Our improvised racks had been constructed from what little woody growth there was in the valley — mostly brush and spindly saplings — and now they were beginning to collapse under the heavy use to which they had been subjected.  Our firewood was almost gone, so we burned the racks during our final night at camp.  We would return to Gray Elk's cave the next morning.

Even though we were thoroughly exhausted by then, we still had to take turns keeping watch all night.  We had an enormous quantity of smoked meat wrapped in hides and packed in hide-bound sacks, and everything else one could harvest from the rhino, too, and it was likely that there were many creatures that would like to claim our hard-won bounty.  Sure enough, throughout the night, many bright eyes stared at us from across the fire, but none braved our defenses.  When at last it was my turn to lie down, I slept a dreamless sleep.

* * *

"Puh-Puh," a voice called, "Puh-Puh, wake up!"

It was my daughter Lily.

"Puh-Puh, Running Buck says we will soon leave," her sister Raven told me.

My eyes still burned from the copious exposure to smoke and from shedding many salty tears. I was rather surprised to find that my eyes did not want to open. I rubbed them to loosen the grit that had accumulated around them and finally pried them open with my fingers.

My daughters were staring at me, mouths agape.

"Puh-Puh, are you all right?" Pony asked.

"I am well enough," I answered, my voice sounding raspy. I was hungry and very thirsty.

"I will get you a drink," Pony volunteered, as she left us for a moment, returning with my water bag. "Here, Puh-Puh. We do not have much water left, but Grandpa Tor says we will refill our water bags on the way back to the cave."

"Many thanks, Pony," I said to her, trying to smile at her reassuringly. My girls still gazed upon me as though they had woken up an old bear rather than their father. "I think we may stop to wash up after we fill our water bags."

"That would be a good idea," Raven agreed. "We are all very dirty."

"We smell like a smoked rhino," Lily added.

"That is true," I concurred, still sipping at the water, trying to wet my dry mouth a little at a time. There was no way I could swallow anything until I managed to sufficiently moisten the inside of my mouth, or I feared the food would just stick there like a fly caught on a spider's web.

By now, everyone else in camp was awake, although some of us had not yet arisen from where we had slept. I sat up with a groan. If I was this sore, I wondered how

Puh, Ria, and Black Wolf felt, given that they were all much older than was I. I groaned again as I slowly pushed myself to my feet.

Karno's necklace swung a bit as I moved, giving me a poignant reminder of my lost friend. I fingered the necklace and thought of the man whose neck it had adorned. I had never owned a necklace before. This one consisted of a leather thong with an oblong pendant of smooth black stone. Within my clan, necklaces were something women wore, but this was a gift I was proud and honored to wear.

The more I moved my body, the less it ached. Soon I was able to help deconstruct our shelter and then load the sleds while feeling only minimal discomfort. We broke our fasts as we worked. We wanted to begin our journey back to Gray Elk's cave as early as possible, in order to reach our destination by nightfall.

* * *

The sun had dipped below the horizon when we heard a chorus of dog's barks. It was Gray Elk's menagerie of canines; they could not yet see us, but they must have sensed our impending arrival. It was likely that the aroma of the smoked meat and our still rather malodorous bodies had been carried downwind to their damp black noses. We had attempted to wash when at midjourney we encountered a stream. However, while the cold water had cleansed us of the most offending filth, we did not have time to have a thorough bathe.

We were welcomed not only by the dogs, but also by some the cave's inhabitants, including Morning Star and our youngest children. Morning Star greeted me with a hallo, and a warm hug and a kiss, but she must have noticed our haggard demeanors. She appeared perplexed.

"You have come back with a huge harvest," Morning Star stated. "But yet you all look so serious." Morning Star looked around, as though to account for all who had departed to make sure they had all returned.

"Pleasant evening to you, Muh-Muh," Fox said. He paused just long enough to hug his mother quickly as he carefully pushed through the mob of canines, running a hand over some of the dogs' heads as he went.

"Hallo, Fox," Morning Star responded. "Pleasant evening to you, Tor," she said to Puh.

Puh nodded in return.

"Pleasant evening to you, Morning Star," Puh answered.

Puh and I were still in the sled's harness, and we were blocking much of the entryway. I knew those behind us were eager to complete the journey.

"I will tell you of our trip after we are all settled inside," I said to Morning Star.

Puh and I brought the sled down the long passageway, to the main chamber. There, the evening meal was in various stages of preparation. Gray Elk reclined on his pallet by the hearth.

"Hallo!" Gray Elk called out to us. "How glad I am to see you all! We had hoped you would return to us this day, so I asked that a large meal be made ready. Travelers always arrive with a hearty appetite."

Morning Star now looked worried, especially after viewing her father's countenance. Black Wolf had the dispirited visage of one who was acutely suffering.

Karno's death had seemed to affect him greatly. The two men had sometimes been at odds, but just the same, Black Wolf was deeply saddened. Those who had stayed behind at the cave slowly came to realize that all was not well, but we were not pressed for information just yet. We placed our sleds at intervals just inside the chamber's main entryway, and the rest of our procession, who were loaded down with heavy packs, shrugged off their burdens and set them near the sleds. We would unpack later. For now we found places in which to seat ourselves by the fire.

We were brought water. We were quite parched and eagerly drank the proffered gourd cups full of liquid. The cool water revived me considerably, but my empty stomach craved food.

Morning Star asked me to hold Owl while she helped to complete the evening sup preparations. Fox sat by me, and Daisy climbed onto his lap, her ever-present doll in hand. Our older girls, even little Willow and Fawn, assisted their mother, just as they usually did at home. I was amazed at the stamina of Pony, Raven, and Lily; they had labored hard at the camp and then hiked all day today while carrying heavy backpacks, and yet they still worked with their mother as though they had not done anything out of the ordinary in the previous days.

When at last all was ready, each family had their meals brought to them by a few individuals from their group. Morning Star and Pony brought our trays of food. I was pleased to see that my sister Mi brought a tray to the Wolfmen. They smiled to her gratefully. Morning Star sat by me. She also observed Mi as she served the Wolfmen.

"Where is Karno?" Morning Star whispered to me.

I tried to speak, but I was unable to form a reply. I touched the necklace Karno had given me. I fought to articulate the words. *Karno was dead.* I could not say it.

Morning Star gazed at me with sympathy shining in her eyes. She wrapped her arms around me, awkward as it was while I still held the baby, and she gently pushed stray strands of hair back from my face.

"You do not have to speak of it just now," Morning Star said softly.

Morning Star momentarily grasped the pendant Karno had given me. Somehow she had guessed its significance.

No one spoke of Karno that night, but he was present, nonetheless. He was absent in body, only.

* * *

In the following days, a summer storm lashed the mountainside with strong winds and heavy downpours. The tempest arrived amid the rumbles of thunder. Even the dogs retreated from the cave's entryway, where they usually enjoyed the cooler air, to the safety of the passageway and inner chambers. I thought this fortunate, as it gave us a chance to assess the many young pups and make our choices. The puppies would not be ready to leave their mothers for some days, but I did not mind this extra time at Gray Elk's.

The children played with the dogs happily, and I was pleased they had a diversion to take their minds from the mostly subdued and saddened adults. Karno's story was eventually told.

"Who will lead the Wolfmen now?" Ty asked Artok and Brumo.

The two Wolfmen exchanged glances.

"That will depend upon Jura's baby," Artok replied. "If she has a boy, he will take Karno's place when he comes of age."

"But that will not be for many years," Black Wolf pointed out. He himself was acting as Head Elder for his people until his son Oak reached maturity. "And what if she has another girl?"

"I do not know," Brumo responded. "We will have to present the situation when we return home and let the clan consider it. If they do not find a solution, we may have to come before you at the fall Gathering and ask that you make a determination for us, Black Wolf."

"If that should come to pass, I will do my best," Black Wolf said, smiling sadly. "I will miss Karno at the Gathering. I never thought of it, but I will also miss being called *Back Woof.*"

Smiles came to our lips as well.

"There can never be another like him," I stated quietly.

"That is true," Brumo agreed. "I am most grieved that he is not here."

"It was his unwavering friendship that brought about this tragedy," Artok added. "When we saw the wounded rhino, he insisted we embark on a hunt; he wanted to harvest the horns for us so that we might be paired again. He should have lived to reach an old age. He would still be alive if we had not . . ." Artok broke off his sentence, unable to go on.

"I understand that you feel sorrow," Puh said after a momentary silence. "But Karno was fated to this end. He lived his life in search of adventure. You know of my nephew Bror; he was named for my eldest brother. The two men could not be more unlike one another. Inasmuch as my nephew is stolid and steady, my brother sought excitement. He thoroughly enjoyed all challenges that included danger and feats of strength and daring. He was killed in a mammoth hunt. We had found a mammoth bull that was bogged down in a massive snowdrift. The dense snow supported most of our weight, but not the great weight of the bull. We felt it relatively safe to attack the creature, and Bror dashed in to strike it, but the beast was not as immobile as we had hoped. If Bror had hung back with the rest of us as we tested the bull, it was likely he would not have been killed. But that was not Bror's nature. It was not Karno's nature. Both men were very strong and very brave. Too brave. That is why Karno is not here. It is not your fault."

Again, quiet settled over the chamber as we absorbed this notion.

"I believe you are right," Artok told Puh. "We will leave as soon as the weather clears. Jura and the rest of the clan must know what has happened as soon as possible."

"But the puppies will not be ready to leave so soon," Gray Elk pointed out.

"We have spoken of this," Brumo replied, indicating himself and Artok. "Karno wanted dogs, but I do not think Jura will be pleased to cope with young puppies while she is caring for a new baby and three small children. Besides, it will be all we can do to tote those great horns and a quantity of meat the distance. I am sorry not to trade for dogs, but perhaps we can make a trade another day."

"Whenever you are ready," Gray Elk assured him.

Running Buck and Sky Fire seemed to be conferring together.

"We will accompany you home," Running Buck said to the Wolfmen. "Those loads will be too heavy for two men."

"We thank you," Artok told them, appearing relieved. "I was not looking forward to the journey, but now I am grateful to know we will not have to do it alone."

Fox suddenly stood up and crossed the room. He stopped where Sky Fire was seated and knelt at his side for a moment. They exchanged a few words and then left the chamber together.

* * *

The turbulent thunderstorm passed, but the rains went on unabated the next day. I took advantage of the inclement weather and returned to the Talking Stones and my unfinished portrait of Morning Star. In the flickering lamplight, I scrutinized my work. Having not viewed it in the light for a number of days, the sight was markedly underwhelming. Now I could understand why Morning Star had not received the drawing with any enthusiasm.

I took care to adjust the curve of her face, to add fullness to her lips. And just a hint of a smile. I thought the image was beginning to look a little more like her.

I then heard approaching footsteps and looked to see Fox enter the room.

"What are you doing, Puh-Puh?" Fox asked.

"I am drawing your mother," I answered. "Well, I am trying to."

Fox gazed upon the Talking Stones, taking in the many wondrous pictures, finally pausing at my contribution. He did not speak for a moment and I waited, hopeful that he might have something encouraging to say.

"It does look a little bit like Muh-Muh," Fox said. "She is very colorful compared to the other drawings. But why is her hair all around her? Is it windy?"

"Gray Elk suggested I add color. About her hair, it is not the wind," I hesitated, wondering how best to explain that it was how she appeared to me when we lay together. "Her hair is loose. She is lying down."

"Oh," Fox said blandly – but a moment later, he said, "*Oh!*" He blushed.

"You spoke with Sky Fire," I said, changing the subject.

"Yes," Fox replied. "That is why I came to you. I asked his permission to court Misty. I told him . . . I told him that I love her . . . and I want to take care of her and the children we might make. He has given me his consent to pursue her. I wanted you to know."

I nodded and smiled as I now dabbed a little more red ochre on my drawing to add life to Morning Star's cheeks and waited for Fox to go on.

"I hope to have an understanding with Misty by the time we leave," he said.

"I wish you both well," I told him, unsure of how best to respond. This seemed weak. "I am hopeful she is receptive," I added quickly.

"Do you think I am doing right?" Fox asked suddenly, as though on an impulse.

"I think you are the only one to know," I answered. "Misty is a fine young woman, and she belongs to a fine family. If you feel strongly about her, you are doing the only thing you can do: following your heart. To me, that is right. Are you worried whether or not you are embarking on the correct path?"

"I am less worried than concerned; I see what you and the other men endure, and I wonder if I can do as well," Fox said. "As I promised Sky Fire, I want to take proper care of his daughter and the family I one day hope to have."

"All men have the same concerns," I informed him. "At least, most men do. All we can do is to do our best."

"But our family's lives and well-being will depend upon what we can provide for them," Fox said. "I have come to see that the hunts are not just entertaining diversions to challenge us and keep us occupied; they are an unrelenting occupation that will take up our lives for as long as we can still hunt. It is this weight of the future that weighs upon me."

"I find it is like eating a mammoth," I told Fox, who looked at me with confusion in his eyes. "You can only eat it one bite at a time. Just the same, you can only live one day at a time."

* * *

The remainder of our stay at Gray Elk's cave was pleasant and, for the most part, uneventful. The Wolfmen, Sky Fire, and Running Buck departed soon after the rain ended, leaving behind the rest of us as we waited for the puppies to grow old enough to become weaned. We spent much of that time hewing wood and hauling it up the mountainside to help replenish Gray Elk's supply of fuel.

Finally, the time came when we could select our dogs. Fox was the one who was really eager for a new pup, but he generously let Daisy select which animal would accompany us home. More than that, he let Daisy name the creature, which she called *Doggo*. Doggo came to spend much of his time with us, rather than with his littermates. He was a large, fluffy canine that reminded me much of my boyhood dog, Rooph.

Puh choose a dog that had a dark gray coat but a white muzzle, feet, and belly. While discussing what it should be named, Mror had an idea.

"He looks like a white dog that is lying in the shade," Mror observed. "We should call him *Shadow*."

Puh and Ria smiled at this. I also smiled at the suggestion. Morning Star had once said Fox's Ena should have been named Shadow because she never left his side. I hoped that this dog would be as faithful.

"That is a good name," Ria said. "He does look like he is in a shadow."

"I like it as well," Mi agreed. She tended to dote on her little half-brother. "It is a clever name, Mror."

This left only Black Wolf to choose his dogs. He had seemed rather distracted lately. He was normally quite decisive, but on this, he dithered over the choices. We wanted very much to help, so one day Black Wolf, Oak, Ty, Puh, and I stood amongst the mob of young canines, looking down at them critically.

"That one is very large," Ty said, pointing it out to Black Wolf. "It might grow into a good hunting dog, or at least a dog big enough to easily pull a sled."

Black Wolf made a noncommittal noise.

"This one is a sweet little female," Oak said, holding up a plump furry bundle, which promptly licked his face. "She would allow you to breed your own dogs."

"Hmmm," Black Wolf responded. "If I bred my own dogs, then I would have no excuse to stop in with my cousin and his family."

"Your excuse could be to simply visit them," I said. "I suppose that since they do not often come to the Gathering, it is the only way you can see them."

Black Wolf did not reply right away.

"As much as I am eager to go home, I hate to leave here," he finally responded.

"It is a pleasant place to stop," Ty noted.

"I dislike leaving as well," Puh spoke up.

Puh and Black Wolf traded significant looks.

"Yes," Black Wolf began, "you understand my meaning. I fear this is the last time I will see Gray Elk. He is old and fragile now. When I help him stand or walk, he is almost as light as a child. It was bad enough to find Buttercup gone, and then to lose Karno ... the idea of losing Gray Elk too is unbearable."

"It is quite hard," Puh agreed. "Buttercup was a lovely woman. I have missed not seeing her this visit. But as for Gray Elk, we can only enjoy our time with him while we can."

"That is true," Black Wolf uttered solemnly. "*Ack!* When did I become so brooding? It seems I feel losses more than I used to. I must be getting old."

"Not old, just older," Ria said to comfort him. "Like all of us."

Black Wolf smiled down at Ria fondly.  He was a very tall man, but next to little Ria, he appeared a giant.  He reached to touch her shoulder appreciatively.

"You are kind, Ria," Black Wolf told her. "But the days and moons fly by, more quickly now than ever. I feel a sense that there is much to be done as each of the seasons run their course." Black Wolf paused. "Perhaps I think too much. Such is not good." He sighed. "When we do go home, I want to try to make things right . . . with Little Fawn. It has been many years. Perhaps she can forgive me now."

We were rendered momentarily speechless at this news.  Black Wolf and Little Fawn had not lived together as real mates in a very long time.  And even when they had, it was often a fractious union.  Would they find happiness, or at least contentedness, at long last?

"She loves you," Ria assured Black Wolf. "I believe she has always loved you."

"Except when she hated me, but never mind." Black Wolf's mood lightened in spite of his words.  He seemed genuinely affected by Ria's declaration.  Black Wolf bent and picked up two puppies, one in each hand. "What say you, little ones? Do you want to go home with us?" The puppy in his right hand then peed on the cave's floor. "I will take that as a yes. We will take these. Oak, you pick out two more."

* * *

The final full day of our stay in Gray Elk's cave was at hand. We had loaded our sleds with all but the things to be packed last-minute and positioned them so they would be ready to be dragged down the long passageway to the outside. We would leave early the next morning.

The evening sup would be a special occasion. The mates of Gray Elk's daughters had returned that day with the meat, hide, antlers, leg bones, and sinew from a red deer. They had also collected a number of onions, garlic, roots, and tubers. I did not know these men well; they spent most of their days harvesting food or hewing wood, the same as Running Buck and Sky Fire, thus they were seldom in residence. They were pleased to be at home with their families, even though it would be for only a few days. Their families were also glad at their arrival, and the men were treated with affection and plied with copious amounts of food and water. They seemed grateful to settle down by the fire next to Gray Elk, to rest, talk, and take sustenance.

"Were you able to find good shelter during that big thunderstorm?" Black Wolf asked.

"Yes," one of the weary hunters responded. "We took cover at a camp that we set up under a large fallen tree. We were able to stay fairly dry, but the elk we had taken down was exposed to the warm, wet weather and the meat spoiled. We salvaged what we could but had to go after another animal. Fortunately, this red deer came along a few days later. As you can see, we smoked most of his meat . . . what we did not consume, that is. We were almost out of stores by then. Most of the greens are becoming tough and bitter now, but the onions and all, with the venison, made for a number of very nice meals."

"Some of the lightning came very close," the other hunter added. "I was worried for more than the loss of the elk's meat." He then looked around to make sure his mate and children were otherwise occupied with meal preparations and would not overhear his remark. I could understand this; I did not like my family to know all I experienced when I was away from home. They, especially Morning Star, had enough with which to concern themselves without fretting over my misadventures.

"I am glad we returned in time for us to see you, Black Wolf," the first hunter said. "We have not seen you for many years – you, too, Tor. I hope you will excuse me if I do not stay up to chat. It has been a long outing and I am most eager to lie down after I have finished my sup."

"It will be the same for me," the other added. "But I will be ready to go again after two or three days. It is very pleasant to be home, but when you spend most of your time out in the fresh air and sunshine, the cave seems dark and confining. Even if the weather is hot, cold, or wet, I would rather be out there." He gestured toward the outdoors.

I mused that I would rather be outside, as well. I liked to visit Gray Elk, but I could not say I would like to live in a cave, even one as spacious as this. The two men finished their evening sup and soon left us.

The rest of the cave's inhabitants now sat around Gray Elk, lingering over the remains of a sumptuous meal. Gray Elk appeared sad. I suspected that he would miss the company of his visitors, particularly his cousin Black Wolf and my father. He had known both of them from the time they were boys. Gray Elk summoned a smile.

"That was a wonderful meal. Thank you!" Gray Elk announced to the many cooks. Many of us chimed in our thanks, as well.

The families then split into groups, the children taking advantage of their last opportunity to play, and their mothers, the chance to socialize.

"Now speak to me those names I do not often hear," Gray Elk requested. "There are not many who still remember them. My father, my brothers; my cousin Eagle Owl, who was one of the bravest men I ever knew. And Tor – of your father, your brothers. Most of them are gone."

"That is true," Black Wolf said. "Since I was the youngest of a long line of siblings, I did not know my father's father. But I knew most of your brothers. And, of course, Eagle Owl. How I miss him. He gave his life trying to protect my family. I am glad that Tris and Morning Star have named their youngest son for him." Black Wolf sighed heavily. "The fall Gathering is when I most often see my older sons and our extended family. Even if the business of the annual Gathering is tedious, I am glad it draws so many of us together. But every year there are fewer familiar faces. I do not often dwell on times past, but recently it is more often I think of years gone by."

"When we are young, we are always looking ahead," Gray Elk commented. "It is only when we grow older that we consider and cherish what we have left behind."

Black Wolf sighed again.

"We leave so much behind. Too much," he said, looking indeed pained. "I think of Willow every day. I wonder how I have survived this long without her and how I will continue to live out my days. I know I must make the best of it. Most of my children are now grown with children of their own, and Oak must one day take his place as Head Elder." Black Wolf gazed across the chamber to where Oak sat among the other young people. Oak was quite tall, and his shining head of glossy black hair stood out from among his smaller companions. "And my youngest daughter still needs to find a mate. Also, I think I must make amends with Little Fawn. I will approach her when we return home. Who knows how much time we have left to do all we wish to do."

"You intend to reconcile with her?" Gray Elk seemed surprised. "I wish you every luck. As I remember Little Fawn, she was a person with very firm opinions and she was not afraid to vocalize them. Little Fawn is a good woman, but not one of whom I would care to be on the wrong side."

"She can have a tongue like a skinning blade," Black Wolf agreed. "But that is perhaps an ironic turn of phrase, when one recalls those ridiculous old rumors that she was a cannibal. How they started, I cannot say. However, now she is not as ill-tempered as she was in her younger years. I have not made things easy for her, and I often gave her reason to berate me. I know she deserved better. Especially when I consider how good she has been to Oak. After Willow died and Oak came to live with me, Little Fawn has never shown a moment's resentment of him. She has raised him as though he was her own. So I will ask her to forgive me. To forget the past and live with me again as mates.”

“I have not wanted to forget the past, but I guess there are times when it is best,” Gray Elk said, nodding. “The past can bring with it many terrible memories.”

“The past can be either good or bad,” Puh said. “The bad times, they are too heavy to carry. The good memories, they are the only ones worth taking into your heart.”

We then talked of many good times; of my Uncle Mror, the Keeper of Stories, and his lively sense of humor, his great strength, his loyalty, and his love of family; Uncle Bror, and his wild adventures. And other loved ones, all long gone. But they were happy remembrances. Everyone was smiling when we bade one another a pleasant evening.

 **Chapter Twelve** 

*At last, the tunnel opens to a huge chamber. As with the passageway, it is filled in places with piles of loose rock where the walls have given away. A draft of cool fresh air wafts across my face and I look up to see blue sky shining through an opening in the chamber's ceiling. Suddenly, I hear something scrabbling over the debris. I am not alone.*

We had finished packing our last-minute items on the sled and we were ready to take our leave of Gray Elk and his family. Before I departed our room, I paused at my drawing of Morning Star, holding up a lamp to illuminate the image. I had left the charred sticks, pieces of ochre, and bits of ash near the wall so I could work on the drawing when inspiration struck or time allowed, and now I was fairly pleased with the final result. Morning Star seemed flattered that I wished to capture her likeness. She was honored to be included amongst the Talking Stones, but she had not expressed anything other than a polite but disappointingly tepid reaction to my rendering of her. I did not mind very much. I liked the image.

When we said our farewells to Gray Elk, he had tears in his eyes, even as he squinted against the bright early morning sunlight. Like Black Wolf and Puh, he must have thought that this would be the last time he would see us. He had asked for assistance to be brought to the mouth of the cave so he could say his goodbyes there. He hugged us all in parting, smiling, but his eyes were streaming. His final embrace was for Black Wolf.

"I am sorry to see you go," Gray Elk told Black Wolf. "But I am grateful to have this extended visit with all of you. While you have been here, I have pondered my many good fortunes that have allowed me to live such a long life; the security of a large cave in which to reside, a family that is willing to take care of me in my old age, a good trade in raising dogs. Thank you, Black Wolf, for all you have done for me and my clan, and for your many years of friendship. I wish you well."

"Thank you, Gray Elk," Black Wolf replied, his eyes also wet, "for sheltering us during our stay, your warm hospitality, the unknown quantity of dogs we have taken from here, and of course, for your friendship, too."

We were now ready to set off, but I noticed that Fox was still talking to Misty. He was aware that our procession had already started to move, but he was reluctant to break away. Finally, he embraced her and quickly kissed her lips. Misty looked stunned as he walked away, but then she smiled and waved.

Everyone before us had already started down the trail, and it was time for Puh and me to start moving our sled. I glanced back at Gray Elk. He was still waving goodbye. Puh and I waved too, and we stepped forward onto the trail.

* * *

Our journey home was favored with fair weather. The puppies were too young to make the long trip on foot, so they were often carried or rode on one of the sleds. In fact, they were small enough so that we had to protect them from possible attack by predators. They might be a mere snack for a large creature like a lion, but a lynx would think a fat puppy to be a nice prize, indeed.

During the time we had been on the mountain, summer had progressed from a season of verdant green to one of ripening fruits and maturing foliage that was just beginning to change color. True autumn was yet a moon away, but still, we now needed to hurry home to prepare for the fall harvest and the annual rut. There would be much to do, and besides, those left at the compound would be anxious for our return. They were sure to have been working hard to keep the homestead going, and they would be running low on meat by now. There was the lake and its fish and shellfish to supplement their diet, and they were apt to set snares to catch small game, and they had various plant foods to forage, but these were not good substitutes for the nutrients we gained from big game. Fat was essential to our survival, and the best source of that was large animals.

Additionally, as had been the case at Gray Elk's, much wood needed to be hewn before winter was upon us. Firewood was not only essential for heating our homes and cooking our food but also served to preserve our foods; harden our spear shafts, throwing sticks, and tool handles; smoke hides; temper stone prior to knapping; and bake items made of clay. Thus, this important chore would take up much of our time when we were not hunting and foraging.

* * *

We arrived at the compound on a sunny but breezy day. Puh had whistled loudly as we neared our homes to announce our arrival. Our friends and family met us as we came off the trail and greeted us warmly. Our loved ones were obviously happy to see us, but it was the puppies that were welcomed with the most enthusiasm. The pups trembled with fear at the throng of strangers who all wanted to hold and pet them, but they soon realized that there was no peril and they began to frolic amongst the many children. Black Wolf's two older dogs looked on with dour expressions, obviously not pleased with the new additions to the clan.

Ty's mate, Aessa, kissed and embraced him, even with a baby on her hip, and then she looked him up and down, as though to assure herself that he was really and truly well.

"You look so fit, and your color is so strong," she said, referring to the tan Ty had acquired after becoming sunburned while we were hunting on the open grasslands of the valley where we had sought the rhino, and on our long treks to and from home. Ty's skin had burned and peeled several times since our departure from the compound.

"I feel very fit," Ty replied, grinning down at her. "I have so much to tell you. This has been an amazing adventure."

"Has it given you a taste for excitement . . . for a life away from home?" Aessa asked anxiously, appearing as though she feared his answer.

"No," Ty shook his head. "It has made me appreciate more than ever that my life here amongst my family is a good one. I am so very glad I went, but I am even happier to be back."

Aessa smiled broadly at his reply.  I did, too.  I was pleased that Ty had satisfied his urge to experience the life of a hunter and to venture far from home.

Twie, Bewok, and their children were on hand to greet us as well.  Bewok used a walking stick to help him get around, but he was smiling, and he did not seem to be in too much discomfort.  I disliked the thought of informing him that his lifelong friend Karno had perished. Bewok seemed to sense that something was wrong, and his smile faltered as he took in our visages.

"Was it a successful trip?" Bewok inquired, looking hopeful as he gazed at our loaded sleds and the six puppies we had brought back with us.

"We will speak of it later," Black Wolf replied gently.

Bewok visibly swallowed.  Black Wolf was not typically known for his mild temperament, and his subdued answer seemed to alarm Bewok more than if he had received a more forthright reply.  But he did not ask for more information. Bewok only nodded.  Those who observed the exchange also seemed to guess there was some significance to Black Wolf's reluctance to declare that we had returned from a completely successful outing. I could see the many eyes casting about as though to count heads, to reassure themselves that all of the travelers had come home.

We were each embraced by our friends and family, and then we brought our sleds to our homes, where they would be unloaded after a brief rest. Morning Star was eager to go into our home and ready it for the family before night fell. We still had plenty of daylight in which to accomplish this.

"Morning Star, please sit," I said to her, patting a spot next to me on the matting by the compound's large central hearth. "You must be weary."

"I will feel better about sitting once I know our house is in order," she responded. "But it will be helpful to me if you can watch our little ones while Raven, Pony, and Lily help me at home. It will not take us long. I might even lie down for a bit when we are done."

"I will watch them," I promised. "Do get some rest."

Morning Star leaned over me to bend down and kiss my forehead, and then she walked away, taking our older girls with her. It occurred to me how much I still enjoyed the view of her. Even after all our time together, my pleasure at the mere sight of her had not diminished.

"We are the lucky ones," Puh said to me.

"Oh?" I was jolted from my trance. "What makes you say that?"

"It is the way you look at Morning Star that makes me say that," Puh began. "And the fact that I have been so fortunate in my pairings. Your mother was all one could have desired, and after she passed, I was fortunate to find

Ria. We are the lucky ones because we have great happiness with our mates. Perhaps even more so because Awna and I were not supposed to be together. Her parents did not want her to become paired with me, and after all we had to endure to be mates, we sincerely appreciated one another. It may be the same for you and Morning Star, considering that at that time, Old Ones and The People did not often allow such pairings."

"I am glad that such is not the case now," said Weasel as he sat down with us, his little daughter in his arms and grinning a grin that exposed his lack of front teeth. His mate, my sister Saree, sat awkwardly down with him. She was now heavily pregnant, so he held out a hand to steady her as she eased herself to the ground.

"What case would that be?" Saree asked, having missed most of the conversation.

"The old way of only pairing with those who are of your own people," Weasel replied. "As for me, I care not for one clan over another, but I do tend to prefer women who are petite."

"Up until recently, I fit that description," Saree said with a laugh. She rubbed her protruding stomach. "I am the size of a mammoth these days."

"Only a very tiny baby mammoth," Weasel told her, putting an arm around her shoulder and giving her a squeeze.

Saree turned serious.

"Puh, why was Black Wolf so mysterious when Bewok asked about the trip?" she queried. "Did something go wrong?"

"I think Black Wolf plans to tell everyone about our excursion when we are all together for the evening sup," Puh answered.

"But a simple yes would have set his mind at peace," Saree countered. "Now everyone is worried. We can see that all of you have returned, so we can only guess it must be some news from Gray Elk's or possibly something about the Wolfmen."

"There is much news to impart," Puh said simply. "Both happy and sad. Let us wait until everyone is present to hear it."

Saree nodded, apparently resigned to await the moment when Black Wolf would reveal all. There was no special reason that Black Wolf would be the one to address our little community; he was acting Head Elder of his own tribe until Oak was of age, but he did not attempt to act as Head Elder on our compound. I, for one, would be relieved if he were willing to give an account of our trip, so that I would not have to be the bearer of bad tidings. And it made sense to tell everyone all at once so we would be there to comfort one another and so the sad news would not have to be repeated over and over again until everyone was informed.

As the evening wore on, more and more residents gathered around the hearth, both to prepare the nightly meal and in anticipation of consuming it. When Morning Star and our older girls returned, Morning Star sat down by my side without any encouragement. Most evenings she would help with the food preparations, but not this night she chose not to.

"Where are our little ones?" she asked me.

"They are playing with their cousins." I pointed to the gaggle of youngsters, some of whom were now on each side of Owl, holding his hands as he took wobbly steps and dodged the new puppies. "All is well at our home?"

"Yes," Morning Star replied. "There was not too much to do. We aired the bedding and matting, spread herbs along the walls, and made sure no mice had moved in, in our absence. After we put the beds back together and laid down the matting again, I am afraid we took naps. But I feel much better now."

"I am glad you rested," I said. "It was a long journey; a long way to carry a large baby."

"It is not as though I do not have to carry him much of the time, regardless of where we are," Morning Star said with a laugh.

Morning Star then began to chat with Saree about Saree's pregnancy. My thoughts turned inward, as they often did. It was good to be home. I was looking forward to sleeping in my own bed this night.

* * *

Most of the smoked rhino meat had stayed at Gray Elk's or left Gray Elk's cave with the Wolfmen. However, we had brought home enough to provide a small portion for each of the compound's residents.

Black Wolf had disappeared after he and Oak stepped out of their sled's harness and did not reappear until the food was ready. As always whenever Black Wolf was home, he carried Little Fawn from their dwelling and set her down in her customary spot. In recent years, much of the fight had gone out of her, but just now she seemed especially pleased. She smiled benignly as Black Wolf struggled to navigate the small entryway of their home, encumbered as he was with her long frame. I could only guess that Black Wolf must have broached the subject of forgiveness, and she was at least considering it.

By the time the meal was through the stars were alight, and a waxing moon was rising. A wolf howled in the distance, soon answered by a few other wolves. Black Wolf's two old dogs scarcely lifted an ear at this, but the puppies cocked their heads, and they uttered little howls. Daisy clapped her hands delightedly.

"Puh-Puh," she said to me, "did you hear Doggo? He can howl!"

"Why do they do that?" my daughter Willow questioned.

"They howl to call to one another," Fox told her.

"Perhaps they howl to share news," Oak added.

Despite the lighthearted conversation, the howls made me think of Karno. He had sometimes vocalized in such a way. When he was courting my sister Ru and she had told him that she would not accept him, his howls that night had been indeed mournful. I suspected that Black Wolf would begin to speak to the assemblage sometime soon. I dreaded the coming revelation to the group that Karno was dead. Bewok, Karno, and Mino had been inseparable since boyhood, and now Bewok was the only one of the three still alive.

Black Wolf cleared his throat loudly.

"I will speak now, if all have finished their sup," Black Wolf said, his voice projecting easily across the compound.

"We have been waiting to hear about your journey," Saree responded.

"Yes, we are eager to hear what has transpired," Ru added.

Black Wolf nodded and he looked at Ru for a long moment before going on. Did he wonder if she would be saddened to hear about Karno, even though she had chosen to be paired with another man?

"As you know, we were able to procure a number of dogs from Gray Elk," Black Wolf began. "We were pleased to stay with Gray Elk for half a moon or so, even though we found him to be in a frail state. He is still strong of mind, but his body is tiring. We were very sorry to find that his mate Buttercup had passed. It is sad, too, because she would have been delighted to know that her granddaughter Misty Morn and my grandson Fox now have an understanding." Black Wolf paused and looked at Fox. "For a pairing that is to take place next summer?"

"Yes," Fox said, beaming with pleasure at the announcement.

The gathering now erupted in congratulations to Fox. I was glad that Black Wolf chose to divulge the news of the impending joyous occasion, to offset the tragic news of Buttercup's passing. When everyone had settled down again, Black Wolf continued.

"You will know from our meal that we found a woolly rhino; not just the wounded rhino that Karno set out to find, but another one as well." Black Wolf looked around the faces that all gazed up at him attentively. He seemed reluctant to go on. "The wounded rhino was dead when he was located. But later we found another that was a healthy specimen." Again Black Wolf paused. "It . . . it was very vigorous. Karno . . . the rhino gored him." Black Wolf blinked back tears. "He was very brave. Bewok, Karno has asked that you sing for him."

Bewok had risen to his feet when Black Wolf started to speak in order to get a better view. At this news, he gaped, and then he slowly slumped over his walking stick.

"I cannot just now," Bewok choked out the words. And he turned and walked away. Twie quickly rose to her feet as well, and she hurried after him.

My heart ached for Bewok. We looked after him in silence. Black Wolf fell quiet. He was done speaking.

"Poor Bewok," Morning Star murmured.

I then glanced at my sister Ru. She was sitting with her family, her most recent infant in her arms. She appeared stunned.

"I will go to Ru for a moment," I said to Morning Star as I rose to stand.

Ru was staring straight ahead, scarcely blinking as her mate Bror spoke to her softly. I settled myself next to them, catching Bror's eyes for an instant. He and Karno had vied for Ru those many years ago. Karno had steadfastly refused to refer to Bror by name most of the time, instead calling him *Bear-Wrestler Man*, because of Bror's powerful build. All the same, the two men had been amiable enough since that time.

"Ru, are you all right?" I asked her.

Ru started as though surprised at my words. Her eyes were damp, but she did not weep.

"I am," she said. "Many thanks for thinking of me, Tris. I am very sad to hear of Karno's passing, but I cannot say the news was unexpected. Karno was never going to die of old age. If anything, I am amazed he lived as long as he did."

"I suppose that is so," I mused. "But he also had incredible skill, strength, and luck. Somehow, I thought he would triumph over all."

"No one triumphs over death – not indefinitely," Bror observed quietly.

I could only nod in agreement.

"I will return to my family now," I said. "I just wanted to let you know I too feel his loss."

When I took my seat next to Morning Star again, Daisy sat herself down on my lap, thumb in her mouth and doll in her arms. She wordlessly snuggled in. Like many of us, she was very tired from the long trek. Black Wolf soon joined us.

"I have asked our sons to unpack the sleds," he announced in a tone considerably lighter than the one he had used just a little while ago. "It will be good practice for them, and it will spare our backs."

"That is well," Puh remarked. "I was not looking forward to the chore."

"Nor I," Black Wolf concurred. "The last thing I have to lug into our home will be Little Fawn. I guess I could ask Fish Hawk to do it; he was the one to do it while I was away, but somehow it does not seem appropriate this night. I have asked her to take me back; she has promised to think about it. My request will not seem quite as earnest if I am not sufficiently attentive. However, she must know that I am in a position to pursue other women if I so choose. But I want her. She has been my mate for many years and, in spite of my behavior, she has stayed true to me and raised a fine family. If she will have me, I want the rest of our lives together to be pleasant ones. I regret my former thoughtlessness. Now I see that I should have given her the same devotion that Gray Elk gave Buttercup. That you and Tris give your mates. That I most willingly gave Willow." Black Wolf paused. "I still miss her every day. I cannot have her now, but I can learn from the many lessons she taught me and pass them on to Oak. One of the lessons is to honor those who have stood by you. It is my hope that Little Fawn will allow me to be her mate once again, to honor her in the way she deserves."

"Mama certainly looks pleased," Morning Star pointed out.

"She is pleased that I was the one to ask to be taken back," Black Wolf laughed ruefully. "I better understand the Wolfmen and their rhino horns now. What woman could turn down a man with a rhino horn? But I hope she is pleased at the thought of having a true mate now."

"Da," Black Wolf's youngest daughter Dewdrop called out to him from across the compound. "Mama wants you."

"*Ack!* I am being summoned," Black Wolf grinned. "It begins already! I bid you all a pleasant night. We will speak soon, I am sure. We will need to hunt in a day or so."

Black Wolf stood, groaning and flexing his back as we returned his farewells for the evening.

"*Ack*," he said again as he walked away. "I feel my age! And my feet!"

"Poor Da and his aching feet," Morning Star said, watching her father walk away. "But I think he will have success with Mama. She may make him wait a while before she gives him her answer, but I believe she will accept him."

"I hope so," I responded.

"I believe she will, too," Ria joined in. "Their saga has been an ironic one. Black Wolf did not meet Willow Woman until after he and Little Fawn had become estranged, but it was his great love for Willow that taught him what it was to be wholly dedicated to another person. I think he wishes to have that once more."

* * *

*Something has followed me into the rock-strewn chamber. I scramble across the rubble, the stones rolling under my feet. I find another passageway, where I take cover. I look back to see a blaze of light moving to and fro, splashing its brilliance on the stony walls of the large room.*

I awoke in a daze to a puppy licking my face. It was Doggo. I petted him briefly and sat up carefully so as not to disturb Daisy, who had nodded off in my arms.

Morning Star laughed.

"You fell asleep!" she informed me. "I did not have the heart to awaken you, especially since I had already indulged in a nap this afternoon."

I rubbed my face, in part to dry it after Doggo's display of affection, and in part to rub the sleep from my eyes.

"Many thanks," I replied. "I did not realize I was so tired."

"The children are weary as well," Morning Star stated. "We should put them to bed. Will you take Doggo on a tour of the bushes before he is brought in for the night?"

"I will," I said, "but I will carry Daisy inside first."

The rest of the compound's inhabitants were also taking their leave of one another for the day. We said our goodnights as we ushered our families toward our homes. Fox was quite tired after his labors unloading the sleds with Mror and Oak, and he was on his bed moments after entering our abode. I set the still-slumbering Daisy in her bed, arranging her doll in her arms and covering her with a blanket. I then picked up Doggo and my spear and I turned to the doorway.

"I will be back shortly," I said to Morning Star, who nodded in return.

Doggo was put down near a clump of brush, and I stood by, hopeful that he would relieve himself without too much of a wait. Doggo plodded along with his waddling gait, sniffing his surroundings with interest. I thought that maybe if I urinated on a tree, he would get the idea. Doggo watched but did not seem inclined to imitate me. We walked a little farther.

I did not dare take my eyes off Doggo for more than an instant, but the cool breeze ruffled the tree branches overhead, causing me to look up. The moon was now fully risen among a field of bright stars. I remembered the spectacle of the falling stars we had seen while we camped in the valley.  I had never experienced anything like that before, and I suspected I never would again.  It made me think of Karno, and his wide-eyed enthrallment during the event.  It somehow seemed fitting that he had been laid to rest in that valley.

All at once, the night air was broken by the sounds of an anguished heart pouring its sorrow into a song so achingly beautiful it pained me to hear it.  It was Bewok, singing Karno's Last Farewell.  The song was the Wolfmen's lament for their dead.  We did not understand the words, but the depth of feeling was unmistakable. Bewok was always the one to sing this song; his compelling voice and the wonderful notes it produced were uniquely apt for this mournful rite.

Bewok could not have been far way, so I went in search of him.  I soon found Bewok leaning on his walking stick, standing alone at the edge of the compound. He had finished singing and he was looking up at the sky with tears coursing down his face.

"Bewok," I said gently. "Karno would be so pleased that you have sung for him."

Bewok turned toward me suddenly, evidently startled.

"Tris," he responded. "I did not hear you coming. I am glad it is you."

"Better me than a hungry creature," I said in a weak attempt at jest.

"I have seen you eat," Bewok returned, with a slight smile. "And I am happy you do not eat humans or I would be worried. I see you have a beast with you, however."

I picked up Doggo and held him out to Bewok, knowing Bewok's fondness for dogs.

"This is Doggo," I told Bewok. "I was instructed to take him out before we go to bed."

"I see," Bewok willingly took Doggo from me. "I am glad. I was feeling very sad just now. I did not think I wanted company, but now that you are here, I see that I do. I . . . I cannot believe Karno is really gone. Even though I no longer saw him very often after Twie and I became paired, I still liked the thought of him out in the world, living as only Karno could live . . . ever in hopes of bringing down another big kill. And I think of Jura. Who will care for her and their children?"

"Karno asked Artok to take care of her and the children," I answered. "His last words were about you. Karno asked that you sing for him. He wanted you to have his bracelets. I believe Black Wolf is holding onto them for you."

"I had hoped I would never have reason to do it, but I have sung for him," Bewok said sadly. Bewok cuddled Doggo, who promptly began to lick the salty tears from his face. After a moment he went on. "Tris, do you ever think about what will happen to our peoples? That is, the Old Ones and the People of the Wolves? There are not many of us left."

"That is true," I agreed. "But we are having more children. Fox will be paired with Misty next year, and they will bring another generation to add to our families."

"But their children will not be Old Ones," Bewok pointed out. "Fox is only half Old One. His children will only be half of that. The same for my children with Twie.

They will only be half Wolfman, and every generation will be less and less. How many generations before our peoples are effectively gone? Who will sing our songs? Tell our stories? You and I could be among the last of our peoples."

I pondered this. I had not thought on this before.

"I do not know what will become of our clans," I replied. "I would like to think our stories will continue to be told and the Wolfmen's music will still be played and your songs will be sung. I do not often speculate about my Dreams: some show me the past, some hint at the present, and some even take me to times that seem to be in the future. Perhaps someday I will have one that will indicate whether or not some bit of us will carry on."

"I have been in awe of your gift of Dreaming," Bewok told me. "Even though I know it can be a weighty gift. I hope this Dream will one day come to you."

"The Dreams can do more than disrupt my sleep; they sometimes also disrupt my peace of mind," I said. "But when I am tempted to bemoan them, I remember the times when they have made a vital difference. The first Dream shook me to my core. At the time, I was not sure if it truly was a Dream – the kind of night visions my Gran had. All I knew was that I felt an overwhelming conviction that I had viewed a scene through my Puh's eyes when he and my uncle were being attacked by a bear. If I had not had the Dream and therefore had not gone to Black Wolf to accompany me in search of Puh and my uncle, Puh would not be alive today. And then there were all the other events that Dream set in motion, like my pairing with Morning Star. So I must be grateful that these Dreams sometimes visit my sleep."

Doggo began to squiggle against Bewok's grasp, so Bewok set him on the ground. Doggo sniffed around a bit more and finally found a place to empty his bladder and his bowels.

"Success at last," I said. "Good dog!"

"Let us go home now," Bewok suggested.

* * *

I found Morning Star by the hearth, tending the fire within.

"I was beginning to worry," she said to me as I entered with Doggo. "You were gone longer than I expected."

"Doggo was slow to cooperate," I responded. "And I was speaking with Bewok."

"I heard him," Morning Star said with evident sadness in her bearing and her voice. "How terrible for him to endure the death of his dear friend."

"It is," I agreed. "He talked about Karno, but he also talked about our peoples."

"*Our peoples?*" Morning Star repeated. "In what way?"

"He mentioned that there are not many Old Ones and Wolfmen left," I replied. "And he said something I had never thought on before, that our children with other peoples will be only half Old One or Wolfman, and their children, if they are also paired with others, only half of that. Bewok said that eventually we Old Ones and Wolfmen will cease to exist. I believe he is right, but I hope something of us will always be remembered."

Morning Star approached and put her arms around me. I too embraced her.

"One can hope," she said, looking up at me. "Our children are our future. We must instill in them a strong sense of who they are and from whom they have descended."

"I guess there is not much else we can do," I mused. Then, changing the subject, "You must be glad to be home. I know I am."

"Wherever I am, so long as I am with you, I am home," Morning Star said, tightening her arms around me. "So you must be sure to always come home to me."

"Nothing this side of death will ever keep me from you," I promised. "Let us go to bed."

Much later, we lay on our nest of bedding, still breathless.

"I love you," I told Morning Star. "I will always love you."

"And I, you," Morning Star returned. "There was never going to be anyone but you."

I kissed her long and deeply. I was amazed at the capacity of the heart; I never knew it could hold so much. As I had many times over the years, I pondered our good fortune in our love and our growing family. How had all this come about even amongst all life's perils and uncertainties? How had our hearts and our bodies borne it all?

As we settled down to sleep, I felt comforted by our exchange of words. I kissed Morning Star's forehead and touched her long black hair, as it lay splayed out around her head on the bedding.

* * *

Crunching footsteps echo off the walls as they follow me through the chamber. My heart beats so hard I can feel it thumping within my chest. I continue onward, hoping to evade this intruder, at least until I can discover whom or what it might be. I meet with another wall. I turn to the right, still surrounded by darkness that is illuminated only by the mysterious circle of light that precedes me wherever I go.

Then I see it. There are animals sketched on the wall. They are faded, but I realize I know these images. There are deer, mammoths, wolves, and much more, all depicted in wonderful detail. Nearer the floor, there are cruder pictures of a bird and a human figure.

It is then that I hear the other being enter. Now that his steps no longer echo, I can tell by his gait that he is a human. I cannot see him because a blinding light emanates from the place where his head should be, but he is speaking words I do not understand. He seems to be calling to me. My mind races as I try to comprehend what is happening.

Suddenly, I feel a shift of consciousness unlike any I ever felt have before. It is as though I am not only seeing events through the eyes of another, but I am part of this being. I sense his confusion. He is mystified at his inexplicable familiarity with these images.

The other man who has just entered the chamber is still speaking, and all at once his words become clear. "… This may be a bear! And these must be mammoths!" he exclaims. Now that he is closer, I have a shadowy view of him. He is wearing very strange and colorful clothing. On his head is something that looks vaguely like a large tortoise shell, only the shell emits a beam of bright light. "And look here! This appears to be a representation of the sun!"

I move to stand next to him and all at once an irresistible impulse makes me reach out to touch the drawing. As my fingers make contact with the cold stone surface, immediately a myriad of memories flood my mind, each one coming and going in a flash: my boyhood home, learning to hunt with Puh, becoming paired, the birth of a child, and many others, as well …

and in that drawing see MorningStar, staring at me across the vast ages of time.

"No," I said. "It is a woman."

*Fini*

# Author's Notes

It all started back in February of 2015, when *The Dreamer* mysteriously appeared in my brain. Tris's experiences were a powerful and vivid presence. His world came alive: I saw the characters: I heard their voices; I felt their emotions; their weariness, their determination, their will to survive and provide for their families. I had no idea where the story came from, but I knew I had to write it.

I thought it would be one book, but as I continued to type it soon became obvious that it would not be completed in just one volume. I divided the chronicle into eight books, which took more than eight years to produce. I have thoroughly enjoyed putting his adventures into words and I must say that I am genuinely sorry to be at the end of the series. I will miss being immersed in Tris's tale and spending time with my beloved characters.

* * *

Before I forget, I should add the obligatory disclaimer: no one portrayed in this book is based on real a person. Resemblance to anyone living or dead is purely coincidental. If anything, it is more likely that there may be a little bit of me in my characters. Like Tris, I tend to be a simple person. I deeply value family and friends. And if I'm tired, I can fall asleep just about anywhere. Due to dyslexia, I can empathize with some of Karno's struggles with numbers and language. Like Puh, I tend to be a quiet and introspective person. Like Ria, I have a love of archery and I'm generally horrified any time I see my reflection. And so on and so forth.

* * *

While I wouldn't compare my experiences to those of early humans, I am hopeful that my life experiences have given me insights into what they must've endured throughout their existence. I was raised by an avid outdoorsman and I've always had a keen interest in science – particularly paleoanthropology and zoology – and history, especially natural history. As part of adding layers of realism and plausibility to my books, I have done extensive research and undertaken both formal and independent study. It's still fiction, of course, and my research can only be as accurate as my understanding current science allows. I hope you will forgive any inaccuracies and the occasional stretching of historical timelines to accommodate the plot. And, please forgive the times when I worked from my imagination to fill voids in order to flesh out details that science has not yet provided.

In addition to gathering pertinent information for the time period, I also had to learn to leave behind the modern mindset. My personal opinion is that people are people; their era and settings may change but humans don't alter much over the eons. That being said, so much of what steers our perceptions about life and our fellow humans is based on modern ideas, many of which must be put aside to understand the perspective of ancient humans. Many of today's people are far removed from the food chain, and may not give much thought to where their necessities of life actually originate, but until fairly recent times humans were forced to procure for themselves everything they ate, wore, and utilized. Long-term survival was a group effort; dependence on one another and cooperation were essential.

This was especially true during the last Ice Age, from which many species did not successfully emerge. Of course, humans can be prone to bickering from time to time, but my guess is that they were likely to be more polite about it in prehistoric times, since for the most part, they could ill-afford to alienate their family, friends, and neighbors. It may be that the only way humans ultimately survived a time in history that some other forms of flora and fauna did not, was by working together, and possibly, due to admixture between Homo sapiens, Neanderthals, and Denisovans (and possibly other unknowns, as well); given the notion that hybrids are often considered to be hardier than their parents.

* * *

As mentioned on the Dedication page, I have dedicated this book to my mother. Sadly, Mom passed away some years ago, but I am eternally grateful for her loving devotion as a parent and her steadfast camaraderie after I became an adult. She was reserved with those she did not know, but for the rest of us she was witty, a fabulous cook, a talented artist, and sometimes a bit of an adventurer. And, like my father, she was one of the most intelligent people I have ever known. After she and Dad became empty-nesters, they lived on their schooner and ran charters out of a New England harbor during the summers and the Florida Keys during the winters, until their retirement many years later. Through it all, she always read my manuscripts and offered moral support and feedback. None of those books was ever published, but writing is a solitary pursuit and it meant so much to me to have her as a sounding board and an enthusiastic one-woman cheerleading team.

I would like to take a moment to recognize a few more people, as well. My Aunt Carol has been a huge help in producing these books. She has volunteered her labors as a proofreader and offered valuable constructive criticism and advice. I can never thank her enough for all she's done! Next, my copy editor, Julie Lipkin (Books III – VIII) and Journal Ready, USA (Books I & II) have done an amazing job cleaning up my manuscripts! Lastly, special thanks to my friend Paula Krugerud, whose gorgeous photos grace the covers of my books. I believe her images give my books a distinctive look and feel, and I'm indebted to her for so kindly letting me use her photographs.

* * *

The series ends with a revelation, but more than that, it muses on the fates of the Neanderthal and Denisovans. It's my opinion that there was no one cause that brought about their demise, rather that many things contributed toward their dwindling populations. However, my best guess is that interbreeding with Homo sapiens was the strongest factor; they simply absorbed the smaller populations of Neanderthals and Denisovans until they were no more.

And finally, the end of the series is not the end of Tris's life. Like me, he's older and a bit worse for the wear, but he's still very much alive. It is simply the end of the yarn, written it exactly as it came to me in 2015. I've left out some back-story and parts that I didn't think added enough to the plot to be worth including, but otherwise, the original tale is unchanged. The inclusions of the Dreams are a mystery to me. I'm not really a fan of supernatural or fantasy literature – I'm rather skeptical of anything that asks me to believe that which cannot be scientifically explained. I've had some dreams that made me wonder if they did in fact represent something more than usual, but thus far I've chalked it up to coincidence. Nevertheless, I am willing to admit that science still has much to uncover and I'm happy to learn from each new discovery.

* * *

This saga has meant so much to me. Not only is it a product of my mind, but also my heart. My books have taken me on a literary odyssey that has brought about many serendipitous consequences. I have had the good fortune to see the spark of engagement in school children while giving a presentation about prehistoric peoples. They are my most enthusiastic audience and so full of questions. I love talking about paleoanthropology, prehistory, and natural history and it is so gratifying to me to speak to an assembly that can't get enough of my favorite subjects! I was also thrilled and honored to have an opportunity to meet some scientists and historical experts whose work I have perused for many years. Additionally, I'm always delighted to hear from readers who kindly take the time to write to me and let me know what resonated with them about my books. The fact that people are inspired to reach out humbles me. I often feel unworthy of their generous words, but it reinforces my belief that most people are good. Some readers have even become friends through our correspondence – at least, I consider them to be my friends, even if I have never met them in person. I love that they send photos of themselves to me, of a moose that passed through their yard, of the woodlands near their home. I am genuinely delighted that they want to show me something of themselves and their world.

* * *

In closing, I can only hope that those who have followed Tris's story have enjoyed the journey as much as I have. After all, for what do we exist if not to enhance the lives of others? If I have helped some of my fellow humans to pass the time in a pleasant way, I am pleased. Thank you for reading.

With best and warmest regards,

E. A. Meigs

## Index of European Ice Age Animals

**Antelope** (Saiga Antelope) These small antelope (24 to 36 inches tall at the shoulder weighing approximately 80 to 140 pounds) ranged over a good part of the northern hemisphere. They are exceptional in appearance due to their unusual muzzles, which feature a long, flexible snout that looks much like a truncated elephant's nose.

**Aurochs** (Extinct) Predecessor of domesticated cattle. Size varied between 61 to 71 inches at the shoulder, with weights of 1500 to 3300 pounds. Their horns could reach up to 31 inches in length. Sometimes aurochs is spelled "auroch", but from

my readings, I am lead to believe that but the "s" is often included even when the animal is referred to in singular form because it is an alternative form of spelling "ox" and isn't intended to indicate plurality.

**Boar** Wild boars are the plows of the animal world. They are built for digging. Their heads and massive

shoulders make up a good part of their bodies and their large, sharp tusks, which continue to grow throughout the life of the animal, are very effective at turning over soil. The largest adult male boars can reach weights of nearly 800 pounds and attain a shoulder height of 49 inches. Sows (females) are much smaller and they lack the mane and thick shoulder/back "shield" of the boars. Their tusks are also of a more modest size. The coloring of their coats varies from anything between white and black, but most tend to run towards darker shades.

**Brown Bear**
(Eurasian Brown Bear) Although this bear is called a "brown bear" its color can range from black to a tawny light brown. Males average 550 to 650 pounds but very large specimens can exceed

1000 pounds. Females weigh 330 to 550 pounds. During pre-history, the brown bear did consume some plant matter, but it was generally carnivorous.

**Cave Bear** (Extinct) This was a very large, stout bear. The average male weighed in at 880 to 1100 pounds. Females averaged a little over half that (495 to 550 pounds). Despite their size, bone analysis and other indicators suggest that cave bears were primarily herbivores.

**Cave Lion** (Extinct) (European Cave Lion) These efficient feline predators were some of the largest known cats in animal history. Based on skeletal

remains, it is speculated that the males may have reached 11 ½ feet in length from nose to tip of the tail, and weighed over 880 pounds.

**Chamois** A medium-sized goat/antelope. They are 28-31 inches tall at the shoulder and range in weight from 55-132 pounds. Besides being a fine source of meat, their hides were used to make garments.

**Crow** (Carrion Crow) A large black bird, approximately 18 to 21 inches in length with a large, heavy beak that is well adapted to catching and eating small prey such as mice, frogs, insects, etc., and scavenging off the kills of other animals.

**Elk** (Eurasian Elk) ("moose" in North America) A medium-sized elk/moose, now extinct in many parts of Europe. They average from just over 600 to just over 1000 pounds, with shoulder heights at 5.6 - 6.9 feet.

**Fallow Deer** A medium-sized deer, about 30 to 37 inches at shoulder height and weighing 66 pounds (small doe) to 220 pounds (large buck), although unusually large bucks may tip the scales at 330 pounds. Their winter coats are brown, but they are  freckled with white dots on their backs and sides during the summer.

**Giant Deer** (extinct) (Irish Elk) The giant deer was one of the largest deer ever to walk the earth. Commonly, it has mistakenly been called an Irish elk, although it was neither exclusive to Ireland nor an elk.

This huge deer averaged nearly 7 feet in height at the shoulder and carried antlers with a spread that could span 12 feet. They are estimated to have weighed nearly 1200 to just over 1300 pounds but larger individuals could have reached upwards of 1500 pounds.

**Horse**  The Eurasian Ice Age horse came in many

different varieties. They were more than likely the size of modern ponies and appeared in all colors, spots and stripes. They may have resembled the Przewalski's horse that still exist today or the now-extinct Tarpan horse.

**Ibex** (Alpine Ibex) A moderate-sized, dun-colored mountain goat. The bucks' horns sometimes reach 39 inches in length. The does' horns may grow to a length of nearly 14 inches. Similarly, bucks achieve a much larger body size (35 to 40 inches at the withers and weighing from 150 to over 250 pounds) than the does (29 to 33 inches at the withers and 37 to just over 70 pounds).

**Lynx** (Eurasian Lynx) The biggest of all species of lynx. Approximately 24 to 30 inches at the shoulder, and including its short tail, it may be 31 to 51 inches in body length. The largest males weighed nearly 100 pounds, but the typical lynx will run between 18 (very small female)  and 66 pounds (good-sized male).

**Marten** (European Pine Marten) A small, weasel-like animal with dark brown fur, often with blond markings or a blond bib on its chest.  At a little less than 3 ½ pounds and about 21 inches in length, the marten was hunted for its beautiful, silky fur.

**Mink** (European Mink) A small mink,

even the largest is just under 20 inches in length and only about 1¾ pounds. They have been prized for their dense, luxurious winter coats.

**Porcupine** (Old World Porcupine) This rodent wears an impressive coat of quills, some of which may be up to 14 inches in length (Crested Porcupine). These species of porcupines come in a variety of sizes: the smallest adults run from 11inches to 34 inches long, and may weigh between 3.3 to 60 pounds.

**Red Deer** (European Red Deer) Another very large species of deer. The buck weighs in at 350 to 550 pounds (48 inches at the shoulder) and does run 260 to 370 pounds (45 inches at the shoulder). These deer, unsurprisingly, are known for their

reddish coats. During autumn, the males often have a short mane on the backs of their necks.

**Red Fox** The biggest of the fox species, the adult ranges from 14 to 20 inches tall at the shoulder and weigh from 5 to nearly 40 pounds. These animals were often harvested for their  fine fur.

**Reindeer** (Also known as caribou) This important game animal consists of several different subspecies and varied in size from 120 to 550 pounds. Color varied as well, but all subspecies shared many of  the same basic characteristics, such as a fairly

impressive set of antlers (in most reindeer, both the bucks and the does grow antlers) and a two-layered coat of fur, featuring a woolly undercoat that thickens dramatically each winter and an overcoat of longer, coarse, hollow hairs.

**Roe Deer** (Western Roe Deer) This small deer averages just over two feet to two feet, 6 inches at the withers, and a mere 33 to 77 pounds. Nonetheless, they were an important source of meat for prehistoric humans.

**Sheep** The actual breed(s) of ancient sheep that roamed Ice-Age Europe are unknown, but it is recognized that sheep were hunted and eaten by early man. It is possible that the Mouflon (shown in image) is the modern day link to prehistoric sheep. The Mouflon have a shoulder height of less than 3 feet and weigh from 75 to 110 pounds.

**Snow Leopard** This beautiful cat is well adapted to life in a cold, mountainous habitat. It has a stout build

and long, dense fur that varies in color from white to pale gray, with dark gray to black spotted markings.  It is about 24 inches at the shoulder with a weight of 60 to 120 pounds, although larger males have been noted at 165 pounds. Their fur was considered to be very desirable and they have long been hunted for their pelts.

**Vulture** (Eurasian Griffin Vulture) This large scavenging bird may have a wingspan of over 9 feet and weigh as much as 33 pounds, although most individuals range from

14 to 25 pounds. It is known that early men consumed the meat of vultures.

**Wisent** (European Bison)  An impressive animal, the  wisent is the heaviest land animal that still resides in modern day Europe. Fully grown specimens range from 5 to 6 ½ feet at the shoulder and weigh 660 (small female) to more than 2000 pounds (large male). The wisent was an important source of food and hides for prehistoric humans.

**Wolf** (Eurasian Wolf) These are the largest of the  European or Asian wolves. Their sizes vary greatly from 70 to 212 pounds. Although their coats could be black, white, or even reddish, by far the most common color was a grey/buff and white combination of medium length, dense fur.

**Wood Grouse** (Western Capercaillie) This Eurasian bird is the largest of the grouse species, weighing as much as 15 pounds. The cocks have an average weight of 9 pounds and a wingspan of 36 to 48 inches. The hen is  considerably more modest in size, with  a  weight  of  approximately 4 pounds and a wingspan of 28 inches.

 **Woolly Mammoth** (Extinct) This large mammal lived in Eurasia and North America, and was similar in size to today's African Elephants, but with considerably longer tusks, a shorter tail, and  much  smaller  ears. The males of this huge species could attain heights of up to 11 feet at the withers and weigh over 12,000 pounds. Females were somewhat smaller, although still impressive in size at up to 9½ feet at the shoulder and weights up to nearly 9000 pounds. Their hairy hides came in a wide range of colors that could be anything from blond to quite dark. They were protected from the extreme Ice Age weather conditions by a double fur coat that consisted of a short, dense, woolly undercoat and strands of long outer guard hairs.

**Woolly Rhinoceros** (Extinct) Looking much like a

modern rhinoceros in a heavy fur coat, the woolly rhinoceros sported two horns on its long snout and carried its thick body on short, stout legs. This animal averaged about 4000 to 6000 pounds, with a shoulder height of about 6½ feet. The larger front horn that grew from the woolly rhinoceros' nose could reach lengths of 24 inches.

# About the Author
# E.A. Meigs

I was raised on Cape Cod (Brewster, Massachusetts, USA) at a time when the Cape was still a rural area made up of woodlands, marshes, beaches, streams, and ponds. There, my life was divided between the land and sea. My father was a commercial fisherman, backyard boat builder, and an outdoorsman; so I had an early introduction to boats, working in the commercial fishing industry and spending lots of time in the local fields and forests. When I wasn't on a boat or roaming around the great outdoors, chances are I was reading or writing. I have been a compulsive writer literally since I could first put words on paper, producing my first full length novel at ten years old. Even at that age, my goal in life was to someday find a way to combine my love of nature, the outdoors, and writing.

After raising a family and embarking on a long and varied career that included many years working on and around boats and in the commercial fishing industry; a stint with Florida Fish & Wildlife in a small field office; and other jobs that actually allowed me to use my writing skills, I awoke one day with *The Dreamer* in my head. I began writing the novel with the intention of producing just one book, but as the story progressed it became apparent that the plot would require much more than one volume to tell the tale.

I have two wonderful adult daughters and nine delightful grandchildren. I am an avid camper and I strive to get out hiking as often as possible, daily, when my schedule allows.